Other Works by
James Carlos Blake

RED GRASS RIVER: A LEGEND
IN THE ROGUE BLOOD
THE FRIENDS OF PANCHO VILLA
THE PISTOLEER

BORDERLANDS

SHORT FICTIONS

JAMES CARLOS BLAKE

AVON BOOKS NEW YORK

AVON BOOKS, INC.
1350 Avenue of the Americas
New York, New York 10019

Collection copyright © 1999 by James Carlos Blake
Cover photograph by Bill Timmerman
Interior design by Kellan Peck
Published by arrangement with the author
ISBN: 0-380-79485-3
www.avonbooks.com

First Avon Books Trade Paperback Printing: April 1999
First Avon Books Special Hardcover Printing: April 1999

AVON TRADEMARK REG. U.S. PAT. OFF. AND IN OTHER COUNTRIES, MARCA REGISTRADA, HECHO EN U.S.A.

Printed in the U.S.A.

QPM   10   9   8   7   6   5   4   3   2   1

ACKNOWLEDGMENTS

On initial publication, most of these works appeared in slightly different form.

"The Outsider: An Introductory Memoir" copyright © 1998 by James Carlos Blake appeared previously in *The Los Angeles Times Book Review*.

"Runaway Horses" copyright © 1994 by James Carlos Blake appeared previously in *Saguaro*.

"Three Tales of the Revolution," copyright © 1993 by James Carlos Blake appeared previously in *The Sun*. Portions also appeared in *Quarterly West* as part of the novella, "I, Fierro."

"Under the Sierra" copyright © 1994 by James Carlos Blake appeared previously in *Fine Print*.

"Aliens in the Garden," copyright © 1987 by James Carlos Blake appeared previously in *The Sun*.

"The House of Esperanza," copyright © 1988 by James Carlos Blake appeared previously in *The Sun*.

"La Vida Loca" copyright © 1998 by James Carlos Blake appeared previously in *Gulf Stream Magazine* with the title "Small Times."

"Referee" copyright © 1998 by James Carlos Blake appeared previously in *Smoke*.

"Texas Woman Blues" copyright © 1991 by James Carlos Blake appeared previously in part (Perdition Road) in *A Long Story*.

FOR
NAT SOBEL

WHERE DO WE GO WHEN WE DIE? HE SAID.
I DON'T KNOW, THE MAN SAID. WHERE ARE WE NOW?
—CORMAC MCCARTHY, *CITIES OF THE PLAIN*

WHAT NEED IS THIS
WE FOLLOW INTO RAMSHACKLE TOWNS . . .

LISTENING FOR A WHISTLE
TO CALL US BY NAME,
WAITING FOR A NIGHT TRAIN
TO CARRY US OUT.
—MARTI MIHALYI, "TRANSIENCE"

NEVER EAT AT A PLACE CALLED MOM'S, NEVER PLAY CARDS WITH A MAN
NAMED DOC, AND NEVER GO TO BED WITH ANYBODY WHO'S GOT MORE
TROUBLES THAN YOU DO.
—NELSON ALGREN

CHARACTER IS FATE.
—HERACLITUS

CONTENTS

BORDERLANDS

THE OUTSIDER

An Introductory Memoir

I

I've always been an outsider, a stranger in every tribe. That's neither boast nor complaint nor plea for sympathy. And it's certainly not a condition uncommon to others. It's the sense of remove from the world around him that defines the outsider, but this feeling of apartness goes beyond mere geography. Even in his own country, among his own fellows, in the midst of his own family, the outsider feels himself a stranger, a keeper of an alien heart.

Some feel like outsiders for obvious reasons, some for reasons more complex, some for reasons utterly and ever unknowable. In my own case, blood heritage and a borderland childhood no doubt played their parts.

I am the fourth generation of men in my family to be born in Mexico, all of us descendants of an American who himself was sired by an English pirate. But I'm the sole member of those generations who was raised in the borderlands—that long brute region flanking both sides of the Mexican-American frontier for roughly a couple of hundred miles in either direction and ranging for more than two thousand winding miles from the mouth of the Río Grande at the Gulf of Mexico to its western terminus at the California shore of Alta California. All along this frontier the outlands of two countries come together to form a culturally sovereign province. It is almost entirely desert country, stark and shadeless and short on mercy, and, with few widely scattered exceptions, sparsely inhabited. From the scrublands of South Texas and Coahuila to the fierce basins and ranges of the Big Bend and Chihuahua to the desert dunes of Arizona and Sonora, its people are mostly of a nature less wholly Mexican or American than an amalgam of both, a nature as distinct and remote and isolate as the borderlands themselves.

II

The pirate was my great-great-great-grandfather Robert Blake, the black sheep of a landed English family. He left Olde England for the New one and lived for a time in

New Hampshire, where he was married and fathered a son before sailing south to plunder in the Gulf of Mexico. He was captured in 1826 and executed in Veracruz and was thus the first Blake buried in Mexican ground. His son John married a woman of established New England family whose fortune derived from paper mills, and he gained appointment as U.S. consul to the Mexican state of Jalisco. Thus, like his father before him, did John Blake venture to Mexico, albeit to a better fate. He fell in love with the country and established a profitable mill he named the Hacienda Americana, which remained in the family until the Revolution of 1910. He sired three sons but only one, Carlos Enrique, lived to maturity. Carlos was already managing the mill when his father was stabbed to death on the church steps one Sunday morning by a foreman with a grievance. A photograph of great-grandfather Carlos shows a quintessential patrón whose stern mustached visage and hard eyes bespeak no tolerance whatsoever for fools or disrespect. He is flanked by his family—by his four daughters, his two sons, and his Creole wife, Adela Arrias, born in Mexico of pure Spanish bloodline and the first Mexican woman taken to wed by a Blake. One son, Tomás Martín, would be killed at age eighteen when his mount fell on him. The other, Juan Sotero, was my grandfather. He rose to the rank of colonel in the Mexican army engineering corps, married a Creole poet named Esther Hernández, and begat two sons—Juan Jaime and Carlos Sebastián. Carlos would become my father.

III

My father was, like his father, a civil engineer, more particularly a builder of roads. He loved the profession not only for itself but as much for the way of life it allowed, and he reveled in that life for ten years before he got married. It was fitting that he built roads, for he loved to travel on them, loved to drive his Model A Fords, his Buicks, his Packards—all the cars he came to own in those wild free years—loved to drive them hard and fast over roads however rugged and raise great plumes of dust behind him.

As a young man, he went to work for his father in the borderlands and over the next few years built roads to Piedras Negras, just across the Río Grande from Eagle Pass, Texas; to Villa Acuña, across the river from Del Rio; to Ojinaga, across from Presidio. He built roads in various portions of the Sonoran desert including the brutal Desierto de Altar, comprising the whole of the region between the southwest corner of Arizona and the Sea of Cortez. He had by then formed his own company, and he and his crews played as hard as they worked. Whenever there was a town within thirty miles of their camp, they would head for that town's cantinas at the setting of the sun and there drink and gamble and frisk with the girls and fight with other construction crews and generally have a fine time. He loved the desert towns—Agua Prieta, Nogales, Sonoita, Mexicali. Loved Baja California above all places on earth, loved Tecate and Tijuana and Ensenada. Sometimes they went to towns on the American side of the border—Calexico, Tucson, El Paso, Las Cruces—just for the novelty of it, to flirt with the blondes. At a time when few Mexicans traveled more than fifty miles from home in their lives, my father and his crews were men of vastly traveled experience, worldly men of the borderland, and not one of them yet thirty years old.

Sometimes there was trouble with the American Border Patrol, and on one occasion my father was jailed in Tucson for a night as a result of a misunderstanding involving an American girl he'd taken for a visit across the border. So bitter did this experience make him for a time toward all things American that he refused to speak English, poorly as he did, for nearly a year afterward. And several years later when the U.S. State Department sent him a notice that, according to the Nationality Act of 1940, he was entitled to claim American citizenship on the basis of his American parental lineage and had only to fill out the enclosed forms to do so, he tore up the papers. In Mexico City his brother Juan received the same forms and also threw them away. They knew themselves as Mexican and no argument about it.

IV

He met my mother, Estrella Lozano, at a dance in Brownsville, Texas, and the ensuing courtship was whirlwind. She'd grown up the only child of a Mexican horse rancher whose ranch encompassed thousands of acres just south of the border in Tamaulipas state. But her mother hated ranch life, and so her father bought them a house in Brownsville. She attended Brownsville schools and learned to speak English so well that her mother, who spoke no English at all, often chided her for learning it better than Spanish. She became a true borderland Mexicana—did the jitterbug and sipped black cows at the drugstore and thought Clark Gable was the living end.

And then she met my father, and next thing she knew, she—who had never ventured farther from Brownsville than her high school graduation trip to Galveston Island— was waving goodbye to her grimfaced mother as her husband of less than three days gunned his yellow Buick from her house on Levee Street and toward the international bridge. Two weeks later she was in Baja California, as far from home as the moon.

She was at first thrilled by the adventure of it all, but my father often had to leave her alone in whatever house he rented in whatever pueblo was closest to the construction camp where he had to spend most of his time. Sometimes they were apart for days, and she'd become terribly lonely. Her only companions were the young maids my father hired to help around the house. The maids were sympathetic to my mother's plight and tried to keep her entertained with stories of the region, with accounts of ancient legends and tales of the haciendas that had long ruled that portion of borderland Mexico. In years to come my mother would tell those tales to me.

Yet there was no assuaging her loneliness, and in one of her frequent letters home to her mother she signed off by writing, "Sometimes I feel like this is the world," and drew a long arrow pointing to a circle the size of a quarter at the top of the page—and then drew another arrow down the margin of the paper to point to a tiny pencil dot at the bottom of the sheet: "And this is me." The first time I saw that letter I was a grown man, but the sense of isolation it conveyed struck me with a keen recognition. It well described how I'd felt most of my life, except that I had no idea where that large circle at the top of the page—which for her was both her father's ranch and her mother's Brownsville home—would ever be for me.

My father came home from the job as often as he could. Sometimes he could stay a few days, sometimes only for hours, for even less time than it took to make the drive from the camp. But whenever he and my mother were together they had wonderful times. They went to nightclubs if there were any in town, to cantinas if that was all there was. They drank and danced and made each other laugh, these young lovers who were as much in thrall to their passionately romantic natures as they were to one another, whom in truth they hardly knew. In photographs from those days my father is deeply tanned and lean-muscled in his short-sleeved workshirt. His hair is black and curly, his grin bright white. He sports a roguish pencil-thin mustache, and his eyes are full of daring. My mother's pictures show a *girl*, dark-haired and fair-skinned, sensuously slight, beautiful. She looks as if she could ride her father's strongest stallions with a sure and easy grace.

They lived in various towns in Baja California during their first six months of marriage, but my mother's favorite was Santo Tomás. Set on a tableland flanked by high jagged sierras, it was more a hacienda than a town in those days, and in later years she often described to me the region's spectacular golden sunsets and blood-red cactus flowers, its strange mountain winds, its richly green vineyards so beautiful in their contrast to the surrounding desert and mountain rock. In that old borderlands estancia I was conceived.

My mother was large with me when my father took her to meet his family in Mexico City. She wanted me to be born in Texas, but my father was still smarting from his experience with the gringo legal system in Tucson and was not keen on this ambition. They were still at odds on the issue when they departed the capital for the Gulf coast, where my father had to attend to a brief business matter—and where the highway to the border awaited their decision about my place of birth. I can envision them as they drove down the winding mountain roads and debated the nationality I should be born to, my mother arguing for the U.S. and all the advantages of American citizenship, reminding my father of his own Anglo roots; my father countering with assertions of his Mexican character and nationality and the necessity of his son being Mexican as well—and knowing he was losing the debate. I see him stealthily choosing the least direct routes toward the coast, in no hurry at all to reach the highway to the north, hoping, perhaps, that given more time my mother might yet capitulate. And then nature resolved the matter by nudging my mother into early labor. They rushed to the hospital in the miasmic and piratical port of Tampico, and there I was born Mexican.

I can imagine my mother's disappointment, my father's wide grin around a celebratory cigar.

V

We lived in Tampico but a short time before moving south to other coastal towns—Veracruz on the bay of Campeche, Salina Cruz on the Gulf of Tehuantepec— where over the next few years my father built roads along various shorelines. We did not live anywhere for longer than four months in the first six years of my life.

My earliest memories of the natural world are of seashores with tall palms and long sand beaches and trees full of squalling parrots, of wet heat and dense foliage dappled with green sunlight, of a series of different houses and all of them white and bright and high-ceil-inged, with wide windows open to the sea and the sound of breakers. I was often in the charge of mestizo maids who laughed like little bells and had brilliant white teeth and warm brown skin that smelled faintly of sugar and smoke. They would take me to the beach to play in the surf and at naptime sang me to sleep with songs I would never hear anywhere else thereafter.

I was still shy of school age when my father moved us to the western frontera he so dearly loved, and I can recall my wonder at the dramatic change in the look and feel of the world. The land was now barren and sand-blown and dust devils rose and whirled across it. Long red mesas shimmered in the rising heat. The desert stretched to the ends of the earth under skies of stunning vastness, under a demonic sun that made blood of the horizon at every rise and set. During the following year, we lived in many of the border towns already familiar to my parents; but now, whenever my father went off to the camps and left my mother behind at home, I was there, as well as the maids, to keep her company. Some of the servant girls were from the high country and said they had come to the frontera to get away from the earth-quakes that so often shook the mountains. I never forgot the tale one of them told of a temblor that opened the ground of her village and swallowed her family's hut while her brothers were yet inside.

Sometimes when my father was home from the job for a day or two, he'd take us to the nearest town for dinner in a restaurant; and sometimes, as we were driving to or from town along those isolated roads, we'd see groups of people—usually all men but sometimes there were women and children among them too—trudging over the desert hardpan with rope-lashed bundles and small bags on their backs. The first time I saw such a group I was amazed that anyone would be walking so far out in the desert and I asked my father who they were. "Mojados," he said. That's what they were called along the eastern region of the border, all along the Río Grande, "mojados" or "espaldas mojadas"—wetbacks—because they got soaked in their illegal crossing of the river to get to the American side. But most of the western region of the borderland was open country and without fences and people could simply walk through the desert and into the United States. My father thought all of them, no matter how they sneaked across, should be called estúpidos for wanting to go to the U.S. in the first place.

On that car trip I heard for the first time about the desperate risks some people were willing to take in order to get to the United States, to el norte—to what they were sure would be a better life than they would ever know in Mexico. Before long we would move to Texas, and I would see them—my countrymen, yet as different from me as moonpeople—stooped and dragging long bags behind them in the cotton fields, picking vegetables on their knees, toting boxes of produce on their shoulders from field to truck. There would come a day in South Texas when my mother would see me looking out the car window at a field of cotton pickers and she'd say, "We're lucky, Jaimito. We're very lucky."

VI

My mother was now trying to instruct me in the rudiments of English, but I was steadfastly opposed to learning the language of Americans. I'd often overheard my father and his friends talking about them—gringos, they called them, enunciating the epithet like it had a bad taste—and I refused to learn the language of such a mean and brutish people. No amount of my mother's reasoning against such bigotry could sway me. Whenever she tried to teach me so much as a phrase in English, I would put my hands tightly over my ears and sing Mexican songs at the top of my voice. It maddened her no end and vastly amused my father.

One day, shortly after we settled into yet another rented house, my mother took me with her on a shopping trip to Calexico. It was my first time on the American side of the border, and there I saw gringos by the dozens and heard their growling language everywhere. And I couldn't help but remark that most of them looked more like me than most Mexicans did.

In a small eatery whose air was thick with strange wonderful smells, my mother bought me my first hamburger. As he set our plates in front of us, the American proprietor said something to me in English and then smiled and spoke to my mother, who laughed and said something to him in return. When he went to wait on another customer, I asked her what he'd said. She started to tell me, then stopped short and smiled sweetly and said she'd be glad to teach me a little English so I wouldn't have to depend on others for the rest of my life to find out what people around me were saying.

The ploy worked. In the remaining months before we left the western borderland and moved to the lower Río Grande Valley, I learned to speak English well enough to make my mother smile and my father shake his head and mutter.

VII

We moved to the United States—Brownsville, Texas, the geographical bottom of the republic—for two reasons: I was of age to begin my formal schooling, and my mother was again pregnant. She not only insisted that her next child would be born American, but also that I would be educated in American schools. I didn't like the idea very much, but for reasons it would take me years to understand, my father had come to agree with her. So we settled into a house on Zaragoza Street in a dusty oak-and-mesquite neighborhood at the edge of town and I was enrolled at St. Joseph Academy.

Now did I begin to learn about the complexities of nationality. Even though about half of the families in the neighborhood were clearly of Mexican descent, many of their members had been born north of the border and were therefore Americans, whom I had always thought of as fair-skinned people who spoke only English. *Those* people, I would soon be informed by my Mexican friends, were called Anglos.

The Anglo kids of Zaragoza Street—most of them native Texans, all of them Southerners—were the first I'd ever known, and my acquaintance with them roused deep confusions about my own identity. My first exchange with them was in front of our new house on the day we moved in. When they asked where I was born and I said Mexico, they thought I was joking. When I insisted on my Mexican birth, some of them got irritated, and one said, "Then how come you don't look like it nor talk like it neither? You ain't like *them*." He pointed at a bunch of kids watching us from the front porch of a house down the block, a group of mestizos, typical brown-skinned Mexicans of mixed Spanish and Indian blood, and to these Texas boys what all Mexicans looked like. They didn't believe I was Mexican because I didn't look or sound like one. And they had not yet met my parents, not yet heard my pale-complexioned mother addressing me in Spanish, not yet caught an earful of my father's movie bandido accent, which the years would never abate.

"If you *really* Mexican," one said, "let's hear you *say* something in Mexican."

Now *I* was getting irritated at having to prove to these peckerwoods who I was, so I said: "Ustedes son una bola de tontos." They looked at each other as if any among them might certify that what I'd said had indeed been said in "Mexican." But none in the group had any under-standing that I'd just called them a bunch of dummies. I turned to the Mexican kids down the street and hollered, "¿Qué tal? Me llamo Jaime Carlos y ahora vivo in este barrio también."

The Mexican kids showed white grins and hollered back their welcomes, and the Texas boys' mouths hung ajar. For a moment nobody said anything, and then blond Danny Shaw, my new next-door neighbor, said, "Dang if you ain't the unmexicanest Mexican I ever seen."

VIII

They never really knew what to make of me, the Anglo kids, both in the neighborhood and at school. Although they didn't often mingle with Mexican kids, they didn't shun me at all even after I'd proved to them I was a Mexican myself. And so I was able to pal around with both groups. Before long, I was speaking the slangy singsong border Spanish of the Mexicans when I was with them, and falling into a Texas accent whenever I spoke English in the company of the Anglo kids. It was the start of a lifelong habit of trying to fit in with the people around me by assuming their modes of speech, a practice reputedly common to misfits, con artists and liars of all sorts, which of course includes writers.

Over time, some of the Mexican kids came to resent that I buddied with the Texans so often and so easily. And some of the Texans were always ready to remind me that I was not truly one of them. Although my English was improving in school every day, I often made mistakes with the language during my first years with it, and the Texans would leap at the chance to make fun of me for it. Sometimes they merely laughed for a moment and I merely felt embarrassed. Sometimes it went past that and the fight was on.

The first time it happened was on my neighbor Danny Shaw's front porch, when I was looking on with him and Nicky Welch at a magazine cover photo of a horse wearing a beautiful saddle. Without thinking, I said, "That's a pretty chair."

The two of them gave me puzzled looks and Danny asked, "*What* chair?" I pointed to the saddle—in Spanish called a *silla*, which also is the word for chair—and they burst out laughing. "That ain't no *chaairrrr*," Danny said, "that's a *saaaddddle!*"

My face burned with the vocabulary error, one which seemed all the worse to me because I was grandson to a horse rancher. And then Nicky Welch, who always went for the extra bite whenever he could, said, "Only some stupid greaser would call a saddle a *chair*."

My father had been teaching me to fight since before I entered school. He knew what would be in store for me with the Texan kids sooner or later and knew he couldn't protect me from it, he could only prepare me. Whenever my mother had seen him showing me how to deliver a proper punch, how to use knees and elbows in a fight, she'd chide him for it and he'd stop—until she left, and then we'd resume our lesson. I always suspected that she knew we continued with them, and that she secretly approved. In fact, the first time I ever heard the word "greaser" was in her company. We were in Mexicali and heard an American yell it from his car at a Mexican cab driver who'd nearly run into him. The cabby didn't even look the man's way, but my mother glared at the Anglo and muttered that somebody ought to smack that damn gringo's face—and my mother rarely used the word "gringo" and even less frequently swore.

I had been in little-kid fights in Mexico, a lot of shoving and wrestling and no real meanness intended, but this was my first fight with anger in it, with a desire to inflict pain. Nicky Welch was bigger than I was, but he fought in the clumsy awkward manner of the beefy and untutored, and by the time Mr. Shaw came stomping out of the house to pull us apart I had pretty well bloodied Nicky's nose and puffed his eye and, best of all, had him bawling. Mr. Shaw demanded to know what the fight was about, and when Danny told him, he just sighed and looked away and softly told Nicky and me to get on home. I felt sorry for him because I knew him for a kind man and I could see that the word "greaser" embarrassed him. But what I mostly felt was exultation, felt it all the rest of that day and through the evening and as I lay in bed that night looking out my window at the stars. The next afternoon I saw stars of another sort when Nicky's big brother Ruben got hold of me as I was coming home from buying a comic book at the drugstore. My mother nearly shrieked at the sight of me when I limped into the house.

There were plenty of other fights to come. I had more fights with gringo kids than my Mexican friends did for the simple reason that I spent more time with them than they did. Whenever some Texas kid made a crack about greasers or spicks in my presence, I usually shrugged it off because I knew that was how Texans talked and there was no personal insult intended. I thought only fools got angry at insults not directed at them personally. I still think so. When the insult *was* personal, there was of course nothing to do but fight. Sometimes, though, as I was punching and kicking and scrabbling around in the dirt with some other kid, I'd hear the Mexicans cheering in Spanish and the Anglos rooting in English and I'd have the strange feeling that the only one in the fight was me.

The fights fell off over the next few years, and one reason for that was my growing facility with English. The better I got with the Anglos' language and the more I sounded like them, the easier it was for them to accept me as one of their own. By the time I was in fourth grade even the Anglo kids were asking me for the answers on spelling and grammar tests.

In the brief rest of our time in Texas, I was fully at ease in both cultures, was fluent with both languages, and had more of a sense of being at *home* than I've ever had since.

IX

One day my father announced that we were moving to Florida for reasons of business and within the month I left the borderland behind me.

But not really.

In the years to follow I would lose my ties to my native country, lose my ease with my native tongue. But I had not, I would learn, left behind the truest of the borderlands—the remote world of the outsider.

I would come to understand that a borderland is as much a region of the spirit as a physical locale, that some of us are born to it and come to know it well in childhood and inhabit it forever after, no matter where we might be on the map.

And I came to understand that even though I am hardly alone in lacking a sense of place in the world, I always *feel* that I am.

So do all outsiders feel.

So do many of the characters in these stories feel.

RUNAWAY HORSES

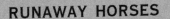

"Our passions are ourselves."
—ANATOLE FRANCE

From the bars of my high window I can see the shimmer of the Río Zanjón through the trees, and beyond them the dark Sierras de San Antonio. The mountains are especially beautiful under a full moon, even though on those nights a crowd always comes out from town and gathers by the iron-barred front gate to be entertained by our howling. I have heard their raucous laughter, their mock howls and drunken derisions. I have imagined their bright faces and delirious exultation not to be among us. Usually, however, on those evenings of the full moon I am oblivious to their echoing caterwauls because I am howling with the other inmates, and when I howl, I am aware of nothing but the brute events that brought me here.

At first I was permitted to visit the gardens behind the main building twice a week, like most of the others. But before I'd been here a month I attacked another inmate. We tumbled into a rose bed, snarling and grappling in the dirt. I got my hands hard on his throat and his eyes bulged like red plums. I would certainly have killed him if the guards had not rushed up and clubbed me insensible. When the warden pressed me for an explanation, I told him the fellow had been singing about a woman named Delgadina, which was the name of my wife.

"But señor," he said, "there must be *hundreds* of women called Delgadina. Why do you believe he was singing about your wife?"

Bastard. Addressing me as "señor" rather than "don." I knew all about him. He came from a family of sucklings to the viceroy—bureaucrats, administrators, a line of glorified *clerks*. My family had been the better of his by leagues since long before the founding of New Spain. *We* had come wearing armor—not, like his people, lace and rosewater. Now this smiling, bloated pig sat reveling in the circumstance that put him in official authority over me.

"That *isn't* what I believe," I said. "And if *you* say her name again, I will tear out your tongue."

I have not been allowed from my cell since.

I do have periods of lucidity—this moment is proof of that. Sometimes they last for days, but I have yet to pass a week without relapsing into . . . what shall we call it . . .

my spectacular dementia. I've been told quite explicitly what I look like in the throes of my lunatic fits. I tear out my hair—what's left of it. I slaver like a sunstruck dog. My eyes roll up in my head. I beat my fists on the heavy wooden door, on the stones of the walls and the floor. I howl for hours. In this place of iron and shadows and sweating stone, I become the madman of theatre. I lack only the rattling chains, but I expect they'll come soon enough.

My howling has rent my voice to a croak which some of my keepers find amusing. My battered hands often look like spoiled meat. They brought a mirror to me last week, thinking, I suppose, the shock might do me good. I saw eyes like firepits, a beard gone wild, facial bones jutting sharply against skin the color of lemonwater. I roared and smashed the glass, and the officious fools bolted from the room like spooked mares. If I were given to religion, or to self-pity, or—worst of all—to the sentiments of Romance, I might say that I have come to know hell. But such talk is the idiom of fools, the self-pitying locution of stage plays and poetry, and I will no more indulge in it myself than I will endure it in others.

Forgive me: I tend to ramble in these periods of respite from the dementia. Insanity of this sort is more than mental torture, it is abject humiliation. How I envy the steadfastly insane all around me. They are spared such recurrent seizures of sanity as I must bear, spared these periodic realizations of where we are, and why.

Suicide? Bah! Some choose it, of course. Not a month goes by without at least one wretch found hanging in his cell or drowned in one of the garden ponds. Cowards, all of them! Suicide is contemptible, the final refuge of the true poltroon. (Like Rojas, that bastard slyboots!) But not

I. I will not kill myself, not ever. I am insane, but I am no coward.

Again, I beg your pardon. I not only ramble like a fool, I shame myself with gross discourtesy. My name is Don Sebastián Cabrillo Mayor Cortés y Mendoza. I am patrón of the Hacienda de la Luna Plata. My family has owned this region of Sonora since Coronado marched through it on his way to search for the Seven Cities of Gold. The first of my New World ancestors, Don Marcos Cabrillo, was a lieutenant in Coronado's expedition. He lost a foot in a battle with Yaqui Indians and was left behind when the column moved on. With a following of four other maimed soldiers and a handful of converted indigenes, he laid claim to all the land visible from the bloodstained mesa where he had been crippled. He named his portion of the earth after the region's dazzling silver moon—La Luna Plata—and over the next three and a half centuries the hacienda expanded to more than a hundred square miles. It took sharp steel to conquer this country of cactus and rock, and an iron will to rule it. It took hardness—as each generation of Cabrillo men was taught by the one before it. As my father taught me. "Hardness," he told me repeatedly through my youth, "is *everything*."

By the time my father became patrón of La Luna Plata, his authority, like that of hacendados everywhere, was enforced not only by his own pistoleros but also by the powerful Guardia Rural, the national mounted police. Since the rurales' wise creation by our esteemed president, Porfirio Díaz, bandits no longer pillage the countryside so freely as they once did, and reports of peon insurrections are now quite rare. Like Don Porfirio himself, the rurales well understand the efficacy of hardness. They are authorized to make arrests on their own suspicions, incarcerate suspects indefinitely, interrogate by any means necessary to encourage the truth, and confiscate a suspect's property as legal recompense to the state. And under the provision of the Law of Flight, they may legally shoot dead any man who attempts to escape their custody. Thus does that highly efficient police force often spare the state the cost and inconvenience of extending judicial formalities to those undeserving of them.

Malefactors on La Luna Plata have always received swift punishment—the branding iron, the lash, or the noose, depending on the severity of the offense. My father was renown for tailoring the penalty to the transgression. As a descendant of devout apostles of the Inquisition, he owned an imagination well-suited to the invention of punishments. There was, for example, the arrogant mestizo foreman who set his mastiff bitch onto a group of Indian children for no reason but sport. My father sentenced him to kill the animal, skin it, and hang the carcass from a tree in the main plaza for a week. He then had to eat the dog's hindquarters, raw and rotten, with the villagers looking on. He also had to forfeit half-a-month's pay to each of the families of the children his dog had savaged.

There was a band of drunkards whose loud cursings in the street disturbed the village mass every evening until the priest complained of it to my father, who had the men arrested and sentenced each one to receive a live coal in his mouth. He ordered a rapist to be conveyed to a pigsty, there castrated, and made to watch the swine consume his severed parts before he was hanged. He permitted the father and brother of a young woman who had been beaten to death by her bad-tempered husband to take the killer into the desert and do with him as they thought proper. Among other things, they flayed his skull, and on their return to the ranch they nailed the entire headskin to the crosspiece over the corral gate, where it was shortly devoured by birds and ants. After a few days, only the scalp remained, and it stayed up there for months, a withered testament to the hard certainty of Luna Plata justice.

I was my father's son in every way—educated by the Jesuit fathers, skilled in the arts of weaponry, easy in the saddle. I was confident in command of men, versed in the social graces, and wholly comfortable with my privilege. And I was guarded in my passions, or so I believed.

On the matter of women my father was as adamant as on all else in life. I was still a boy when I discovered he kept a rawhide quirt on his bedroom wall, and I intuitively perceived how my mother came to bear the small dark scar on her wrist which she tried to conceal under lace-cuffed sleeves. I do not presume to judge my father on that point, though I have dwelt upon it.

Understand: I loved my mother. She was a lovely woman of grace, refinement, and generous spirit. Yet who but my father can know what she was like as a wife? Whatever he felt in their most intimate moments, whatever urges she inflamed in his soul, whatever image of her he carried in his heart—such were the things he surely had in mind when he warned me of the perils of passionate love. In my boyhood he encouraged me to indulge my young appetite for women as freely as I wished. His own casual indulgences had produced a scattering of blue-eyed mestizos among the peons of La Luna Plata. "Enjoy your lust," he advised me, "but beware of love. It is the most perilous of the passions."

A few days before my wedding, as we took brandy in his study, he advised me once again. He had arranged the marriage when Delgadina Fernández Ordóñez was but six years old. "She was an awkward, bony child," my father told me with a smile. "Legs as spindly and knobby as sugarcanes, eyes like a baby owl's. Your luck is pure gold, Sebastián. Who would have thought she'd bloom into a rose of Castile?"

It was indeed a matter of luck—a bartered bride's beauty, or her lack of it, is of no significance in these arrangements. My father's sole concern, of course—the only concern of any don seeking a bride for his son—was to secure some sort of economic or political gain for our family. My union with Delgadina would increase both the expanse of our land and the strength of our political influence in Hermosillo, the capital, where her father, Don Antonio, had powerful connections. "Your dowry," my father said proudly, "is the most admirable I've heard of since my own."

He paused to light a cigar and regarded me over the flame. "I am told," he said, "that she is spirited and quick of wit. Somewhat saucy. Occasionally even impertinent. Such qualities in any woman can be amusing, sometimes charming. It is natural to desire a beautiful woman, but if she also possesses charm and a proper wit, well, then love is certainly possible."

He stood at the window and stared for a long moment at the distant San Antonios. "But listen, my son," he said with sudden gravity. "Of all the misfortunes a man might meet in life, none is more terrible than to become subservient to a woman. That is a perversion of the natural order. Yet it can happen when a man loves a woman with more passion than he can control. Passion is like a powerful stallion champing at its bit. We must keep a tight rein or risk losing control of the beast. A man on a runaway horse, Sebastián, is both a dangerous fool and an object of ridicule, a thing of scorn in every man's eyes—and to all women. Such a man's own wife will look on him with contempt. If she is a worthy woman, she will curse the day fate married her to a weak, unworthy man."

He had leaned closer to me as he spoke and now was gripping my forearm hard. "Passion, Sebastián, is like fine brandy—a joy, a great pleasure to the man who knows how to drink. But it is an infernal cruse to the fool who gulps without restraint. This you *must* remember."

He was suddenly aware of his own intensity and stepped back, smiling awkwardly, and then busied himself refilling our cups. Without looking at me, he said, "Never give her reason to question even in her own mind who is master and who is maid."

I respected my father above all men, but I was not as guarded as he, as suspicious, as—let us speak bluntly—as *fearful* of the heart's strong passions. I had the arrogant confidence of youth. Unlike him, I was absolutely sure of my self-control, utterly confident that my love for Delgadina would never prove a weakness. Indeed, even as he counseled me in his study, he did not know that I was already in love with my bride-to-be. I had been since the first time I'd seen her, a little more than two years before, when she was yet fourteen and I five years older.

It was at my cousin Marco's wedding reception. I was in the main patio with another cousin, Roberto Luis, a handsome but salacious fellow who would be killed in a duel a year later in consequence of publicly insulting the daughter of a don. He asked if I knew that my betrothed was in attendance, and then laughed at my look of surprise. "Over there," he said, pointing to a group of girls standing in the shade of a willow at the far end of the patio, protected from male encroachment by a clutch of sharp-faced dueñas. "The sleek thing in the green dress. You lucky prick! A little skinny, maybe, but look at the melons on her!"

She was laughing with the others at some amusement, then turned in a sudden swirl of copper hair and caught me staring at her across the crowd. She smiled boldly and held my gaze—and I felt the breath sucked out of my heart. One of the crones spotted the look between us, and in the next instant the dueñas hastily herded them all into a side patio and out of sight.

We were formally introduced on the morning of her quinceañera—the ritual occasion of her fifteenth birthday, which marked her coming-of-age. I was appointed her escort for the day's festivities. She was even more beautiful than I recalled from my glimpse of her at Marco's wedding. She delighted in banter and laughed with ease, her eyes at once impish and full of warm promise. Our betrothal was made public two months later.

We were officially engaged for a year. A few weeks before the wedding, as we were walking in the garden one late summer afternoon (and trailed closely, of course, by the ubiquitous flock of chattering dueñas), she told me that even before Roberto Luis had shown me who she was, I had been pointed out to her. Had she not known I was the man she was promised to, she said, she would never have regarded me with such open audacity at Marco's wedding. "My God," she whispered in mock horror, "you must have thought me *wanton*!"

And so we were married. But although I loved her dearly—and rejoiced in the beauty of her flesh—I never abandoned myself to my passion for her, not fully, not even in the most ardent moments of our conjugal intimacies. Understand: I relished the affection she lavished upon me and the way she so much enjoyed receiving it in return. We were tenderly solicitous of each other—and avidly amorous mates. Indeed, the fervor of her lovemaking sometimes shocked me, even as it thrilled. Yet I always held a portion of my passion at a distance from my love for her, posting it like a marshal at a fiesta who is forbidden from enjoying himself but must keep a watchful eye on the proceedings and prevent things from getting out of hand. That restraint was the source of my confident self-possession. And as I was first and foremost Cabrillo don—and the next patrón of La Luna Plata—self-possession was imperative. Hardness was everything.

And she? She deferred to my wishes in all matters, of course—though not always without some feigned expression of rebellion: an exaggerated pout that presented her lower lip like a succulent wedge of fruit; a quick, saucy show of her tongue, followed instantly by the giggling smile she could never suppress; a sassy toss of her hair and an impudent sidewise look. Such gestures endeared her to me all the more. I kept no quirt on the bedroom wall.

Our first three children were girls. My father joked about it, but in his eyes I saw the same desperation that was gnawing at me. Then came Hernán—and the fiesta celebrating his birth roared for a week. We hoped for still more sons, but Delgadina inexplicably turned barren and our efforts over the next two years were fruitless. My disappointment was huge, but she gently impressed upon me that I should not permit greed to rule my soul.

"We have a beautiful and manly son, Sebastián," she

said, softly stroking my beard. "Are we not truly blessed?"

Each day brought me some new or deeper comprehension of her beauty, a beauty that transcended the exquisite configuration of her flesh, that went beyond the artistry of her eyes and breasts and hair. Her morning smile, her laughter, her regal serenity and sometimes mysterious gaze, her whispered endearments and touches in the night—everything about her brightened my soul like spring sunlight.

My father was now confined to a rolling chair, both legs ruined under a fallen horse. His hair and mustache had gone white and his hands were palsied, but his eyes were yet dark and hard and sharp. One afternoon, as we took a private glass of wine in the garden, he said, "The first time I saw you look at her, I knew you would never be able to lift your hand to her in reprimand, no matter how strongly she might provoke you. I feared for you. Now I see I had no cause to worry. She loves you dearly, and she seems determined never to give you cause to regret your benevolent nature toward her."

He raised his glass in a trembling hand. "I salute you, my son, you and your remarkably good fortune."

Had he lived two years more, he would have changed his opinion of my fortune. But within a few weeks of my mother's mortal collapse at the church altar one morning as she was receiving Communion, he caught a severe illness of the lungs after sitting outside in the patio during a rare rainstorm while I was away in Nogales on business. He had refused to be rolled under the shelter of the veranda while the cold rain and rough wind lashed him, and he cursed the servants for wanting to treat him like a piece of sugar candy to be guarded against a little rain. He was

bedridden the last nine days of his life. I was at his bedside the night he expelled his final breath, a rasping exhalation that sounded like . . . "hard."

A few weeks after his funeral, I faced the first public
test of my fitness as the new patrón of La Luna Plata.
Captain Reynaldo Ochoa and his local troop of rurales
brought before me a man charged with stealing horses
from one of my herds. I conducted the trial in the main
plaza of the hacienda, as my father always had, in the
shade of the hanging tree. It was a sultry morning smell-
ing of dust and hot stone, and the women in the crowd
were all fluttering fans against the heat.

As Ochoa presented the details of the case against the
man, I scanned the faces of the spectators. They were
watching me even more closely than they looked at the
accused, their eyes bright with eager curiosity. I knew
they were wondering if the customary character of Cabrillo justice—swift, fitting, and unsparing—would obtain
at La Luna Plata under the new, young patrón. Everyone
knows that sometimes the son is but a short shadow of
the father.

The rurales had intercepted the thief near the northern
boundary of the hacienda as he was heading toward the
border with eight horses bearing the brand of La Luna
Plata—probably, as Ochoa surmised, intent on selling
them to North American buyers. Throughout Ochoa's pre-
sentation of the charges and evidence against him, the
thief stood slouched over the hitching post he was tied
to, spitting idly and smiling like a man at an entertainment. He was precisely the sort of arrogant vermin my
father had hated above all other kinds. "They make it a
pleasure to pass sentence on them," he once told me. But
then had quickly added: "But never let your pleasure

show. No man is so feared—and therefore so respected—as he who dispenses punishment with no show of emotion."

I asked the defendant if he had anything to say on his own behalf. He leaned back against the post and shrugged with his palms turned up in a theatrical gesture of befuddlement. "Hey, patrón," he said, "I *found* those horses. Anybody could see they were lost horses. I'm a stranger here, so I didn't know whose brand they had. I thought I should take those lost horses to the next town and try to find the owner, maybe get a nice reward for returning them, you know? I was only trying to do a good thing, and these hardworking officials"—he gestured at the rurales—"they didn't understand." He looked at me and saw my smile. "Hey, patrón, do I *look* like a goddamn horse thief?"

In that moment, I had an inspired vision of his punishment. I condemned him to hang, naturally, but not from the tree in the plaza.

"Any man who steals from La Luna Plata must be properly punished," I said, speaking loudly enough to be heard by everyone present. "But punishment should serve a higher purpose than mere retribution. It should serve as moral instruction, as well." I smiled at the thief. "Through you, I will show many others in Sonora the consequences of stealing from me. Of course, you yourself will learn little from your punishment other than the difficulty of drawing a breath while hanging by the neck from a rope." There was a chorus of merry laughter from the spectators.

I decreed that the instrument of his execution would be a gallows erected on a stout flatbed wagon hitched to a strong team of mules. He would hang on that mobile gallows all the way from the hacienda to the border, fattening the crows as he went. In every village along the road from here to Nogales, people would see what happened to horse thieves on La Luna Plata. "At the border," I said, "my boys will cut down what's left of you and feed it to the eels in the Río Alisos."

The crowd was impressed. There was much nodding and murmuring of approval. The thief himself grinned broadly and shook his head slowly and muttered, "God *damn*."

On the following day, as soon as the wheeled gallows was ready, he was hanged. Then an escort of a half-dozen men took him away, the corpse jouncing and swaying at the end of the rope with every jolt of the wagon.

Ten days later a mail rider from the north arrived with the news that the six men I'd sent with the gallows were all dead. They had been attacked by a gang of bandits a few miles north of Laguna Seca. According to what the mail rider had heard in a local cantina, their bodies had been stripped and left in the desert, but the hanged man's corpse was gone. The name of Juan Rojas was mentioned repeatedly in the cantina talk, and it was generally supposed that the hanged man had been a member of his bandit gang, although no one could say why they had bothered to take away the body. The Rojas Gang were not known to care about the niceties of proper burials, not even for one of their own men.

"*Rojas!*" my chief foreman said. "That son of a bitch is harder to kill than a cockroach." A year earlier it had been rumored that Texas Rangers had killed Juan Rojas near El Paso, but then Rojas and his boys raided a ranch in eastern Sonora and made off with a herd of cattle. A few months later it was said that Rojas had been hanged in Fronteras, but once again the report of his death was proved wrong when he robbed a mining company of its payroll near Santa Teresa.

I sent a detail to retrieve the bodies from Laguna Seca and ordered a requiem service for them all. As for Rojas, my boys made inquiries everywhere, but no one had seen a sign of him, and after a few weeks we had to assume he was no longer in Sonora.

So then. Time passed and life was good. Delgadina's attentions to me were distracted only once—by the death of her father, Don Antonio. He retired to his bedroom early one evening, complaining that he did not feel well, and in the morning he was as cold and stiff as the brass bedposts. He had sired three sons and three daughters, but the first two boys died in infancy, as did one of the girls, and at age fifteen the surviving son was taken by the black fever. Then Delgadina's remaining sister, her elder, rejected the marriage Don Antonio had arranged for her and instead eloped with a man he regarded as beneath her station. Don Antonio never spoke her name again. He bequeathed all his property to Delgadina (and thereby to La Luna Plata), with the exception of a tiny hundred-acre parcel called La Querencia, which he left to his wife. She had him buried there, behind the house overlooking the Río Magdalena.

Delgadina had loved her father dearly, and for several weeks after his death she dressed in black and went about the house in silent red-eyed grief. She spent hours in the church every day, lighting candles and praying for his soul's salvation. Then at last she dried her eyes and put away the mourning dress and came to me in the night, her hair loose and gleaming redly in the moonlight, her nipples hard as stones, her tongue greedy in my mouth, on my flesh. She gasped at my touches and panted hotly with her brute pleasure. She sighed in enveloping contentment. In the morning she awoke smiling. "You are my *life*," she whispered in my ear. And though I did not say it, she was mine.

For eight unsurpassable years I was married to Delgadina Consuelo Fernández de Cabrillo, and, as with superior wine and high art, our union improved with age. But *now* . . . now I pace from the barred window to the bolted door and back again, going to and fro in my cell and walking up and down in it, damned to the memory of all that followed. . . .

A few days before his fourth birthday, little Hernán drowned in the river. What do the details matter now? What did they matter one instant after he was dead? Of course I demanded details *then*. He had been playing with some other children near the trees and well away from the riverbank. Then he went out of sight for a moment while his nanny chatted with her friends, and then someone was crying out that a child was in the water and swirling downstream. Horsemen sped downriver with ropes. And then they had him and pulled him out of the river and he was dead.

Those were the details his young nanny was able to tell us through her stuttering, choking sobs before my fist shattered the side of her face. My boot stove her ribs. Then Delgadina was atop her, shielding her, saving the bitch's worthless life.

I rode into the desert and galloped in great circles, shrieking at the mountains, howling at the moon. I rode the roan stallion to death. The next day a search rider found me walking over the cracked earth. I yanked him out of the saddle and rode back to the hacienda, then locked myself in the candlelit room with the boy in his open coffin. The windows were hung with black drapes, and a chill draft shook the candle flames so that the shadows wriggled like snakes on the walls. I howled curses at God till the candles burned out, till my voice broke to a rasp and finally gave out completely, till the finality of my son's death filled the room with its stench.

When I at last opened the door, she stood there, waiting to embrace me. The agony in her eyes stunned me with the realization that mine was not the only sorrow keening under our roof. Her quiet grief helped to placate somewhat the fury of my own, but although she pleaded with me over the following months to make apology to God for having cursed Him, I would not do it, not even in the face of her argument that if I asked His forgiveness He might yet permit her to conceive another son.

"*Damn Him!*" I thundered. If hope for another son depended on deference to a God who would so blithely take from me my only man-child, then I spat on all hope. Hardness! Hardness was all!

No. I lie. I am a damnable liar and I confess it. Hardness was not all. Delgadina's love had become no less vital to me, no less a shield against life's brute possibilities, than my own hard will—though I could never have admitted it, not then, not even to myself, for fear of admitting weakness. But in a life full of uncertainties—even the uncertainty of preceding your son to the grave—her love for me was as certain and abiding as the sierras, and I wore it like an iron skin against the world.

And then, early in winter, Delgadina conceived. When she told me, I refused to believe it. If she proved wrong, I was afraid the disappointment would make me insane. I simply nodded and said, "We will see if it's so."

Her smile was as softly radiant as a sunrise. "It's so, Sebastián," she said, placing her fingers against my lips. "It's so."

I waited two months more before believing that it *was* so, and then my exultation soared. We would name him Alvaro, in honor of my father. Four months later her belly was beautifully rounding and she was lovelier than ever.

As in the past, her mother had planned to come to La Luna Plata to assist with the birth, but then the old woman's health took a bad turn and she was unable to travel. Delgadina asked my permission to go to her mother's house at La Querencia to have the baby.

"Mamá has been so alone there," she said. "The memory of a grandchild's birth under her roof will comfort her for the rest of her days."

She knew I had spring brandings to oversee and dozens of stock buyers to receive in the coming weeks, but she assured me she felt strong and quite able to make the rugged three-day journey to La Querencia without me. I was loath to grant permission. The road to La Querencia traversed a portion of the most desolate region of La Luna Plata, and there was but a single rude waystation on the route.

"For goodness' sake, Sebastián!" she chided me. "Mamá has made the trip a half-dozen times, accompanied only by the driver and an old man with a rusty gun who sleeps on the coach roof most of the way. Am I less able than my mother? With attendants at my side and your pistoleros all around the coach?"

She gave me that look of hers—sidewise, half-smiling. "Do you think," she said in a stage whisper, widening her eyes in mock fright, "the *Yaquis* might get me?"

No one had seen a Yaqui Indian on La Luna Plata in

years, not since the rurales had tracked down the last of the renegades. A few had escaped into the mountains and would hide there forever; the rest had been killed or sent to the henequen plantations in the Yucatán. But mothers still threatened wayward children with the warning, "If you don't behave, the Yaquis will get you."

The truth of the matter was that I did not want her to go because I knew I would miss her terribly. But it was the foolish sentiment of a lovesick boy, and I would have felt worse than foolish to speak it. My father's old warning rang in my head like a bell. Against such sentimental impulses of the heart, he would have admonished me to stand hard.

And so I gave consent. And on an early pink morning in May, I stood in the main courtyard and returned her farewell waves as her coach—escorted by six armed horsemen—rolled out the front gate. I smiled and smiled, but I already missed her so much my chest felt as empty as an open grave.

We exchanged several letters a week through relays of dispatch riders. She reported that all was well at La Querencia. She felt strong and her mother and the midwives were taking good care of her. She wrote of the stark beauty of La Luna Plata's western reaches—of the blazing whiteness of its vista and the dazzling blue depths of its desert sky. She wrote of the brilliant flowers and tall green willows along the Río Magdalena, all the lovelier for their contrast with the rough, surrounding landscape of pale rock and sand. I had seen it all myself since childhood, of course, but never before so clearly as through her wondering eyes.

"But sometimes the wind blows hot and hard," she wrote, "and affects the spirit strangely. At such times I miss you so terribly my heart hurts." In her final letter she wrote: "It's a son, my love, I know it is. He has spoken to me in the night, when we comfort one another with our thoughts of you."

One morning the mail rider didn't show up. I sent men to search for him, thinking his mount might have quit him somewhere in the wild country. By the following afternoon, none of them had returned. I kept watch on the western horizon from an upper window of the house, but I was tired after a sleepless night and dozed off in my chair.

When I opened my eyes it was almost dusk, and a horseman—one of the searchers I'd sent—was at the courtyard gate, speaking in obvious agitation to the hacienda foreman and several guards. I bolted downstairs, but when he saw me running toward him, he reined his mount around and gave it the spurs. I raced across the courtyard, yelling, "Stop him!" The guards worked the levers of their carbines but seemed uncertain of what to do, and the foreman shook his head at them and gestured for them to lower their weapons.

I was breathless with fury as I reached the gate. "Damn you!" I shouted at them. I pointed at the fleeing rider and ordered, "Shoot that horse! Shoot it!"

The guards again raised their rifles, but the foreman again made a gesture against my order. "There is no need, Don Sebastián," he said.

I grabbed him by the shirtfront and raised my fist to strike him—but the look on his face stayed my hand. His eyes were full of terrible news. "He feared you would punish him," the foreman said. "For being the one to tell you what has happened at La Querencia."

And so he told me.

We set out at a gallop under a thin yellow moon and rode straight through the night and all the next day, and through the night after that, using up one horse after another from the string of reserve mounts we trailed behind us. We paused but once, to refill our canteens at the way-station. Those who slept did so in the saddle.

On the second sunrise we caught sight of a thin plume of smoke in the distance, and I howled once and dug in my spurs. An hour later we arrived at the blackened ruins of La Querencia.

A small band of rurales was grouped around a camp-fire. On a low rise behind them lay a line of bodies covered with blankets. Captain Reynaldo Ochoa nodded to me as I dismounted, then led the way to the arrayed dead, his big spurs chinking. He said he had not yet buried the corpses because he knew I would want to see them for myself. I quickly went down the line, snatching away blankets and raising hordes of flies. Most of them were servants and their children. The six guards I'd sent with her were among them. And her maids. And her mother. But she was not.

"They took her," Ochoa said. He was rolling a cigarette, affecting casualness but watching me warily. "Her and some of the other young women."

I took a step toward him and my face must have been something to see—he dropped the cigarette and put his hand to his saber hilt and took a step back. "Juan Rojas, Don Sebastián," he said. "It was him and his boys. The stable boy got away and rode to our post at Tres Palmas. We got here as fast as we could, but . . ." He gestured vaguely toward the bodies.

I tasted blood and realized I was biting my tongue to keep from howling. I forced myself to breathe deeply, to think clearly. My head was filled with images of Delgadina—of my little son curled inside of her. I spat blood and asked how he knew it was Rojas.

"Because one of them told us," he said, smiling for the first time. "Your boys did all right before they went down. They killed seven of the pricks and shot two others so bad they got left behind." He pointed to a flock of buzzards alighting behind a rocky rise. "I had the dead ones thrown in the arroyo back there," he said. "Let the scavengers have them. My boys don't dig graves for killers of children."

"Where are they?" I said. "The ones wounded—*where*?"

One was a survivor no more, he said. A couple of the rurales recognized him as a wanted violator of young girls in southern Sonora and couldn't be restrained from dealing with him on the spot. He was now with his friends in the arroyo. The other bandit said he knew the rurales were going to kill him, too, so why tell them anything. "He wanted to die like a tough guy—you know, with his mouth shut," Ochoa said. "My half-breed Apache persuaded him to change his mind. He's a very good persuader. In fifteen minutes he had the fellow jabbering like a parrot. The only reason the whoreson is still alive is I knew you'd want to talk to him."

"*Where?*" I said.

I followed him back toward the group of men at the fire, feeling the blood pounding in my temples. The prisoner was sitting with his hands tied behind him, propped against a cactus stump and staring dully into the fire. He had a tourniquet around a badly wounded leg. His other foot was a bootless, black-and-red chunk of charred meat.

Ochoa kicked his wounded leg and said, "Hey, prick, the patrón wants to talk to you."

His face remained empty of all expression as he answered my questions. Yes, it had been Rojas. No, they hadn't planned it, they didn't even know this place was out here. They'd come across it simply by chance. Yes, they'd taken some of the women. Rojas thought they might be worth ransom, or be valuable as hostages if the rurales should catch up to them—both possibilities depending on who their fathers or husbands might be.

In response to my next question, he grinned and said, "*Molested?*" as if he found the word amusing. "Damn right they'll be *molested*. Rojas himself will *molest* each one till her nose bleeds!"

I kicked him in the mouth so hard I was afraid I'd broken his neck. Ochoa tugged on his ears to revive him and pulled him back to a sitting position. Speaking in a thickened voice through raw bloated lips, he said yes, they'd headed west, toward the sea, but whether they would turn north or south he didn't know. He thought maybe there were ten or eleven of them left, he wasn't sure. He was sure they had taken four women.

When I was satisfied the prisoner had given me all the information he could, I told Ochoa to see that he was given his fill of water and that his tourniquet was sufficiently tight. I did not want him to pass out from thirst or bleed to death. I wanted him taken to the arroyo and staked down naked among the dead.

Ochoa glanced toward the buzzards and vultures flapping heavily into the arroyo and gave a small snort of unmistakable disdain—as if he found my mode of punishment too elaborate, too much an excess of the rich. The rurales preferred to shoot a man and be done with it.

Impudent mestizo bastard! His barbarous Indian ancestors cut the beating hearts out of sacrificial victims—women as well as men—and then ate their flesh. *He* would take exception to my means of executing this filthy vermin who'd ridden with the kidnapper of my wife? I dared him with my eyes to speak his objection, but he only shrugged and turned to relay my order to his men.

We set out to the west shortly before sunset, following the route taken by the rurales Ochoa had dispatched in pursuit of Rojas before my arrival. His orders to them had been to split up if they reached the coast without having spotted him. One bunch would go north to the village of San Andrés, the other head downcountry to Puerto Lobos. Rojas would have to go to one place or the other. There was nothing else in any direction but desert or the Sea of Cortez.

At dawn we arrived at a rocky escarpment within sight of the sea and stopped to rest the horses. "Here's where my boys split up," Ochoa said. "Which direction do you want, Don Sebastián?" I went south with six rurales and he went north with the other five.

There are no words to describe what I was feeling as we rode. Every phrase I fashion has the sodden impact of banality. Every description I attempt sounds like cliché from some foolish romance. Nothing, *nothing* ever said by anyone anywhere can convey what I was feeling. *Christ,* what pathetic things words are! Their insufficiency is as smothering as a lack of air. The congestion of wrath and anguish throbbing in my veins could never be expressed by words. It could only be felt. It could only be dealt with.

Late that afternoon, we met a half-dozen of Ochoa's advance rurales on their way back from Puerto Lobos. No one had seen riders anywhere in the vicinity. Rojas had to have gone north, to San Andrés. The advance rurales led a string of fresh mounts, having expected to meet some of their comrades coming from La Querencia to assist them. We switched our saddles to the extra horses and galloped off to the north.

As we rode hard to catch up to him, Ochoa met with the other rurales he'd sent ahead. They'd been waiting for him a mile south of San Andrés. Scouts had confirmed that Rojas and his men were in the village and unaware of the rurales' nearness. Ochoa didn't want to lose the advantage of surprise, so he didn't wait for the rest of us to get there before he attacked. But even though the bandits were caught off guard, they put up a fierce fight, killing two rurales and wounding several more. Ochoa's boys killed six and took two prisoners. The only one to escape was Rojas himself, who had abandoned his men in the middle of the fight and ridden away into the open desert.

All this I learned from Ochoa when we reached San Andrés, after he answered my first breathless question, after I learned Delgadina was dead.

She had been found tied to a bed in the small back room of a cantina. "Mistreated" was the word Ochoa used. She'd been mistreated but was still alive when he found her. From the look of things she had miscarried only shortly before.

"I told her you were on your way to her," he said. "And she heard me, Don Sebastián. She smiled. She tried to hold on, to wait for you, but she could not." He had ordered some women to remove her to another room and clean her before I arrived. He took me there.

When I saw her, I felt my soul leave me like something on wings. I put my fingers on her face, but it was like trying to touch a star, like trying to dry your eyes at the bottom of the sea. I insisted on seeing the room where she'd been found, and there I saw the bloody mattress, the thick red stain that had been my son.

I wanted the two captured bandits burned alive, but Ochoa said it was too late, they had been shot while trying to escape. I whirled on him in a rage, but he held his ground and said, "*They* did not steal her, Don Sebastián. *They* did not touch her. That I know. For them a bullet was proper and just."

"*Damn* you!" I shouted. "You dare to tell me what is proper—what is *just*?"

His eyes flashed with anger but he quickly got them under control. "I already sent some of my boys after him," he said. "We'll get the bastard, Don Sebastián. Sooner or later. You'll see."

I was trembling with the urge to strike him, but I was afraid that if I hit him even once I would not stop until I'd killed him. At that moment I was afraid even to curse him: I feared that if I opened my mouth I would start howling and never stop.

I took Delgadina back to La Luna Plata and buried her in the sprawling flower garden behind the main house. I dug the grave myself. I called for a priest to pray over her only because she would have wanted it, but when he tried to commiserate with me afterward, I told him to go to hell.

And then I waited. I could do nothing else. Ochoa had his rurales roaming everywhere in search of Juan Rojas, and he had sworn that when they caught him they would deliver him to me. But I lived with an unremitting fear that Rojas might die before they could catch him. He might even choose death to being taken alive. If he resisted arrest, Ochoa's boys would surely shoot him. Or he might get killed in a drunken brawl in some cantina or whorehouse. He could be thrown from his horse and break his neck. A jealous woman might stab him in his sleep. He might be captured by the army and stood against a wall, or caught by Texas Rangers and hanged from the nearest tree. He could be bitten by a Gila monster or a rattlesnake. He could drown while trying to ford a river, or be swallowed by quicksand. He could get a sickness and die in bed. There were so many ways he might die before I could get my hands on him—and some of them such that I would never even know he was dead—that I chewed my lips bloody resisting the urge to howl. My fists rarely unclenched. I spent hours every day pacing from one top-floor window to another, my throat so tight it felt snared in a noose.

Two weeks passed, and then four, and I thought of nothing but Juan Rojas and the vengeance I would wreak on him for having trespassed so grievously against me. When I was not pacing I was working in the cellar, making special preparations for him. He had robbed me of Delgadina and my unborn son—of my life, if not my breath—and the sole purpose of my continued existence was to make him suffer for his sin. For the first time since boyhood I prayed. I apologized to God for all the blasphemies of my life. I beseeched Him for a single concession and promised I would never ask another: I pleaded with Him to deliver Juan Rojas to me alive. I prayed and prepared for him and I paced, my jaws clenched against the ceaseless urge to howl. And I waited.

Late one afternoon, nearly two months after Delgadina's death, one of my vaqueros came back from a visit to the whorehouse in San Lorenzo with the news that Juan Rojas was in jail at the rurales' outpost in Tres Palmas.

All the whores had been talking about it, he said. They'd heard the story of the arrest from a rurales sergeant the night before, one of Ochoa's men. The sergeant said the rurales had been tipped off by a barkeeper from Sahuaro who'd been sentenced to thirty days in jail for watering his tequila. The barkeep had been in the jail only a week when he heard that his wife had run away to Sonoita with a friend of his, and he was enraged. For more than a month he had been permitting this friend, who was in trouble with the law, to hide in the back room of his cantina, and this was how the friend repaid his kindness—by stealing his wife. On learning of this treachery done to him, the barkeeper in turn betrayed the friend to the rurales. The friend was of course Juan Rojas.

The rurales had gone to Sonoita and entered the pueblo after nightfall. They searched stealthily from place to place, carbines ready, and found him in a cantina, singing to himself with his head on the bar. Although Ochoa had repeatedly assured me that when his boys found him they would do everything possible to capture him alive, I knew the rurales never took chances with their quarry. If he'd made the least show of resistance, they would have shot him a hundred times. The sergeant told the whores he himself eased up behind Rojas and clubbed him in the back of the head with his carbine. He hit him so hard that Rojas didn't wake up until Sonoita was thirty miles behind them. Chained hand and foot, he made the journey to Tres Palmas in a goat cart. He had now been in jail, my man said, for nearly a week.

It was after midnight when I arrived in Tres Palmas, my horse blowing hard and dripping lather. I had insisted on coming alone, had shouted down my importunate foreman's pleas to take an escort with me. I had been wild with exultation and, I admit, not thinking clearly. I had bellowed some half-witted foolishness about the moment being *mine,* and I would share it with no one. I told the foreman I would kill any man who tried to follow me. But the hard ride through the cold desert night had cleared my mind sufficiently to regret not bringing an escort. It had finally occurred to me that Ochoa had violated his pledge to bring Rojas to me—and, for whatever reason, might yet be disinclined to hand him over.

Tres Palmas was little more than a scattering of adobe buildings on either side of a sandy windblown street blazing whitely under a full moon. I tethered the foundered horse in front of the jail and slipped my carbine from its scabbard, worked a round into the chamber, and went inside.

The windowless room was dimly lighted, the air thick with cigarette smoke and fumes from the lanterns on the walls. Ochoa and a couple of his boys were sitting at a table, playing cards and sharing a bottle of tequila. Nobody seemed surprised to see me—or very pleased. Directly behind them, the door of the only cell was shut, but I could make out the indistinct form of someone standing close to the bars. I held the rifle loosely at my hip, the muzzle jutting vaguely in the table's direction.

Ochoa looked tired and sad. He returned his attention to the cards he was holding, then threw down the hand in disgust. His eyes were bloodshot. "What, Don Sebastián?" he said. "What *is* it?"

I'd never before seen Ochoa drunk, but I was not surprised by the sullen arrogance the tequila effected in him. Strong drink so easily agitates these primitives and sets loose the mob of resentments always lurking in their dark hearts. But I was feeling no more inclined than he toward the social amenities—and in any case I was not the least interested in his damned resentments, whatever they were. I shifted my stance slightly so that the rifle pointed his way less ambiguously. He flicked his eyes at the weapon and sneered.

"You were to bring him to me," I said.

"Ah," he said. He glanced toward the cell. "*Him*. Yes, well, I would have, you see, but I have a duty. A duty to justice."

One of the others laughed, a sergeant, and Ochoa grinned at him and took a drink. The bottle was nearly empty.

"Listen, God damn you—"

"No, Don Sebastián," he said. "You listen. I telegraphed my report of his arrest to headquarters in Hermosillo, and they told me a magistrate will be passing through in a few days. He'll give him a trial and then we'll hang him, all legal and proper. If it will make you happy, we'll use your rope. If it will make you happier, you can have his carcass. You can have him butchered and dine on him every night until there's nothing left but the bones. Hell, you can make soup from the bones till you've had the last miserable drop of him." His two men were grinning whitely, much entertained.

"Damn your lowborn insolence," I said. "I want him *now*."

Ochoa's smile vanished and he spat on the floor. "You *people*!" he said. "I want, I want! You hacendados want *everything*! God damn it, do you think you're the only ones who *want*? You think *you're* the only one who ever got fucked? You think you're the only one who ever wanted to get even?"

The impudent whoreson! Daring to speak to me in that manner! Daring to *refuse* me! Rojas was right *there*, not a dozen feet from me, and this ignorant peon had the audacity to deny him to me. I'd had enough. I brought the rifle up, aimed it squarely in his face and thumbed back the hammer with a loud double click.

"Even a Cabrillo don," he said, looking as if he were about to smile again, "knows what happens if he shoots a rurales captain."

"Yes," I said. "The rurales captain dies."

My hands and voice were steady. The quivering was all in my heart—because I was certain I would have to shoot him, and then, of course, his underlings would all immediately shoot me. They would kill me while Rojas watched from his cell. And thus, from this tiny distance, he would escape me after all. The injustice of it filled me with a raging sadness.

For a moment no one moved, and then Ochoa sighed heavily and threw up his hands in resignation. "To hell with it," he said, and stood up. "You or the hangman, what's the difference? Why the hell should *I* care?" From a peg on the wall he took a large metal key ring with a single key on it and unlocked the cell door and swung it open.

"Out," he said.

Juan Rojas stepped into the light. He was smaller than I had imagined, both short and slight, but he looked to have strength, and his eyes were as bright and quick as a hawk's. With black hair hung to his shoulders and a red bandanna headband to hold it out of his eyes, he looked like an Indian. A Yaqui.

Ochoa ordered him to turn around, then bound his hands behind him with a length of rawhide cord. I lowered the rifle to my hip but kept it pointed at Ochoa, then told the sergeant to fetch two fresh horses, saddled and equipped with full canteens. The sergeant looked at Ochoa and Ochoa nodded.

While we waited, Rojas stared at me inquisitively but without fear. *You'll soon find out,* I thought, looking at him. If he read the hatred in my eyes, he gave no sign of it. Ochoa sat at the table, sipping at the last of the bottle and softly singing a love song.

And then the sergeant was calling from the street. I peeked out the door to see a pair of horses in front of the jail—and a dozen rurales spread out across the street, all of them with carbines.

Ochoa laughed and said, "Did you think he would bring a brass band and girls with flowers to see you on your way?"

I jabbed the rifle muzzle under Rojas' chin and glared at Ochoa. "I'll settle here if I have to," I said. But my heart howled at the possibility that I might be forced to kill him so quickly, with so little pain.

"Jesus, man," Ochoa said. "I hope it never gets me as bad as it's got you."

He went to the door and ordered his men to rest easy. Then we all walked out and Ochoa told a couple of his boys to help Rojas get on a horse. I mounted up and took Rojas' reins too, still expecting Ochoa at any moment to give his men the order to shoot me. But he merely stood with his thumbs hooked on his gunbelt and watched as I led Rojas' mount away at a canter.

A few hours later the sun blazed up out of the distant mountains and layered the rocky landscape with a hard gold light. We rode in silence through the long shadows of the saguaros. Those early hours of the ride back toward La Luna Plata with Rojas in my custody—to do with *as I wished*!—were glorious. Never in my life had I desired anything so greatly as to have this man in my power. I had desired it with all my soul, dreamed of it, even prayed for it. And now, there we were, the two of us, deep in the desert and on our way to the things I had in store for him. Sweet Mary, my joy throbbed!

The sun was high above the mountains when I realized I was laughing out loud. I had no idea how long I'd been doing it. I looked behind me at Rojas and my good humor vanished instantly. The bastard was smiling.

I jerked the lead rope and his horse lunged up alongside mine. Rojas sat easily in the saddle even with his hands tied behind him.

"You think something's funny, you son of a whore?" They were the first words I'd spoken to him.

He shrugged. "A man in the desert, laughing at nothing—that's funny, no?"

I shuddered with the urge to shoot him in his grinning teeth. "Let me tell you some things," I said. "Let's see how funny you think they are."

I talked steadily as our horses paced side by side and the sun climbed higher in the copper sky. I told him—in the most precise and intimate detail—the plan I had for him once we reached the main house. I told him about the little dungeon I'd fashioned in the windowless cellar and the playthings I'd collected there. I spoke to him of scorpions and fire ants and fierce yellow wasps, of venomous spiders whose bite would make a man sick for days. I had jarfuls of all of these things in that dark cellar with the thick stone walls. There were ropes and wires, steel hooks dangling from the ceiling. There were skinning razors and sharp iron spikes, fine long cactus spines and shards of broken glass. There would be buckets of boiling water, pots of caustic lyes. For his thirst, there would be tankards of goat piss. The furnace would burn day and night, and in it were the branding irons.

The more I spoke of it, the faster my breath came. He listened as raptly as a child hearing a fantastic tale. And then he suddenly laughed. "Jesus Christ, man! How many guys do you think I am? You want to do all *that*, you're going to need more guys to do it to, because I don't think I can make it past the first few things you got in mind. What's got you so damned mad, anyway? All this crazy shit—spiders and *goat piss*! *Jesus*! What the hell did I ever do to *you*?"

He couldn't have stunned me more if he'd spit in my face. I could see that he meant it—he did not know who I was, other than somebody of the hundreds who for one reason or another wanted him dead.

It was outrageous.

I drew my pistol and lashed him hard across the face, knocking him off his horse. I slid from the saddle and grabbed him by the hair and pressed the muzzle hard against his eye. I told him who I was in yells, bellowed my complaint into his face. I hit him with the gun again and let him fall into the dust.

With his hands fast behind him, it was a struggle for him to sit up, but he made it. Blood streamed from his nose and fell in bright drops on his dirty white shirt.

"Cabrillo," he said, and ran his tongue over his torn lips as though he was tasting the name. Then he smiled all the way up to his eyes. "*Cabrillo!* Goddamn, man, I know you!" He spat a red streak and laughed.

"A rolling gallows! What kind of crazy bastard thinks up something like that? Man, you know how tight that noose got from him bouncing up and down on that rope? It pinched his neck to no bigger around than my dick. It stretched his neck a foot! Another few miles and his head would've come off—what was left of it. The crows had worked it over pretty good. Ate up his eyes, his lips—"

He choked on blood, coughed and spat red. He grinned at me with his shattered red teeth. He must have seen my confusion in my eyes. "A couple of your boys spoke your name when they were begging me to spare them. They were only following your orders, they said. They were only escorting the gallows to Nogales as you commanded. But I shot them anyway—for being such scared little girls and for not keeping the birds off my brother's face."

I wasn't sure I'd heard him right—or even what I was thinking.

"You goddamn hacendados," Rojas said. "You live in forts. You got an army of guys to protect you. You got the goddamn rurales. How's a guy like me supposed to get even with a guy like you?" He paused to spit again. His grin now turned sly and his eyes blazed like little coalfires. "But you say that little hacienda on the Río Magdalena belonged to you? The beautiful red-haired woman with the mother-belly was *your* woman?" He cackled like a delighted child.

I felt as though I'd been clubbed in the spine. For an instant the white sky whirled. The remote sierras shimmered in the rising heat. His laughter chewed at my ears.

"Believe me, señor," he gasped, choking on blood and laughter, "*please* believe me—I had no idea she was *your* woman."

"You'll pay for it forever!" I yelled. "I'll listen to your screams like music!" My words sounded hollow in my own ears.

"Hell, man, I *never* would have known," he said through his laughter, "if *you* hadn't told me."

"I'll give you pain so great, you'll beg, you'll *beg* me for death!"

He laughed with bloody spit running down his chin. "Thank you, señor," he said. "Thank you a thousand times for letting me know I avenged my little brother after all. Thank you!"

"I'll give you *agony*!" I shouted. I grabbed up handfuls of dust and flung them wildly. I whirled and kicked at the stones around me as though they were hateful things. "AGONY!" I screamed. "Every day! Every night!"

But he was talking right through my raging promises. ". . . skin like milk! And those tits, my God! Like cream candy with little cherry tips. But best of all was her cunt. Soft as—"

I screamed and threw myself on him, clubbing him with the gun. His head fell back and his eyes rolled up in their sockets. I straddled him and shook him by the shirt collar, shrieking, "You'll beg me to kill you and end your pain, you will!" I was weeping now, crying like a child. "Every day you'll plead for your death, you'll *pray* to me for your death! And sometimes I'll say yes, and you'll want to kiss me, you'll call me Jesus Christ, you'll ask God to bless me for eternity for so kindly killing you. But then, you worthless bastard son of an Indian whore . . . I WON'T DO IT!"

He coughed and choked and started coming around, and I raised the pistol to hit him again—and then suddenly realized what I was doing. I jumped up and backed away from him as if he were on fire. I was horrified. In my rage I had been about to destroy the only thing I had left to live for.

He wormed his way a few feet over to a small rock outcrop, panting and grunting with his efforts, and worked his way into a sitting position with his back against the rock. His broken face was caked with blood and dirt.

I hastily holstered my pistol and folded my arms tightly across my chest. Hardness, I told myself, hardness! Maintain command! Steel yourself against the bastard's taunts. The first thing I would do when we got to La Luna Plata would be to cut out his tongue.

"Oh please let my baby son live."

He said it in a high mimicking voice and laughed at the look on my face. "That's what she said to me, you hangman. I stripped her to her earrings and she said, 'Oh *please* let my baby son live.' " He spat blood at me. "Well, listen to this: I put it to her like one of your goddamn branding irons! She was *begging* me to—"

I shot him and shot him and shot him—howling even as I emptied the pistol into his grinning trickster's face, howling with the horrifying realization of what I was doing, howling as the gunshots faded into the foothills . . .

As, here in this house of howling men, I have been howling ever since.

THREE TALES OF THE REVOLUTION

THE SOLDADERA

In 1913 my grandaunt Adela ran away with a boy intent
on joining Pancho Villa's Army of the North. She was
sixteen. The Revolution promised freedom from tyrants
such as Díaz and Huerta—from her own father, the cavalry colonel who venerated them both. The family was
landed, rich, its blue veins but slightly darkened with the

Indio blood it long denied. Only Adela's youngest brother did not disown her. We still have the faded photograph he framed, clipped from a Chihuahua newspaper, showing Villa and Carranza standing side by side and squinting in dusty sunlight and mutual distrust—and there, directly behind them, her arms around the necks of fierce-faced compañeros, her breasts crossed with bandoleers, is Tía Adela. The boy she ran away with is not in the picture. Years later he showed up at my grandfather's door on a crutch, one pant leg folded and pinned to a back pocket. He told tales of Adelita: how she rode on the packed roofs of boxcars jammed with horses and artillery; how she shot more federales in the battle of Zacatecas than anyone else in the brigade; how she danced around a campfire with Fierro the butcher and took a kiss on the mouth from Villa himself. How, at the horror of Celaya, she got caught on Obregón's barbed wire and was shot to pieces by the machine guns.

THE COLONEL

From the veranda of the hillside mansion serving as our headquarters, I watched the firing squad do its work in the plaza below. The wailing of widows and wounded men carried up to mingle with the furious piano music from the ballroom behind me. In the plaza a federal captain stood against the church wall and made a hasty sign of the cross just before the rifle volley shook him and he fell dead on the cobblestones. As a labor detail dragged him away, the next man in the line of condemned stepped up to the wall: a hatless whitehaired colonel who stood at attention. The captain in charge of the executions raised his saber and gave the commands: "Ready! . . . Aim! . . . Fire!" The rifles thundered and the colonel rebounded off the wall and dropped to the ground. And then slowly, awkwardly, as the spectators gasped and began to raise a great jabbering, he got to his feet and slumped against the wall.

The riflemen looked at the captain. The captain stared at the colonel—and then thrust his saber up and yelled, "Ready!" I had never seen one get back on his feet before. "Aim!" The old man pushed off the wall and stood weaving, trying to square his shoulders. "Fire!" He bounced off the wall and fell in a heap. Then pushed up on his elbows. Then made it to his hands and knees. The crowd hushed utterly. People blessed themselves and knelt in the street. I thought, holy shit.

The captain spotted me and yelled, "What *now*, my general?" With twelve bullets in him the old man sat on his heels with his shoulder against the wall. He brushed vaguely at the blood soaking his tunic.

"Once more!" I ordered. "If he's still breathing after the next one, we'll give him a clean uniform and command of a regiment."

The colonel was on one knee and still trying to rise when the next volley hit him. I rued not having spoken to him before he died.

THE TRIUMPH

We looted the city to its bones. Whatever we didn't want or couldn't take we destroyed. Every grievance we had against the bluebloods, the Spanish, the Church, the bosses, against our own fathers, against *life*, we redressed against Zacatecas. The streets ran with blood. We shot military prisoners standing against the wall, priests kneeling at the altars, rich bastards groveling on the floors of their fine big houses. We packed the mineshafts with corpses, piled and burned them in the streets. A little boy watching the flames constricting the tendons of the blackening dead cried, "Look, mamá! They're dancing!" We rode horses into the mansion salons, grinding horseshit into parquetry, shredding Middle Eastern carpets to rags. Into roaring fireplaces we threw books, ledgers, letters, photographs. Not a sculpture in town went unbroken, not a windowpane stayed intact. Our soldaderas paraded the streets in silk dresses, in bridal gowns of delicate lace trailing in the dust. Their feet scuffed the cobbles in satin slippers. We picked the churches clean of their gold and silver. We stripped houses, stores, stables of everything that could be carried away. Toward our trains flowed a steady stream of stock and wagons loaded with strong-boxes, stoves, furniture, clothes, gilt picture frames and chandeliers. Every automobile in town that still ran was driven onto the flatcars. The mules walked stiff-legged under loads of booty. The wagons creaked with the weight of it. The trains groaned. It was our greatest victory in the war against the oppressions of the rich. As we pulled out of Zacatecas the air was heavy with the odors of smoldering ashes, blood-dampened dust, enemy flesh going to rot. All the powerful smells of triumph.

UNDER THE SIERRA

The mountains were blazing under a high sun when the first tremor passed through the cornfield. It rolled lightly over the low hill flanking the cemetery and rippled into the village of Sombra de Dios. It shook dust from the walls and roofs and rattled crockery and tins. All singing, all laughter, all gossip ceased. The animals fell silent in their pens. The only sound was of Paco Cantu's one-eyed white dog, whining and turning in tight circles in the middle of the muddy street. Women at their cookpots took quick account of their children. Girls at the creekbank made swift signs of the cross and hastily gathered their wash.

In the cornfield the men stood fast and tried to sense the earth's intentions through the soles of their feet. Sombra de Dios was set on a narrow tableland in the western range of the Sierra Madre, a region of Mexico which often trembled as if in sudden fright. These shudders were usually brief and harmless, and the villagers had long ago learned to make jokes of them. "The mountain has been startled from its siesta," they might say. Or, "The earth is once again shrugging at one of God's great riddles."

But sometimes a tremor was more than a minor interruption of the day's work. Sometimes it was a warning of imminent worse, an advisement that, for reasons known only to God, the earth was in a black temper, in a mood to bring ruin.

For a long moment the men in the field waited to see if worse was coming. Then somebody uttered a loud derisive curse, and somebody else added to it. A pair of young machos expressing their fearlessness. Now others among them grinned and made dismissive gestures and made fun of each other for their frighted looks. They resumed their slow shuffle along the rows, plucking corn and dropping it into the long bags slung across their chests and dragging behind them.

And then again the stalks rustled queerly. Louder this time. And the ground again quivered under their feet.

Once more the men stopped working. Some slipped off their picking bags and began to ease slowly out of the field, casting anxious glances at the dark wall of the mountain barely fifty yards away.

"It is nothing, nothing!" Anastasio Domingo called out to them. He was a village elder and the foreman of this season's harvest. "A little trembling. It will pass. Don't be such hens and get back to work!"

Standing beside him, his eldest son Benito could feel the ground shivering softly against his soles. He was as eager as the others to abandon the field and put distance between himself and the looming mountain. But his place was at his father's side.

Now a low growl sounded deep in the earth—and the rest of the men threw off their bags and hastened away.

"Father," Benito said, shedding his own bag. But old Anastasio was not listening. He was glaring up at the mountain and muttering darkly.

Its growl deepening, the ground began to quaver. Then it suddenly jarred sharply and men cried out and fell. They scrabbled to their feet and ran. And Benito ran with them.

The ground buckled and men again fell—and again rose and kept running. The earth rumbled. The mountain shook against the sky. It began to shed black boulders. The huge stones bounded down the rockface and cut swaths through the cornstalks.

Benito fell twice before reaching the wide clearing encompassing the village cemetery. Here the villagers were coming together in a terrified herd. Here was the only spot a falling rock had never reached, the only expanse of ground a temblor had never cracked open.

Benito's younger brother Lalo ran up to him, wide-eyed, yelling, "Father! Where's father?"

They searched the crowd frantically, and then someone shouted, "There, Benito! Out there!"

Anastasio Domingo was still at the edge of the corn-

field, all alone now between the mountain and the cemetery, bellowing curses at the sierra, shaking a bony fist.
He tottered like a drunk on the undulant ground. A boul-
der the size of a sow shot past within feet of him.

"Fatherrrr!" Benito cried. He started for the field but
Lalo grabbed his arm and held him back, yelling, "No,
Benny!"

The ground at the base of the mountain wall ripped
open with an explosive burst and a jagged gaping fissure
lengthened swiftly and made directly for Anastasio. The
old man tried to run but he still wore his picking bag and
the load of corn weighed him down. The fissure rushed
up behind him, the ground crackling as it parted, widening like monstrous jaws.

The ground opened under Anastasio and the villagers screamed.

The old man caught hold of the rim of the fissure and
arrested his fall. For a moment he hung in the crevasse,
only his head and arms visible as he clawed wildly at
sand and stones in a desperate effort to pull himself out
against the full weight of the picking bag hanging round
his neck.

Then the ground broke under his grasp and he vanished into the abyss.

This time the village was almost undamaged. Much
clayware had been shattered and a few pens had come
apart and the animals had scattered and would have to
be rounded up. But no walls had collapsed and no roofs
had fallen. The creek had not drained to thick mud, not
this time.

Singly and in small groups the villagers approached
the edge of the crevasse where Anastasio Domingo had

dropped out of sight. They peered into the black void, blessed themselves hastily and hurried away with faces tightly fearful.

The day after the temblor, Father Enrique arrived in the early evening from the neighboring pueblo of Tres Cruces and said a mass for Anastasio's soul. But there was no funeral because there was no corpse to bury. The old priest spoke of God's mysterious ways and of the great need for faith during our brief tenure in this vale of tears called Life. But his words did little to comfort the village men, and after he departed they gathered in the village cantina to drink with urgency and speak forlornly of the riddles of life and death.

The room was draped in shadows and pungent with the sooty smoke of kerosene lamps. The men drank and gestured and shook their heads. It had been such a meager little earthquake, they told each other. All of them had seen at least a half-dozen temblors worse than this one, quakes that left the village in piles of broken adobe and littered with tiles and thatch, that buried entire cornfields under mountain rocks, that ripped open the ground in a dozen places—and yet had killed no one. Then along comes a dwarf of an earthquake like this one, a weak sister of an earthquake that drops only a few big rocks in the field and opens only one big crack in the ground— and yet, just like that, it takes a man off the face of the earth. How, they asked, was a man to make sense of such a thing?

For a time they drank in morose silence. And then Marchado Ruiz spoke up in a loud slurred voice. He said he only hoped they had not held the mass for Anastasio's soul too soon.

Heads turned his way. Marchado Ruiz was a fool and

everyone knew it, but even from him such a remark could not be easily ignored. Eyes narrowed at him in question. Lips drew tight in anticipation of stupidity.

"What I mean," Marchado said, waving his cup for emphasis and spilling pulque on the men sitting beside him at the long table, "is that maybe Anastasio was not yet dead."

Now everyone in the room was staring hard at Marchado Ruiz. Faces clenched in anger and men muttered darkly. What was this fool saying to insult the dead?

"I *mean*," Marchado said in the rising whine of one desperate to make himself understood, "that hole looks pretty damn deep, doesn't it? I dropped a rock into it and never heard it hit the bottom. That's *deep*, no? So, what I mean is, what if it's *so* deep that Anastasio was still falling when the mass for his soul was said?"

The room fell silent as a tomb.

"The mass was supposed to be for a dead man, but if he was alive and still falling, the mass was too soon to do him any good, no? Now, maybe he died of fright as he fell, but I don't think so, not a brave man like old Anastasio. Hey, for all we know, he's *still* falling. It's possible, no?" He looked around at his gaping audience. "I mean, that hole looks pretty damn deep to me."

Marchado Ruiz had never been able to tell a joke properly in his life. The only laughter he ever inspired was derisive and directed at his foolishness. But now somebody burst out laughing—*truly* laughing—and in a moment was joined by somebody else.

And then suddenly everyone in the room was laughing—laughing hard, laughing with their teeth and eyes and belly, laughing with all their heart, roaring with laughter. They pounded the bar and tabletops with their fists and slapped each other on the back and *howled* with laughter. They bought drink upon drink for Marchado Ruiz and they put their fists to their faces and wept with laughter.

All of them—even Benito and Lalo, who could not help themselves and would later pray for their father's forgiveness—laughed and laughed until their bellies were in agony from laughing, until their fists were raw and sore and their jaws ached and their eyes were burning dryly, drained of all tears.

And then every man of them got happily drunk—and later, singing loudly in the moonlight, they went staggering home to their women and their beds. And in the morning, as the sun once more ascended over the mountain peaks, they were back at their work in the sierra's long shadow.

ALIENS IN THE GARDEN

I

There were, Julio thought, some clear advantages to working in the fields rather than in the groves. For one thing, you did not have to climb a ladder to pick tomatoes, so there was much less risk of breaking your bones. And a full basket of tomatoes did not weigh even half as much as a full box of oranges, a difference for which your back was grateful at the end of the day. And in the fields he had seen but a single snake, a little green one said to be harmless except to bugs, but in the groves he had known more than one man who had been bitten by a rattler.

He was working swiftly but with care not to bruise the ripe tomatoes, plucking them from the vines and putting them in the basket, pushing the basket ahead of him along the low row of plants. He paused to wipe the sweat from his face, being careful not to get insecticide in his eyes.

So now he thought of a ladder as a risk, he told himself, of a hundred pounds of oranges as a great burden. Sweet Mother of God, he was thinking like an old man. He felt a rush of anger—followed instantly by confusion because he did not know what, exactly, he was angry about. About being in this dusty field, of course, breaking his back under a roasting sun. Did a man need more reason than this to feel angry? But he knew it was something else, too, something more than the outrage of a life at hard labor, that for the past few days had been gnawing on his spirit like sharp teeth.

"You there! Got to work goddammit!"

Gene, the worst-tempered of the crew chiefs, had spotted him kneeling idly and gazing into space and was pointing at him from six rows away. "This ain't no mothafucken pignick!"

Although he still did not understand much English, Julio well enough understood Gene's commands. Pinche negrito, he thought, as he resumed working. Goddammit *you*. Goddammit all of this. He suddenly wished he was back in the groves, the ladders and snakes and heavy loads be damned. In the grove you at least had some shade and so what if the air could get so thick it was hard work just to breathe? Out here you worked in the sun and you sweat like a mule and you crawled along on your hands and knees with your back bent and your spine cracking. You breathed dust and insecticide fumes all day long. The bug spray burned and stained your skin and you carried the smell of it everywhere, even after you washed. Goddammit! A man had to work hard all his life, yes, but not on his knees. A man was not meant to work on his knees.

Well . . . a priest, maybe, he thought, and strained to smile at his own weak joke.

II

He had arrived in Florida three months ago, crammed into the back of a truck with fifteen other men at the end of a journey that began shortly after they crossed the Río Grande some thirty miles upriver of Laredo, Texas. Guided by a Mexican coyote—a smuggler of illegal border-crossers—they splashed across the river in the middle of a windy moonless night, choking on the muddy water and on their pounding hearts, fearful of being captured by la migra—agents of the American immigration service—or by the Border Patrol. They walked and walked in the night wind under a sky blasting with stars, shivering in their wet clothes, and then just before sunrise the truck came clattering out of the vague gray dawn and found them as planned.

The driver was a freckled Anglo boy of about seventeen who counted the men and then handed the coyote an envelope and ordered them in wretched Spanish to get into the back of the truck and be absolutely quiet for the whole trip if they did not want to be captured by la migra. Watching them from the truck cab was a large pale Anglo in a cowboy hat who spoke not at all. The men clambered up through the rear of the box-shaped cargo compartment and sat on the floor with their backs against the sides. There were several plastic bottles of drinking water and some lidless gallon cans to hold their waste. Then the boy yanked down the rollered door and locked them in darkness.

Julio had been among strangers even then. Most of the other men in the truck were from the same region of Coahuila state and had long been acquainted. A few of the others had come together from Nuevo León, and there was a pair of friends from Chihuahua. But Julio had come the farthest, all the way from Nayarit, a state unfamiliar to the others, and only he had come alone.

The truck's tires droned under them all day and night. The men's excited jabbering gradually trailed off, and soon they were all curled on the floor and trying to sleep, occasionally cursing in the dark when someone made use of the piss cans and his aim was poor, or when a can was kicked over by someone's careless foot or toppled by a sudden lurch of the truck. By the end of the first day every man's clothes were damp and reeked of piss.

Julio slept fitfully, dreamt of his wife's dark eyes, his children's faces. Once, on waking in the reverberant darkness, he felt as if his chest had been hollowed, felt such an abrupt rush of loneliness he had to clench his teeth against weeping.

The truck made stops only for fuel—and every time it did, gasoline fumes rose thickly in the dark compartment, and the men warned each other not to light cigarettes. Sometimes the fuel stops were in a town and they would hear street traffic, and sometimes people shouting, and once they heard children laughing and guessed they must be passing by a school. Sometimes, as they rolled slowly through a town, they caught the smells of food and moaned quietly and told each other in whispers of the meals they were going to buy for themselves as soon as they received their first pay. During a stop sometime in the second day, the doorlock rattled and the door rolled up just far enough for the boy to shove into the compartment a large paper bag containing sandwiches and bags of corn chips. The sudden blazing strip of sunlight under the raised door was blinding, and the brief inward rush of fresh air burned Julio's lungs as it cut through the stench he had become inured to. The sandwiches were made of bologna and dry bread—but every man gobbled his down in a few quick bites.

Late the next day, they felt the truck leave paved road and begin jouncing over uneven ground. Nearly an hour later they came to a stop and the lock sounded and the door flew up on its rollers and the Anglo boy counted out ten of the men, Julio included, and told them to get out. The other six men were again shut inside the truck and the truck departed.

They were in Florida. Julio had always thought it a beautiful name. *Florida!* It conjured visions of a lush land hung with flowers, a world far removed from the starkly rugged sierras where he grew up struggling for subsistence in cornfields full of stones. When he staggered out of the truck and saw the endless rows of rich green trees hung with golden fruit, he felt he'd been delivered to a garden of God.

They were housed in small, battered, unfurnished trailer homes set in a wide clearing deep in the grove, four men to a trailer, and they slept on the floor. They were fed from a mobile kitchen, a camper-backed pickup, that showed up twice a day, at dawn and at dusk. Its rations were the same at both meals—rice and beans, flavorless white bread, bags of corn chips, ice water. They worked every day from sunup to sunset, scaling ladders to pick the fruit at the higher reaches of the trees, dropping the oranges into the canvas bag hung across their chests, descending the ladder to empty the bag into a packing box, repeating the process until the box was full, then lugging it to a truck with a long slat-sided bed and there collecting a ticket from a crew chief before emptying the box into the truck. They were paid in cash every night, forty cents for every ticket, and even after the bosses deducted expenses for shelter and food, Julio was left with more money than he could earn in a week of hard work back home. He allowed himself some money for beer and candy bars and for gambling a little in the nightly dice games, and the rest he kept in a thin roll held tight with a rubber band and tucked in the front of his underwear. Every night he fell asleep with his hand cupping the roll protectively.

As he went about his work he daydreamed of the glorious return he would make to his village of Santo Tomás one day. He recalled the promise he'd made to his wife, Consuelo, that he would come home in the spring, no later than midsummer, for sure. And perhaps he would—if he did not decide to stay in Florida a while longer and make even more money. A promise to a wife was a serious thing, he reminded himself, but subject to change, of course, with the unpredictable circumstances of a man's life. Maybe he would be satisfied with the amount of money he would have saved by this summer, or maybe he would wish to stay a little longer and add a little more to it. Would not a man's wife herself, his children too, be better off with every dollar more he saved? A man's family would be proud of him for such industry. In any case, when he at last returned home he would be rich and respected and envied for miles around.

They had not been in the grove three full weeks before his sleep was shattered one night by sirens and by loud-speakers blaring in Spanish that everyone was under arrest and anyone who tried to run away would have worse trouble. Julio bolted from the trailer into the glare of encroaching headlights and spotlights of cars and trucks with blue lights flashing on their roofs. Cries of "La migra! La migra!" carried through the grove as men fled shouting in every direction. In panic he ran too, ran wildly, trying to escape the blinding lights, the crackling bullhorn voice of Legal Authority. He ran into the grove and was almost struck by a careening pickup truck that glanced off a tree. He jumped onto the rear bumper and held tight to the tailgate. The truck slued onto a narrow dirt trail and he was pulled into the bed and somehow—who could ever say how?—they escaped, five illegals of them and a single Anglo crew chief.

The chief drove through the night, and at sunrise they arrived in the farming town of Immokalee, two hundred miles south of the grove country they had fled. The chief deposited them at the Ross Hotel, a name suggesting amenities far beyond the realities of that dimly-lighted, one-time warehouse of unpainted concrete block. The place was an open dormitory for transient field workers and offered the cheapest bunks in town at three dollars a night, a private locker for a dollar more. It was even more malodorous than the trailers in the grove had been. Cockroaches skittered across the floor and the walls were covered with crude sexual drawings and profane scrawlings in English and Spanish.

"Put bars over the windows," one man said to Julio, looking around, "and it could pass for the jail back home in Sabinas."

III

He had now been living in the Ross for more than two months. He woke every morning before sunup and walked to the Farmers Market where the contractors with fields to be picked called out the day's wages. As soon as he hired on he'd board the crew bus and take a seat and doze off like most of the other pickers around him. The rattling bus would usually get them to the fields just before the sun broke redly over the trees—and even before they were off the bus, the chiefs would be barking for them to get to work, goddammit, get to work.

But the narrow escape from the immigration agents' raid on the orange grove had been a reminder of life's ready perils and that a man had better take his pleasures when he could. He began to accompany a pair of new friends, Francisco and Diego, to a cantina called the Rosa Verde almost every night. The bar was about a mile beyond the edge of town, and sometimes they did not stagger out of the place until the early hours of the morning. And sometimes, after bidding his friends goodnight and heading back toward the Ross, he ended up sleeping in the palmetto thickets alongside the highway where he later woke shivering on the foggy ground with a hangover like an iron spike in his skull. Sometimes he awoke early enough to hurry to the Farmers Market before the crew buses left for the fields, and sometimes he missed the buses—twice last week—but was able to hitch a ride to the fields.

This morning he'd again come awake in the palmettos. He was lying huddled on his side, his clothes damp with dew, and staring into the pink eyes and long whiskered snout of a curious possum within inches of his face. He let a startled groan and the ugly thing scurried into the brush. His hangover was monstrous. With painful effort he got to his feet, clung to a papery cajeput trunk and heaved up the residue of the pickled pigfeet he'd so avidly consumed in the Rosa Verde the night before. He was repulsed by the smell of himself, the rancid taste of his tongue. The sun was already above in the trees and he knew the crew buses had long since departed the Farmers Market. He stumbled out to the shoulder of the road and started walking in the direction of the fields. Not ten minutes later a pickup stopped for him. The driver was a happy Chicano who spoke execrable Spanish and tapped his fingers on the steering wheel in time to the rock song on the radio. He gave Julio an appraising look and grinned and shook his head. "Bunked in the Palmetto Hotel, eh?" he said in English. "Rough, man." Julio didn't understand, and so smiled and shrugged. The Chicano laughed and turned up the radio.

He got out at a crossroads and thanked the driver for the ride and from there hiked another two miles to the tomato fields. The day was cloudless, the broad sky almost achingly blue, the sun already hot on his shoulders. A hawk circled over a cattle pasture and a flock of egrets rose on slow-beating white wings and banked away over the pines. The crew buses were parked in the shade of the roadside trees, their drivers napping or leafing through comic books and nudie magazines. When the black crew chief named Gene saw him heading for the stack of empty baskets by the loading truck, he stalked toward him, yelling, "*You* there! You fulla shit you think you come out here and work any goddam time you feel like. *You!* I'm talkin to *you*, goddammit!"

Julio stood with a basket in his hands and stared without expression at Gene's yelling, contorted face. He didn't need to understand the man's words to know what he was saying. But he knew he would work. All week the order had been for red ripes and the chiefs needed every picker they could get.

"Goddammit, this be the lass mothafucken time, you unnerstan? The *lass!*" The chief gestured angrily toward an empty picking row. "Go-head on, get you sorry ass to work."

The moment he settled onto his knees and started picking, he knew the day would be a mean one. It was not yet midmorning and already the sun was burning into his back and scalp. His blue Kansas City baseball cap was back in his locker at the Ross Hotel and he would have to work the day bareheaded. He remembered a red bandanna balled in his pocket and dug it out. Although he was tempted to wear it capped over his head and tied under his chin, he didn't do it—that was the way the field women wore them. He rolled it and banded it around his forehead. It would keep the sweat out of his eyes for a short while, until it was saturated, and then would be worthless because he could not afford to stop working every few minutes to wring it out.

Each time a picker filled a basket with tomatoes he carried it to the end of the row to be inspected by a checker. If the checker approved the load, he gave the picker a ticket worth the day's rate for a full basket, and then he called for a toter to take the tomatoes and load them in the truck. At the end of the day, the picker turned in his tickets for their total worth in cash. Today each ticket was worth forty-five cents. Last week the call had been for green tomatoes, the hardiest kind and thus the easiest to pick, as well as to check and load. The pickers had been able to work fast and the checkers hardly glanced at the loads before issuing tickets for them, and the toters had dumped them into the truck as casually as rocks. But when the order was for red ripes everybody had to work more carefully and the process was much slower. The pickers had to be mindful to pluck only ripe fruit and the checkers had to inspect the loads closely to ensure nobody was trying to get by with hiding greens and pinks under a top layer of ripes—a deception not unknown to pickers trying to fill baskets as fast as they could. The toters had to be careful not to bruise the tomatoes in loading them in the trucks. The crew chiefs stalked up and down the field, commanding the pickers to work faster, work harder, and the pickers cursed them under their breath. The call for red ripes always put everyone in meaner temper.

The fields were sprayed nightly and Julio's stomach churned at the smell of the oily insecticide gleaming on the fruit. Within the hour his arms would be blackened to the elbows. The air was dusty, and the broken fruit discarded along the rows was already swarming with bulbous green flies, and the pickers had to work with their mouths closed against them. He ached in every muscle. His pulse beat painfully against the back of his skull and his eyes felt too large for their sockets. The insecticide seared the cuts in his hands. Sweat was already oozing from under his headband and rolling into his eyes, and when he wiped at it with the back of his hand his eyelids were left burning. His tongue felt like an oil-caked rag.

A hundred yards away, set on a crate in the middle of the field, was a thirty-gallon water barrel covered with a wooden board. Throughout the day, the workers would go to the barrel and dipper a drink, but none of them ever drank fast enough to avoid a chief's angry order to quit lazing and get back to work. The sight of the barrel roused Julio's thirst like a half-mad dog, but he would not go for a drink, not yet. Not on a morning when he had started work after everyone else and before he had even picked his first basket. No, he told himself, it would be as always: he could not go for a drink until he had picked at least three baskets. It was a rule he had made for himself on his first day in the fields when he'd discovered that many of the pickers were drunkards working only for the money to buy their next bottle. They were the first to go to the water barrel every day, and few of them were ever able to work all the way through the afternoon. Any man who went for water ahead of such derelicts was ridiculed without mercy by the other pickers and deserved to choke on his shame. But Julio knew that by the time he had picked his first three baskets, all the bums would have made their first trip to the water barrel.

Everyone laughed at these bums, but kept their distance from them, too, for they all stank of something more than unwashed flesh and filthy clothes. The bums had a stink such as Julio had never before smelled on a living man, a stench of something dead, and it always made him feel a little afraid. One such wretch was working in the row to his left this morning, a sickly pale and red-eyed man whose grimace showed green teeth. Now and then Julio caught the smell of him and felt a small shiver even as bile rose hotly to his throat.

In the row to Julio's right worked Big Momma Patterson, an enormous Negro woman wearing a wide-brimmed straw hat, knee pads and gloves. She had been about ten yards ahead of him when he got to work, and she had since taken a full basket to the checker and started filling another, and the distance between them was now nearly fifteen yards. She was the best picker in the field today. The only one better was Sammy Bowlegs, a Micco-sukee Indian who was at the moment serving sixty days in jail for setting fire to a woman's hair in a barroom.

Julio's hands and knees were now beginning to achieve their usual rhythm, his picking action gaining smoothness. His hands moved swiftly through the vines, grasping the tomatoes against his palms and snapping them free with a crook of the finger and a twist of the wrist, setting them quickly but gently into the basket. He pushed the basket forward and stepped up behind it on his knees. The same action again and again. When he filled his first basket and stood up, sharp pains ground into his back and his knees cracked loudly. He cursed and spat and picked up the basket and tried to swing it up to his shoulder as he usually did, but the action made him lose his balance and he sidestepped clumsily and his feet tangled in the vines and he just barely managed to drop the basket right-side up before he went sprawling. The derelict picker in the row beside him laughed and said something, and Momma Patterson looked back at him and smiled and shook her head. Gene came stomping down the row, swearing and gesticulating angrily. Julio retrieved the few spilled tomatoes and then jerked the basket up onto his hip and lugged it to the end of the row, ignoring Gene's ranting as he did the flies raging around his head.

While working on his third basket he paused and leaned low over the vines and vomited quietly. He wiped his mouth with his sleeve and was dizzy for a moment and then suddenly felt much better. Well, he thought, *that's* done. By the time he filled the basket, the pasty drunkard in the row beside him had gone for water. Julio carried the basket to the checker, received his third ticket, retrieved an empty basket and took it back to his row, and then went to the water barrel and drank like a drowning man.

IV

Its little bell tinkling, the faded-orange lunch wagon came down the road and parked in the roadside shade as it did at noon every day. The owner and driver of the wagon was a thin-haired fat man named Harold who sweated constantly and had a wall eye. The wide serving window was attended by his busty but plain daughter, Georgia, who never smiled or scowled or showed any reaction to the fieldworkers' pathetic attempts at flirtation except boredom and occasional impatience when one of them slowed up the line. Harold accepted cash or field tickets for his wares, the full range of which consisted of hot pork sausage on a bun, cold cheese sandwiches, corn chips, unchilled cans of soda pop, moon pies, cigarettes and candy bars.

The crew chiefs' whistles shrilled up and down the fields, signaling the half-hour lunch break. Julio was not hungry nor even sure his stomach would accept food without throwing it right back up. But he had to eat something to give himself strength for the afternoon, the longest and hardest portion of the day. As the line advanced toward the serving window it was engulfed by the heavy smell of hot pork grease and Julio fought down a surge of nausea. He paid six tickets—two dollars and seventy cents—for a cheese sandwich and a can of Dr Pepper.

He crossed the road and sat in the grass in the shade of a mimosa tree. He stared morosely at his lunch. Six tickets. He had five left in his pocket. Never before had he picked so few baskets in a morning's work—not even three days ago when he did not arrive at the fields until after nine o'clock in the morning. If he did not do better this afternoon . . .

But of *course* he would do better. Didn't he always do better in the afternoons? By then the pain of his head would have eased and he would have food in his belly and the return of his strength. At the moment, however, he was tired to his bones, more tired than he had ever been after a morning's work. He did not understand it. This was not the first time he had worked in the sun with a tequila hangover. He wondered if he would be able to work through the afternoon without dropping from exhaustion. Then realized it was the first time he had ever wondered such a thing.

The sandwich tasted strongly of oily mayonnaise on the verge of turning rancid, but he forced himself to chew it, swallow it, keep it down. He spied Alfonso de la Madrid standing in the lunch wagon line—and then Alfonso saw him looking and quickly averted his gaze.

Julio's belly tightened in anger. The five tickets in his pocket, together with about eighty cents in coins, represented all the money he had in the world, and the reason for that sad fact was an unfortunate incident on the Sunday just past. And the cause of that incident—and thus the true cause of his present poverty—was Alfonso de la Madrid. . . .

V

"*Stop* for him, man—he's a Mexican!" Alfonso shouted as Diego's rusty, smoke-trailing Plymouth rumbled past a hitchhiker. "Give the poor fellow a ride. Don't be a bastard."

They were on an isolated stretch of State Road 82, a two-lane blacktop flanked by cattle pastures and pine stands and citrus groves, returning to Immokalee from a day in Fort Myers. The red afternoon sun was almost down to the trees. Pine shadows touched the road. The sweet scents of orange blossoms and new-mown grass swept in through the car windows. Squalling blackbirds lined the telephone wires, and a scattering of cattle egrets fed on insects in the pastures.

They had been to a movie and then eaten at a Burger King and then stopped in at several bars. Alfonso sat in the front seat with Diego, both of them wearing new straw hats they had bought at the Edison Mall. Julio rode in the back with Francisco, who was not feeling too well. His eyes were bruised purple and swollen nearly shut, his lips cut and bloated, his nose hugely broken. These disfigurements had come to him in an alley behind a Fowler Avenue bar, by way of a shrimp boat captain at least twice his age. The shrimper had disputed the legality of a shot by which Francisco sank the eight ball to beat him in a pool game and win their bet of a beer. Francisco

had said, "It is a technique much admired in Piedras Negras. I will accept a Budweiser as my prize."

Although he had learned his English in Mexico, Francisco spoke the language quite capably, better even than
Diego, who had been born and raised in Colorado and
learned both English and Spanish in childhood—but un-
fortunately did not learn either very well. His pronuncia-
tions in both languages were often perplexing, and it was
an old joke with his friends that no matter which language
Diego used to call his dog, the confused animal would
simply stare at him from a distance and scratch its head.
"Julio and me, we don't even speak English," Alfonso
had once remarked, "and we speak it better than Diego."

"Well, we ain't *in* no fucken Perras Nigras," the old
shrimper had said to Francisco. "Around here that's a
illegal shot and you lose. Make mine a fucken Michelob."

Francisco winked cockily at his friends at the bar and
said to the shrimper: "Maybe you wish to discuss this
disagreement outside, eh, old man? Under the eyes of
God?"

"Fucken A John square," the shrimper said, tossing
his cue on the table and heading for the back door.

And now Francisco was not feeling so well.

Diego brought the Plymouth to a stop and the hitchhiker came running. Diego looked at Alfonso and said,
"Maybe I should get rid of this car and get a bus, eh? To
all the time pick up the damn people you always want
me to pick up?"

"Your kindness has put a smile on the Holy Mother's
face," Alfonso said. "You are ten feet closer to heaven."

The hitchhiker was breathing heavily when he got to
the car. Julio moved over, permitting the man to have the
seat by the door.

"Many thanks," the man said as Diego put the car in motion. He was tall and lean and hatless, his hair cropped short, like a soldier's. His jeans and jacket still held the smell of new denim, and though his low-cut brown shoes were smeared with mud, they looked new also. On a band slightly too large for his wrist hung a gold watch. He said his name was Luis Blanco. Alfonso introduced him all around. Julio thought the man had eyes like a policeman—quick-moving, taking note of everything.

In answer to Alfonso's questions, he said he was a baker in Fort Myers and was going to Immokalee to visit his girlfriend. He had a car of his own—a nice little Chevy only five years old—but it was being painted this weekend and so he had to use his thumb to get to Immokalee. He didn't have to work tomorrow and would take the bus back to Fort Myers tomorrow night.

He asked about Francisco's battered face and laughed together with everyone else—except Francisco, who glared at them all—when Alfonso told the story of the fight. Julio noticed a small dark tattoo on the webbing between the thumb and forefinger of Luis Blanco's left hand, a symbol shaped like an arrowhead. When Luis Blanco saw him looking at it, he casually covered it with his other hand. His Spanish was much like Francisco's, a borderland region singsong. He was, he said, originally from Mexicali.

When he learned that all of them were pickers but for Diego, who worked as an auto mechanic in a garage, he asked if the pay was good for pickers at this time of year. Did they get paid every day, as he had heard? They must be doing very well to have a car and spend Sunday in Fort Myers and be able to buy new hats. Did they think he could get work in the fields? He missed his girlfriend and wanted to live closer to her.

"Hey, friend, any poor fool can work in the fields," Diego said. "All you need is the strength of a burro and the brains of the same burro. You don't want to quit a clean nice bakery to work in the fields." He glanced at the man over his shoulder. "Pardon me for so saying, my friend, but that would be very stupid, even for love."

"But pickers *do* get paid every day, right?" the man asked.

"Damn right we do," Alfonso said. "We always have money in our pockets. Not like this poor fool"—he gestured at Diego—"who gets paid only on Friday and by Wednesday is broke again."

Diego glared at him and said, "This poor fool has a car. And my friend Luis the baker here, *he* has a car. The only ones I see in this car who *don't* have a car are ignorant pickers."

"You have a *car*?" Alfonso said, feigning surprise. "Well, why don't we use it next time instead of going to town in this donkey cart?"

Diego showed him a middle finger.

The Luis fellow turned to look at the rear window and Julio looked too, his curiosity roused. There was no traffic in sight in either direction. The man now looked at Francisco slumped against the door with his eyes closed, then looked intently at Julio as if he were trying to read his mind, then reached under his jacket and withdrew a small chrome-plated pistol. He held it in his right hand, on the side away from Julio. Julio gaped.

"Stop the car," the man said. "Pull over to the side of the road."

Diego looked at him in the rearview mirror. *"What? Why?"*

The man raised the gun where Diego could see it. "Do it," he said.

"Hey, man, what the hell are you—" Alfonso began, but the man pointed the gun at him and snapped, "Shut up!"

"Oh, God," Diego sighed and slowed the car, eased onto the shoulder and shut off the engine.

"Who told you to cut the motor, you idiot?" the man said.

"What?" Diego said, wide-eyed in the rearview. "I don't know . . . nobody. I always do it because sometimes the motor, it gets a little too hot and—"

"Quiet!" the man ordered. He held the gun low, out of sight of anyone who might drive by, but pointed vaguely at Julio's chest. Francisco had now come awake and seen the pistol and gone pale under his bruises. He sat utterly still against the door.

"I don't want to shoot anybody," the man said, "but I have done so before, so don't try anything foolish, any of you. Understand?"

Diego and Esteban and Francisco nodded. The man looked at Julio and smiled tightly. "Do *you* understand?" he asked. Only now did Julio realize he had been wondering if a bullet from such a little gun would hurt very much. The man angled the pistol so that it pointed up at his face. The muzzle was small and dark and Julio's mouth suddenly tasted of copper. He nodded.

"Very good," the man said. "Now you two"—he gestured at Diego and Alfonso—"take all your money out of your pockets. Do it *now*! And you two"—looking now at Julio and Francisco beside him—"hand it over."

Julio worked his hand in his pocket and extracted a few small bills and some coins and handed the money to the bandit, who accepted it with his left hand and stuffed it in his jacket pocket. Wincing with pain, Francisco leaned across Julio and gave his money to the man.

"For the love of God," Alfonso said plaintively as he handed his money over the seat. "Why are you doing this to us? We are not rich. We are Mexicans, the same as you. If you want to rob somebody, why not rob the gringos? They have all the money. That's what *I* would do."

The bandit stuffed Diego's money in his pocket with the rest. "Oh sure, sure you would. Pancho Villa, that's you. Now, pull your pockets inside out, all of you! Do it quick!"

He leaned forward to look into the front seat and saw that Diego's and Esteban's pockets were showing whitely. He glanced across at Francisco and saw that his pockets, too, hung limply from his pants. Only Julio had not reversed his pockets. The bandit narrowed his eyes at him.

"I gave you all I had," Julio said. "Truly."

"*Truly?*" the bandit echoed, arching his eyebrows. "Well, forgive my lack of trust, my friend, but"—he wagged the pistol at Julio's pockets and showed a large grin—"I insist."

Julio glanced down at the pistol, then stared hard into the man's eyes. If he had been asked at that moment what was going through his mind he could not have said. But something in his face made the man lose his smile. He pressed the pistol against Julio's right side and cocked the hammer. Julio had never heard that sound except in the movies and he marveled at its chilling effect in the world of mortal flesh. He felt his heart beating fast against his ribs.

"*My friend* . . ." the bandit said softly, almost sadly.

A van with dark-tinted windows whooshed past.

Julio pulled his pants pockets out and the rest of his money fell on the seat.

The bandit looked at the clump of bills and then at Julio and then gathered the money with his free hand. "Oh, truly," he said in a mimicking voice. "That's all of it . . . *truly*." He laughed and hefted the fistful of money as if trying to guess its worth by its weight. Julio knew exactly how much it was. Seventy-nine dollars. Five of which he had won at the cockfights on the previous weekend and the rest was all the money he had managed to save during his time in Florida.

"Jesus Christ, Julio," Francisco said thickly through his swollen lips.

"Have you been robbing banks?" Diego said.

"Listen, man," Alfonso said to the bandit, "the rest of us are not so rich like this one. Those twelve dollars of mine are all the money I have in the world. Leave us some little bit of money, eh? Please. Enough for a beer and a taquito tonight, eh?"

"Is this one always so stupid?" the bandit asked as he finished tucking money into his pants pocket.

"Always," Diego said. "But look . . . can't you leave *me* with some money? I'm not like these pickers, man, I have a wife, I have little children. I have—"

The bandit shook the pistol at him. "You're going to have another hole in your goddamn head if you don't shut up."

Diego's eyes widened and he threw up his hands.

"Put your hands down, stupid!" the bandit said, glancing quickly along the road to see if any cars were passing by. "Sweet Jesus, what did I do to get a bunch like you? You fools think you're the only ones with troubles? If I told you pricks *my* troubles we would all drown when this car filled with your tears. Now leave the keys in the ignition and get out, all of you. Out! Now!"

Diego looked stricken. "You are not going to steal my *car*?" He had recently paid one hundred and twenty-five dollars for this ancient six-cylinder Plymouth, having saved the money for it over a period of nearly a year. It had not been easy. Almost every penny he earned went toward the support of his wife and seven children.

"*Steal* it?" the bandit said. "Listen, fool, I wouldn't steal a piece of shit like this. I only steal cars my sainted mother would not die of shame to see me driving. I wouldn't stoop so low as to steal this stinking car."

"I'm very glad to hear that," Diego said, looking both relieved and somewhat injured, "even though I don't think you truly realize what a good car this—"

"I'm just going to borrow the damned thing. Now get out—*every*body! Start walking back the way we came. Move!"

They got out and began walking. They heard the motor grinding as the bandit tried to start it, heard his faint cursing of the recalcitrant engine.

"The son of a bitch is going to have to hitch another ride to make his getaway," Francisco muttered.

"The shoemaker's children go barefoot," Alfonso said, "and the mechanic's car needs a mule to pull it."

"*You* shut up," Diego said, pointing a finger in Alfonso's face. "Don't say another word—not you!"

Alfonso put up his palms defensively and backed away.

The motor finally clattered to life and they stopped

walking and turned to look. A single headlight beam poked out in front of the car into the gathering gloom and then the transmission shrieked as the bandit worked it into gear. Diego groaned and said, "Doesn't that bastard know how to *drive?*"

The Plymouth lurched onto the highway and began a ponderous acceleration, trailing a thick plume of dark smoke and grinding loudly every time the bandit worked the column gearshift. Then the car went around a wide bend in the road toward Immokalee, still some fifteen miles away, and the taillights disappeared.

They spoke little as they trudged along the shoulder of the road. Except for Diego, the only legal citizen among them, they all ducked down in roadside ditches or ran into the pines to hide every time headlights appeared on the highway. One never knew when those lights might belong to la migra.

Diego put his thumb out to every car and truck that came flashing up from behind them. But the Sunday evening traffic was sparse and none of it even slowed down for him. His rage increased with every vehicle that sped past. He shook his fist at the shrinking taillights and bellowed, "Bastard! God damn you! Are you afraid I'm going to *rob* you, you son of a bitch? God DAMN you!"

He swore as fervently every time he caught sight of Alfonso, who was keeping a careful distance behind all of them.

" 'Stop for him, he's a Mexican!' " Diego mimicked sarcastically, glaring back at Alfonso. "You are a stupid shit!"

"I think we ought to hang him from one of these trees," Francisco said, and Alfonso dropped a few feet further behind. He was keeping uncharacteristically mute in the face of his fellows' rancor.

VI

The sky was gray with dawn light when they at last reached the town limit. A couple of ragged men sat on the curb in front of a convenience store and looked upon them with curiosity as they walked by. Julio glanced back just as Alfonso slipped away into the shadows of a side street and disappeared. A little farther on, Francisco said, "Look!" and pointed down the block to their right. The Plymouth was parked at the end of the street. Diego let out a whoop and jogged toward it.

"Good," Francisco said as he and Julio followed after him at a walk. "Now he can give us a ride to the market."

When they got to the car Diego was staring in horror upon the freshly crumpled right front fender. "Look," he said, pointing at the damage. "Just *look* what he . . . what that dirty *prick* . . . look how he did. He steals my good car and can't drive it twenty miles without wrecking it. That son of a bitch should be in prison. *Look!*"

Julio could not help thinking that the right fender now resembled the left one more closely than it had before, but he did not think this a good moment to mention it to Diego.

And now Diego discovered a parking ticket under the windshield wiper. He snatched it up and gaped at it in disbelief. It cited him for parking in front of a fire hydrant. He shivered as if suddenly very cold. He whimpered lowly. He crumpled the ticket in his hand and raised the fist to heaven and shook it as though he would demand an explanation from God Himself.

"What kind of son of a bitch—" he began, then started choking on his bile and outrage and fell to a harsh and prolonged fit of coughing that raised the veins starkly on his forehead. He slowly recovered, hacking and spitting, wiping the webs of mucus from his nose, the tears from his eyes. "What kind of son of a *bitch* . . ." he said breathlessly, brandishing the ticket at his friends, "would give a man a goddamn *ticket* . . . in the middle of the goddamn *NIGHT!*" He turned his face up to the sky. "Oooooh God," he moaned, "what bastards! What injustice! What *injustice* this stinking world is full of!"

The town was coming to life all around them. Several cars and trucks rolled past, their occupants staring out at them—some with amusement, some with indifference, some with disdain. Diego glared balefully at the hydrant, at the car, at Julio and Francisco, then whirled and went to the driver's side and got in and slammed the door shut with such force that the driver's side window shattered and showered him with broken glass.

He let a furious howl and pounded on the steering wheel with his fist. His curses rang in the streets.

The engine cranked laboriously as Diego worked the ignition key, then it began to sputter, then abruptly roared into action and poured black smoke from its exhaust pipe. He wrestled with the shift lever in a series of horrific metallic shrieks until the transmission at last surrendered to first gear. The engine still racing furiously, Diego released the clutch pedal and the Plymouth shot into the street with tires screaming and veered wildly for a moment before he had it under control. He fought the transmission through the rest of the grinding gearshifts as he drove away in a clatter and a cloud of oily smoke, heading home to a wife and seven children who would shriek and squall the whole while he got ready to go to work, sleepless and empty of pocket.

Julio and Francisco watched him until he rounded a corner and was gone.

"We should have asked him for a ride to the market," Francisco said.

Julio yawned hugely and shook his head. "No," he said. "Not this time."

As they were walking to the Farmers Market Francisco said, "At least the son of a bitch left the keys in the car for him."

"That's right," Julio said. "Diego should be thankful, shouldn't he?"

Francisco looked at him and started to laugh—and then winced with the pain of his battered face.

VII

The matter was quite clear to them all: Alfonso de la Madrid was to blame for the robbery. He had been the one who wanted to pick up the hitchhiker and then the hitchhiker had robbed them. The matter was clear enough. Diego had made it known that he did not want to see Alfonso ever again—and if he did see him, he would run over him with his car and then drive back and forth over him until there was nothing left but a stain in the road. Francisco, too, would get narrow in the eyes at the mention of Alfonso's name. None of them had spoken to Alfonso in the several days since the robbery and Alfonso was keeping his guarded distance from them all. He had not even shown his face in the Rosa Verde.

Sitting in the shade of the mimosa, Julio watched Alfonso buy his lunch and then hurry away to find a place to eat it, well removed from Julio's sight. The fool knew damn well it was all his fault.

And yet. . . . Furiously chewing the last of his sandwich, Julio knew that his lingering anger of the past few days did not entirely have to do with Alfonso. It was rooted in something deeper. His friends had attributed his low spirits to having been robbed of more money than they had. He was the only one among them who had managed to save any money, and he had given up every dollar of it. What man wouldn't feel sour about that?

But that wasn't it, either. No. What was eating at his heart, Julio knew, was something else.

It was this: he had done nothing to resist the bandit. He had sat there and let the man rob him.

Why had he not tried to take the little gun away from him? It was a question he had been asking since the robbery.

The robber had let his guard down several times. He had been laughing, enjoying himself, loose with his attention. He had been within easy reach.

He could have grabbed the gun from the man. He could have grabbed it and forced it from him. The man had not looked very strong. He could have taken the gun from him and shoved it up his nose and made him beg for mercy, made him weep with regret for having tried to rob him.

Why didn't he at least *try* it?

Had he been afraid?

Well, now . . . of course he had been a little afraid.

The fellow had a gun, didn't he? Show him a man who was not afraid of a gun and he would show you a fool.

Ah? And why would such a man be a fool?

Why? Mother of God, the question was more than foolish. Because a gun can kill you. Kill you quick.

His rage tore through him.

Sweet Jesus. Was that what he had been afraid of? Of being *killed*? Of being killed *quick*?

The realization made him laugh out loud—and the laughter burned in his eyes.

THE HOUSE OF ESPERANZA

I

The house of Esperanza was a small concrete structure
near the Church of Our Lady of Guadalupe in Immokalee,
a small rugged town in the winter produce region of
southwest Florida. The detail work on the house had
never been completed: three of its outer walls lacked
stucco; pipes and wiring were exposed throughout the

interior, and several windows were still without glass. The roof had been tarred but remained unshingled, and every hard rainfall produced a new leak. Esperanza had informally inherited the house from Salvador Escondido, its builder and her husband by common law, who one morning kissed her goodbye at the front door, left for work in the produce fields and never returned. That had been almost two years ago. The most popular rumor was that he had run off to Chicago with an Anglo waitress from Fort Myers.

II

Chuy came to Florida in a truck crammed with fifteen other Mexican laborers illegally smuggled into the U.S.—wetbacks, they were called in Texas and sometimes called each other. They'd been led across the river one dark night by a smuggler who guided them into the Texas desert and to the waiting truck. Some of them had been taken off the truck in an orange grove somewhere in central Florida. The others, himself among them, had been brought to Immokalee.

He'd been in town almost three months when he met Esperanza while buying beer in the Mariposa Market in the company of his friend Esteban. He saw her at the far end of an aisle, leaning on a shopping cart and contemplating the shelves of canned soft drinks. He thought her the most beautiful woman he had ever seen.

Esteban saw the way he was gazing at her and said, "Forget it, man. That one, she used to do it for twenty dollars—too damn much! Some said this one was worth it, but I never had the twenty dollars to find out. I wouldn't pay twenty dollars for it anyway, not with any woman. Well . . . with Isabel Vega maybe, you know, the movie star—but not with this one. She's too damn snooty, this one. They say she would not do it with you if she did not like you, the way you looked or talked or smelled, *anything*. If she didn't like something about you, she'd say no and that was that." Esteban habitually spoke as fast and voluminously as a man on the radio. "Listen, some-body once offered her *thirty* dollars to do it, a man she didn't like, so she said no. All right, the fellow said, make it thirty-five. No, she says, go away. *Forty*, the fellow says, and he holds up twenty dollars in each hand. She slammed the door in his face so hard she nearly broke his nose. A pair of fools, the both of them—him for offer-ing so much, her for turning it down. Anyway, she got on the welfare and stopped doing it anymore. Now her nose is like this"—Esteban tilted his head back and pushed up on his nose with his forefinger—"like she's looking down at the world and every man in it. Bah! She's a strange one, that whore!"

"Don't call her that," Chuy said without taking his eyes off her. He was enraptured by her proud posture, the liquid blackness of her hair, the play of muscle in her brown calves. He wondered if the children with her—a boy of about six or seven, a girl somewhat younger, and a boy of about three—could possibly be her own. She seemed too firm of breast and lean of belly to have borne three children.

Just then the younger boy accidentally brought a furi-ous slide of canned drinks crashing to the floor. The woman wore sandals and one of the cans struck her ex-posed toes. She gave a small cry and might have fallen had she not been supporting herself on the cart. Chuy rushed to her without thinking and dropped to one knee and tenderly cradled her uplifted injured foot. Two of the toes were already swelling darkly and showed beads of blood at the top rims of the nails. He suddenly envisioned how he must look and felt his face go warm. The children gaped at him. He looked up to meet her eyes, expecting anger at his liberty, scorn perhaps, but her aspect was only of faintly amused curiosity. She made no move to withdraw her foot from his gentle grasp.

"Please, señora," he said, "permit me to help you to get home with your groceries and children." He was astonished at his own boldness, for he was not one to speak easily to women, not even to those of his acquaintance, never mind attend to the injured foot of one whose name he did not know. Up close, he saw that she was even lovelier than she'd looked from a distance.

"Thank you, señor," she said softly. "You are very kind." And she smiled upon him.

And so he took her home. And she insisted that he stay to have supper with them. And after they ate and she cleared the table they drank coffee with sugar and milk and smoked cigarettes and talked and laughed and listened to music on the radio. And after she put the children to bed and led them in their prayers and bid them good night she came out and sat beside him on the living room couch. And after a while, he made bold to kiss her. And she kissed him in return. And then they were touching, caressing, breathing hotly against each other's neck. And then she took him by the hand and led him to the bedroom and there they made love.

And there, as he discovered a few days later when his urine came out scalding, he caught the clap.

III

Her first husband, whom she'd married at age sixteen in
the Church of the Sacred Heart in Brownsville, Texas,
where she was born, had been killed in an oil field acci-
dent outside of Corpus Christi just a few months after the
birth of their son, Raúl. He had carried no insurance and
left her penniless. For the next two years, she lived with
a pair of scolding aunts in Matamoros. She tended to her
infant son and prayed every night for a means to get
away. The means came in the form of handsome Salvador
Escondido, whom she met one morning under the palms
of the riverside park. They'd known each other a month
when he asked her to go with him to Florida. The following day, with Raúl on her lap, they were on their way in
Salvador's rattletrap Chevy.

She loved Florida, its faithful sunshine and verdant
lushness, its comforting long way from Texas and Mexico.
During her four years with Salvador, she gave birth to
two more children, María and Joselito. Then Salvador ab-
sconded and she had been obliged to provide for herself
and the children however she could. At the local welfare
office, she was time and again required to answer count-
less questions, asked for one document after another she
did not have, instructed to fill out endless application
forms she could barely understand even with the aid of
a translator. She was made to wait weeks for official sig-
natures and stamps of approval. During this long and
complex process, she had supported her family by various
means. She had taken in laundry and ironing. She had
taken in sewing. She had taken in men. But she was careless and got pregnant again. With the help of a neighbor
woman skilled in such matters, she was able to end the

pregnancy without any effects more serious than a painful infection that lasted two weeks—and guilt that sometimes woke her sobbing in the middle of the night.

But she was desperate for money, and so she resumed receiving men. Soon thereafter she contracted gonorrhea. Repeated treatments at the local clinic made no headway against the disease, and the clinic doctor, a young Chicano named González with little sympathy for human weakness, asked her how she expected to get cured if she persisted in prostitution. Until that moment she had avoided the word even in her thoughts, and hearing him say it made her rage with shame. She said she was persisting in only one thing, keeping her children fed, and she stalked out of his office.

Not until her welfare payments were finally approved and began to arrive in the mail did she stop seeing men and return to Dr. González and his antibiotics. By the time she met Chuy in the Mariposa Market a few weeks later, she had assumed she'd been cured.

IV

All morning the rumor had snaked through the dusty, sunbaked produce fields: a raid was coming—a raid by la migra, the American immigration agents. Maybe tomorrow, maybe the day after, but soon, very soon. The rumor was not an uncommon one—it went through the fields at least once a week. In fact, la migra *did* make a raid now and then, and it had now been several weeks since the last one, and so this time the rumor carried a feeling of great likelihood. Everyone could feel it.

During the lunch break, Esteban sat with Chuy in the

shade of a roadside tree and chain-smoked Marlboros and gulped two RC Colas and told Chuy he was not going to wait to find out if the rumor was correct. He intended to take the midnight bus to Miami. He had spoken of going to Miami ever since Chuy met him. Many mojados talked of going there but few ever did.

"Miami, Chuy—that's the place for us! The place is full with Cubans, with Latinos from everywhere, from Nicaragua and Honduras and Guatemala, everywhere! I know, man—I have been told by people who know. There are so many Latinos in Miami, nobody knows who's legal and who's not. Hell, nobody *cares*, not in Miami! And everybody speaks Spanish there, man, everybody knows that. In such a big city we will be a lot safer from la migra than we are in this little pueblo of a place where wetbacks are so easy to catch. Listen—in Miami we can be taxi drivers. That's right! In Miami *anybody* can be a taxi driver. I have been told, man."

Esteban put his palms forward as if to ward off an objection, though Chuy had given no sign of making one. "I know what you are going to say," he said. "You are going to say how can we become taxi drivers if we don't know how to drive a car. That is your trouble, my friend—you are always letting little things get in the way of a good idea. The answer to your question is simple: we will *learn* how to drive. There, you see? The problem is solved, eh? Besides, there are many kinds of work in Miami. It is not like this place where the only work is in the stinking fields. We can work in a restaurant if we want to—a fancy restaurant where all the customers are rich. We can work in white jackets, man. We can be *clean* and never again have to sweat for our pay. Think of it! Is that not a thousand times better than working in a field of dust and poison under the goddamn sun and sweating your life away like some burro?"

A thousand times better, Chuy thought. Ten thousand times better. He smiled and shook his head in amazement at the strength of his friend's dreamy faith.

Esteban thought he was shaking his head at his idea. "Ah, Chuy," he said sadly—and then abruptly brightened again. "Listen, man, don't forget about the Cuban women. Miami is *full* of Cuban women. Everybody knows they are the most affectionate women in the world. That's right. They have tits as sweet as melons, the Cuban girls, and asses big and soft like pillows. Oh man, I get dizzy just thinking about them. Jesus Christ, Chuy! Miami is the place for us! What the hell do you have here that is so important you cannot leave it, eh? A donkey job picking vegetables in the goddamn fields. A lousy cot in a flophouse full of drunkards. An appointment with la migra is what you'll have if you don't come with me tonight. It's what you will have very soon."

True, Chuy thought. The man speaks the truth.

Now Esteban tilted his head and his face went sly. "But wait. Can it be the woman? Is that it? Is my good friend Chuy thinking of *her*? No, no, that cannot be. My good and reasonable friend Chuy would never be so foolish to stay here just because of her." And now his face was again serious. "Hey, man, really, not for *her*, eh?"

Chuy averted his friend's eyes and said nothing. He took a bite of his barbecued pork sandwich and sipped from his bottle of Dr Pepper and stared at the fields across the road.

"Ah, Chuy," Esteban said, shaking his head. He picked up a stone and flung it into the palmetto scrub. "You've been seeing her nearly every night for—how long?—almost a month, no? Well, that's good, yes, a man should have all the fun he can. She's damn good-looking and a hundred men in town would give their soul to the devil to be in your place and having such fun." He paused and looked at Chuy sadly. "But it's *only* fun, right, Chuy? I mean, you are not . . . *serious* about her? Hey, man, she was a—"

"*Don't!*" Chuy whirled on him. "Don't say it!"

Esteban made the raised-palms gesture again. "Yes, all right my friend, very well. I'm sorry. I spoke improperly."

Chuy turned away and looked out at the fields again. Esteban stood up and brushed pine needles from his pants and scanned the sky. He cleared his throat. He looked at Chuy and said, "Look, if . . . well, maybe I'll see you at the bus station tonight, eh?"

Chuy said nothing.

Esteban put his hands in his pockets and kicked at a pine cone and started to walk away. Then stopped and turned to look at him again. Chuy looked at him without anger now. He shrugged without knowing what he meant by it. Esteban smiled crookedly and shrugged in return.

The crew chiefs blew their whistles to signal the end of the lunch break.

V

At sunset the crews boarded the field buses for the ride back to town. They arrived at the Farmers Market in the dark, and Chuy went directly to the Ross Hotel, that one-time warehouse furnished in the manner of a ramshackle barracks with worn folding cots and battered surplus wall lockers. Most of its residents were field workers who would be in town only as long as the harvest season. Chuy had lived here since arriving in Immokalee.

He washed up at one of the large industrial sinks of tin and changed his shirt and combed his hair, then went to the long narrow counter by the front wall and re-claimed a shoebox containing his few possessions. Oscar, the evening manager and half-owner of the Ross, re-trieved the cord-bound box from one of the closets behind the counter. The closets were kept locked and only Oscar and Martin—the day manager and other half-owner—had the keys. A month ago Oscar had discovered someone trying to force open one of the locks and he broke the thief's spine with a tire iron. It was said that the closets of the Ross Hotel were safer than a bank.

The moon was round and white and blazing just above the pines when he got to Esperanza's block. He paused across the dirt street from the house and smoked a cigarette and listened to the hymns of the evening con-gregation at Our Lady of Guadalupe down the street. The windows of the house glowed brightly yellow, and the sight of the house infused him with a strangely bitter-sweet feeling, a confusion of yearnings he could not have explained to himself had he tried. Out here was darkness and chill wind and the odor of dirt as ripe as a ready grave. More than once he had staggered back to the Ross after a night in the cantinas with his friends and awak-ened on his cot at dawn with a painful head and this same raw-dirt smell in his nose, a smell ingrained in the dirty clothes he'd slept in and rising off the fresh mud on his shoes. He shivered in a gust of wind. His loneliness felt like a hand at his throat. And then he remembered last night. All day he had refused to think about it, but now, looking at the house, he remembered—and felt a rush of shame.

Now the singing in the church ceased and he heard the children in the house laughing happily. He could faintly hear the music of the little radio she kept in the kitchen so she could sing along to it while she cooked. His stomach growled.

He crossed the weed-and-sand front yard and knocked on the front door. The children's voices rose excitedly, and then the door swung open and they clamored at the sight of him—Raúl, age seven and mop-haired and dark as an Indian; María, nearly five and already destined to break hearts with her beauty; and little Joselito, four years old and both shy and curious. Chuy ruffled Raúl's hair and gave Joselito a quick tickle under the arm, then tossed his shoebox on the sofa and swept up María and swung her around as she shrieked with delight. He set her down again and she gave his leg a tight hug before running to rejoin her brothers at their game of Chinese checkers.

He shut the door behind him and went to the kitchen. Esperanza was at the stove, stirring a pot of beans. She pushed a strand of hair from her eyes and looked at him with serious aspect for a moment before smiling and asking, "Are you hungry?"

"I could eat something, yes," he said.

"Then sit at my table," she said, "and I will feed you."

These had been the first words they'd spoken to each other under her roof, and the exchange had become a ritual on his arrival in the evenings.

The table was already set for him. The children, as usual, had been fed earlier. As she retrieved a bottle of beer from the little refrigerator and set it before him, she said, "Chuyito, are you practicing to be a salesman?"

He looked up at her, puzzled.

"Why else, I wonder, do you continue to knock on the door for permission to enter?" She stood beside him and stroked the back of his neck. "You are hardly a stranger anymore, you know."

He felt his face go warm. "It would be impolite not to knock," he said. "It is your house, after all."

She made a small smile and shook her head, then went to the stove to prepare their supper plates.

She had told him much about herself during the past weeks. She had told him about her girlhood in Brownsville and her father's small tortillería and the long hard hours the five of them—she and her parents and her two older brothers—had worked at making and packaging the tortillas, of the hard days after her father drowned at Padre Island one bright summer day while trying to save her oldest brother who drowned with him, of the loss of the tortillería to creditors, of her older brother's running away from home a year later when he was but sixteen, of her mother's subsequent illness and her long hard year of dying, of going to live with her horrid aunts and then meeting and marrying Raúl and then living with the aunts again after his death on the oil rig, of coming to Florida with Salvador Escondido.

Regarding his own past he had been deliberately vague and was both relieved and curious that she did not question him closely about it. Not until a week ago had he confessed to her that he was in the country illegally, half expecting her to tell him to get out of her house immediately, before she got in trouble with the authorities for harboring him. But she had simply said she knew that. When he asked how she knew, she smiled at him as though at a sweet but slow-witted child and ran her hand through his hair. "Ah, Chuy," she said, "you are so *obviously* illegal, my little son, that the back of your shirt is still wet. It could only be more obvious if you wore a big sign that said, 'I am a wetback.' Every evening that you show up at my door I give a prayer of thanks to God that la migra did not get you that day."

For her part, she had told him even about the whoring. Only women who were ashamed, she said, lied to men, or women who were afraid of them.

And then, three nights ago, as they lay contentedly entwined in her bed after making love, she had kissed his ear and said he ought to give up his cot at that awful flophouse where he lived and move in with her, since he was with her almost every night anyway.

He had declined her offer with the explanation that such an arrangement would put at risk her welfare payments. She said she was willing to take the risk. If she lost the welfare she would go to work, maybe at the Farmers Market as a sorter, maybe even as a picker in the fields. Lots of women worked in the fields, she reminded him. He said that was true, but she had two children not yet of school age to care for at home, and even if she found someone to care for them while she was at work, she should not, for their sake, take the risk of losing the welfare money.

She narrowed her eyes at this suggestion that she lacked sufficient maternal concern, but she held her tongue and tacitly deferred to his reasoning and had not brought up the matter since. And thus had he kept his cot at the Ross Hotel and returned to it every night after leaving her bed—and after stopping at the Corazón for a beer or two with his friends.

But now, watching her at the stove, he thought of the real reasons for his refusal to move in with her. Here was a woman who openly admitted to him that she had prostituted herself—and yet she was raising three well-disciplined children in the ways of the Church, teaching them proper behavior even as his own mother had tried to teach him, praying alongside them every night before they went to bed. Here was a woman who kept a clean house and cooked wonderful meals and showed him respect and fidelity. Here was a woman who had told him frankly and without shame that she could live without a husband—though she would prefer to have one—but not without the comfort of a good man in her house. What was a man to make of such a one? He saw her by turns as fragile and hard, guileless as a child and mysterious as a cat, sometimes saintly, at times beyond redemption. She confused him—and therefore frightened him—more than he cared to admit.

And there was still more to it than that. He sensed that to move in with her would be somehow to surrender something he could not even begin to define, and this feeling only deepened his confusion.

She ladled beans into two bowls and then paused to brush a strand of hair from her eyes with the back of her wrist. The gesture struck him as that of a little girl, and his chest suddenly ached with his affection for her. And then he was abruptly seized with guilt as he remembered the events of the previous evening, a sequence that began when the field bus arrived back at the Farmers Market and his friends asked him to come with them to Corazón for a beer. Although he had not told Esperanza he would join her for supper, he had eaten his evening meal there every night for more than a week, and he knew she would have something prepared for him. And so he'd told his friends he could not go with them now but would join them later, as usual. One of the men had laughed and raised his hands in front of him with the hands bent down at the wrists in the manner of a begging dog, and the gesture drew laughter from the others. They glanced sidelong at Chuy, and among themselves exchanged a look bespeaking humorous pity for one too fearful of his woman to join his friends for a beer before going home. Chuy felt his face go hot with anger—more at himself than at them, for he sensed they were right to ridicule him. "Hey, what the hell," he said. "I *do* feel like a beer. Let's go!" His friends had cheered and clapped him on the back.

But at the bar of the Corazón he had felt stupidly childish for having come for the reason he did. And then felt angrier yet because he did not think he should be feeling stupid for doing as he pleased. And then wondered just *what* it was he pleased to do. He gave hard thought to the question for the next few hours as he drank one beer after another.

He but vaguely remembered leaving the Corazón and making his hazy way to Esperanza's house. He could remember nothing of what followed until he woke in her bed this morning, woke with an aching head to her insistent shaking of his shoulder and her exhortations to hurry or he would miss the bus to the fields. It was the first time he had spent the entire night in her bed and his hangover was weighted with guilt. He evaded her eyes as he hastened into his clothes, then rushed to the Farmers Market and got there just in time to catch the bus.

VI

Tonight she fed him a stew of turkey in a spicy chocolate sauce—together with steaming bowls of beans and rice, platters of warm tortillas and fried green chiles. She opened two more bottles of beer, one for him and one for herself, an sat across from him and watched him eat. The little radio on the shelf over the kitchen sink was tuned to one of the Spanish language stations, which tonight was playing a succession of tunes from the Revolution— "Adelita" and "Valentina" and "Jesusita de Chihuahua" and "Las Mañanitas." "La Cucaracha" was the children's favorite and when it came on she turned up the volume so they could hear it in the living room and sing along with it. They had finished their game of Chinese checkers and were now busily occupied in scissoring pictures out of magazines, photos of models and movie stars and pala-tial estates and automobiles. Esperanza permitted them to tape the pictures on any of the unfinished walls except the ones in the living room, which she reserved for cruci-fixes and framed paintings of the Sacred Heart and of the Blessed Mother.

"I have the medicine for you," Esperanza said, taking a small brown bottle from her apron pocket and pushing it across the table to him. "I'm sorry it took Irma so long to get it, but her friend has had to be very careful." Irma was a friend who had a friend who worked in a pharmacy and was sometimes able to get certain medicines for those in need of it—for a price, of course, but a much better price than one would have to pay to the pharmacy even if one had a prescription. "She says this is very strong. She says to take one pill every morning, one at noon, and one at night when you go to bed. The burning should stop in just a day or two, but Irma says to keep taking the pills until they are all gone, even after the burning has stopped."

"Do you have to take such pills?" he asked.

"No. The doctor is giving me injections."

"Does he think you are . . . seeing men again?"

Esperanza shrugged.

"I don't like for him to think that."

He had not risked going to the clinic himself because it was widely believed that la migra had posted agents there disguised as patients. The radio made daily announcements that such rumors were completely false, that anyone needing medical attention could come to the clinic without fear of being arrested, that no one in the clinic would question any patient's immigration status. Such announcements were also believed to be tricks of the immigration service.

He had a second helping of everything and drank another bottle of beer. As he finished mopping the mole sauce off his plate with a tortilla, Esperanza excused herself and went to put the children to bed. Raúl called goodnight to Chuy from the kitchen door and María dashed in to give him a quick hug and kiss. Joselito peeked into the kitchen from behind his mother's skirt and Chuy winked at him and the boy giggled and ran off down the hall.

While she led them in their prayers he smoked a cigarette and finished his beer. After she tucked them into bed and turned out the lights in the rest of the house, she returned to the kitchen and poured coffee for them both. They sipped in silence but for the music from the radio. After a time she got up and turned down the volume and refilled their cups.

"You are very quiet tonight," she said.

He smiled at her and shrugged.

"Last night you were not so quiet."

He felt his smile dissolve and he stared down into his coffee cup. "I am sorry about last night."

"Do you remember what you said?"

He felt a sudden tightness in his belly and recognized the feeling as alarm but had no idea why he felt it.

"I am told it can be difficult to remember things when one has been so drunk as you were."

"I am very sorry I came to your house in such disgraceful condition," he said, glancing at her and then looking into his coffee again. "Forgive me."

"There is nothing to forgive," Esperanza said. "A man sometimes gets drunk with his friends. What is more natural?"

Chuy sipped at his cold coffee.

"A man gets drunk," Esperanza said, "and he says things. You said you love me."

Chuy glanced at her. He could not read her face. He lit a cigarette and looked into his empty cup and exhaled a long plume of smoke.

"You said you want to marry me," Esperanza said.

She got up and took their cups to the sink and washed them and dried them and hung them on little hooks under the cupboard. She sat down at the table again and took a cigarette from his pack and lit it.

"Oh, Chuyito," she said with a small smile. "Don't look so sad, my son. I will not ask you anything about love. Questions about love are always so foolish. No one truly understands love."

Chuy looked at her and said nothing. He told himself to think of nothing. It was a trick he had learned. If you thought of nothing, nothing could bother your mind.

"But I want to know," she said. "Were you telling the truth? Do you truly want to marry me?"

His cigarette burned his fingers and he quickly snuffed it in the ashtray.

"If an illegal marries a legal citizen of this country, then he too becomes a legal citizen. That is the law. Did you know that, Chuy?"

He had heard that such was so, but had not known if it were true. One heard so much that was not true. "Yes," he said.

"You would no longer have to live in fear of la migra."

"No," he said. Think of nothing, he told himself.

"I can be a good wife, Chuy. I would be, for you."

"I know." It was not so hard to think of nothing.

"The children love you and respect you. I believe you would be a very good father for them."

"Yes," he said.

"Then you truly want to marry me as you said?"

He looked at her. There was no pleading in her voice or her eyes, nor the slightest show of fear. She blinked slowly and waited for his answer.

"Yes," he said. And she smiled.

They smoked in silence for a while. He studied the palm of his hand, its lines, its thick scars, the marvelous manner in which it obeyed his silent commands to open and close.

"I am very happy, Chuy," she said. "But I want you to know that it truly makes no difference to me about love. I give myself to you, Chuy. I give you my family. I give you citizenship in this country. I give you my house where you will always have a home and always be safe. All I want is a good father for my children and a good man in my bed. I ask nothing more. You have my love, of course, but I do not demand yours in return. I can live without love. I have learned to live without it."

VII

They lay on their backs, their shoulders touching, and smoked in the dark. The sheets smelled of their lovemaking.

"Your sleep last night was troubled," she said. "You spoke names. Calles. Muria. Others. Tell me: who are those names?"

He watched the tip of her cigarette flare and cast her face in red light and shadow. The names were of men with whom he had sneaked across the Río Grande into the United States one night several months ago. In another lifetime. Calles had been barely more than a boy. Coughing with sickness in the back of the truck bringing them to Florida, coughing until blood gushed from his mouth, and still coughing until he died. They had buried him at the edge of a swamp in a place called Alabama. And Muria. The tough guy from Culiacán. He had punched a field boss who cheated him on his pay and the boss loosed the big dogs on him and the animals ripped his arms open to the bones and tore his crotch bloody before the other bosses got them off him at last and took Muria away—to a hospital they said—and nobody ever saw him again. That had happened two months ago.

"Nobody," he said. "I don't know. Who can say why he has the dreams he has?"

They put out their cigarettes and she turned on her side so that her buttocks pressed against him. He reached around and held her breast, then slid his hand down her smooth belly. She worked her hips and in a moment they were joined. Joselito began to whimper in the other bedroom. The child was a poor sleeper and given to frightening visions in the dark. By the time Chuy spent himself and rolled away from her, the boy was crying loudly, and Esperanza got up quickly to tend to him. After a time the boy quieted and then she came back to bed and snuggled against him and murmured endearments against his neck as he caressed the curve of her hip. She soon fell asleep.

He lay awake. The wind had come up and he heard it rushing through the trees. Moonlight swept in and out of the room through the open window above the bed. She lightly snored once, smacked her lips and moved in more snugly against him, and breathed deeply once again. A dog barked persistently in the distance.

The moonlight vanished behind the closing clouds. He could smell the rain coming. He wondered what time it was. They had come to bed around nine o'clock, maybe a little later. The wind-up clock was ticking on the small table on her side of the bed but it was too dark to see it.

Maybe you are no different than good-hearted but foolish Esteban, he thought—damned to living on the thin air of stupid dreams. Maybe you will be poor as always, even here, in this country of milk and money. Maybe there is nothing ahead but defeat and more defeat and still more defeat until you are dead. Maybe.

The dog went silent for a moment and then renewed his barking more furiously than before. Chuy gently disengaged his arm from under Esperanza, paused to see if she would waken, then eased out of bed and scooped up his clothes and carried them to the living room.

He dressed quickly. The wind was stronger now, and he could hear the trees tossing. He groped along the sofa in the dark until he found the shoebox, and then took it into the kitchen and flicked on the little light over the stove. He cut the cord binding and removed the top. The box held a deck of playing cards, an empty key ring, a pair of wool socks, a few seashells, a blue bandanna, and a large jackknife he had won from Muria in a dice game two days before the dogs got him. He took out the socks, bandanna and knife, then closed the box and retied it tightly and set it on the shelf over the sink. He emptied his pockets and placed his money on the counter, spread out the bills and coins, made a quick count and then re-pocketed two dollars. He rolled the bandanna into a rope and tied it around his neck. He picked up the knife and admired the clean feel of its onyx grips, then opened it as he had been taught by Muria—with a hard backhand snap of the wrist, so that the blade appeared almost magi-cally. It was six inches long and honed as finely as a shaving razor.

He folded the blade back into the haft and put the knife in his pocket. He scooped the money off the counter—five dollars and some change—and went back to the bedroom and entered on tiptoe. The woman was lying on her side, her face in dark shadow. He carefully placed the money on the dresser and then quietly opened the closet door and took his hat from its hook.

As he retraced his steps to the bedroom door, she said distinctly, "God will damn you for your stupidity."

He did not falter in his stride. He went down the hallway and through the living room and out the front door. He walked fast across the yard and turned down the street into the gusting wind as the first drops of rain stung his face and he left behind the house of Esperanza.

LA VIDA LOCA

THE LOSS

Check it out. I knew this dude worked as a ticket seller for a while at a dog track in T.J. He had a cousin down there got him the job. Dude was living in Chula Vista, crossing to Mexico every day to work this job. A million beaners trying to cross over to *here*, every day, you know, for the American Dream and all that shit—and *this* pocho's crossing over to *there* every day to make his nut. Crazy, eh? La vida loca, man.

Anyway, this dude—Cisco his name was—had a routine for boosting his take-home. Strictly legit, too, man. And tax-free. (*You* tell the IRS everything? Not in this life.) What he did was, every time a guy at the window asked him what number to play, he'd tell him. Every race, there's guys asking him the winning number. He's selling tickets, they figure he's got to be in the know, he's hip to the winner. Assholes, sure, but there's plenty of them in the world—I'm right, que no? So check it out: these guys are asking Cisco what number dog's gonna win and Cisco's telling them. Only he gives a different number to every guy that asks him. He'd go right down the list of entries, man—tell the first guy who asks it's the number one dog, tell the next guy it's number two, and so on. Every time he went through all the entries, he had to be giving the winner to *one* guy for sure. Some races he got asked by so many guys he'd go through all the entries nine, ten times before he closed the window. A lot of those guys never bothered to thank him, but plenty of them were real sports about it. They'd come back to the window with a big grin and kick him a ten, a twenty, depending on the payoff. End of the night it added up. Told me he was taking it home in a wheelbarrow some nights. Pretty good, eh? Fucken bulletproof, man.

The only problem was, some of the guys he gave a bum number didn't take it too good, you know? *They* came back to the window, he'd get an earful, a lot of hard-ass looks. Sometimes he'd shrug, try to look like he'd been fucked too, you know, like *he* got a bum tip. Mostly he just acted like he didn't hear them. Tried not to make eye contact.

One night a couple of pendejos who lost heavy on one of his numbers laid for him. Big mothers, man. And *real* bad losers. Followed him out to the parking lot. Took him off to the last nickel and then stomped him for laughs. Nearly killed him, man. Both arms busted, one leg, his cheekbones, lost some top teeth, some vision in one eye. You name it, man, they did it to him. He was all fucked-up for months. Went broke on the hospital bills.

I hear he's in L.A. now. Sells insurance in the barrios.

THE ROUST

Every man's got his own good reasons to be bitter, but you can't give in to them any old time you feel like it. There's a time and place for everything. The world's any-how not about to give a shit. A lot a these guys have a hard time understanding that, especially the Mexes. Chico, he never understood it for a minute.

There me and him were, killing a pint out by the bridge that runs out to Mustang, and Chico's already a little pissed because there's not but a couple of slugs left and we haven't got enough money between us to buy another bottle. Then here comes this cop car with its siren going and its blue lights flicking and it bounces up over the curb and screeches to a stop right in front of us, damn near runs us both over. Shook me so bad I dropped and broke the bottle and that was it for the last two swallows.

It's just one cop, some Mex kid with wetback parents if he ain't one himself, and here he is in the Corpus P.D. Looks about to piss his pants, too, when he jumps out of the car yelling, "On the groun', on the *groun'*! Hands behin' joor head!" But as he yanks his gun out of the holster he loses his grip on it and the thing comes skidding over to me. Never saw anything like that in my life.

Chico yells, "*Get* it!" and I snatch it up and point it at the cop with both hands. I hadn't held a gun since the army.

The cop's eyes are *this* big. Up go his hands. "Don't choot!" he says. "Don't choot!" He starts talking a mile a goddamn minute and you can hardly understand him, saying they're looking for two guys just hit the McDonald's six blocks away—one Anglo, one Mex—but he can see we're not the same two, so please don't shoot. I can feel myself shaking and I'm wondering what the hell I think I'm doing.

Chico tells him shut up and cusses him good. I'm saying, "Let's *go,* man, let's get *gone!*" but Chico *is pissed.* He picks up a big chunk of cinder block and goes over to the cop's car and POW!—he cobwebs the windshield of the driver's side. I couldn't goddamn believe it.

"*Sick* a gettin rousted!" he hollers. Picks up the chunk of block again and POW!—busts the other side of the windshield. The cop's still got his hands up but now his mouth's hanging open. Mine too, probly.

POW! Chico takes out a headlight, saying, "Fuck it *all!*" Then the other light. Then the party lights on the roof. And all the while he's smashing up the car he's going, "Goddamn cops! Goddamn People! Goddamn Marisol, you whore!"

Marisol's his ex. Got remarried down in the valley last year.

Now we got sirens closing in on us from all sides like walls, but Chico doesn't even seem to hear them, he just goes on busting that cop car all to hell with the piece of cinder block, yelling, "Sick of it! Fucken *sick* of it!"

Forget running. I hand the cop the piece and put my hands behind my back for him to cuff and we stand there and watch as the backups come tearing in. They see what's going down and they all go at Chico with their billies swinging. He made a fight of it for about five seconds before they coldcocked him good and gave him a bunch more for good measure.

I drew six months on the county farm. Chico had a bunch of priors so he got eighteen months in Huntsville.

Probably spending every day of it brooding on all the things he's sick of.

THE HOLDUP

We hit this convenience store in El Paso just off I-10 last Thursday night nearly did us in.

The routine went fine at first. Ramos braced the red-headed chick at the register while I watched the doors and kept the others covered. He worked smooth and fast like always, Ramos, a real pro. Red went big-eyed and said something, probably trying to bullshit Ramos about no key, a timelock, something, but we'd scoped this place good and knew better. Ramos talked to her nice and soft and she nodded and punched open the register and quick started sticking the bills in a plastic bag.

The fat guy by the ice cream freezer was freaked but smart enough to stand fast and keep his mouth shut. So was the big Mexican momma holding a little girl against her legs. They couldn't keep their eyes off the gun. That's why I use the .44. It's a bitch to lug around and try to hide even under a loose shirt, but a cannon like that gets their complete attention and they remember it a lot better than my face.

But there's this guy in a UTEP shirt who's had his head way in the deli cooler from the time we came in and he still doesn't know what's going down. He's already chomping on a sandwich when he turns around and catches the action. Next thing I know he's bent over and gagging and he drops down on all fours and he's making these godawful choking noises and he's turning fucken *blue*. All I can think is, if the sonofabitch dies we've had it. In Texas, somebody dies of *any*thing during a felony— trips on his damn shoelace and busts his head open—it's a murder rap for the perps. We'd worked maybe fourteen-fifteen jobs together and nobody dead yet. Never had to shoot, no heart attacks on us, nothing. Now this guy.

Ramos sees what's happening and I see his lips say *shit* and he quick comes over and gets busy working on the guy—who's now *purple,* starting to twitch, eyes rolled way up in his head, tongue bulging like you wouldn't believe. Ramos hugs him from behind and locks his hands together in the middle of the guy's chest and gives one fast hard squeeze after another. Even as I'm thinking we are royally fucked, I'm wondering where the hell he learned to do that. Everybody's watching him like it's TV.

Suddenly a big glob of sandwich shoots out of the guy's mouth and splats against a *People* magazine in the rack a good ten feet away and the guy starts sucking breath like an air brake.

Ramos runs over to the counter and grabs the money bag and we run out of there like cats with our tails on fire. I wheel the Mustang down the frontage road and onto the freeway and we're gone.

We're halfway to Tucson when Ramos counts the take. Hundred and thirty-two bucks. Jesus, this business. I usually have me two beers every night. That night I quit counting after the first six-pack.

REFEREE

I was best friends with Mato in grammar school, but I wouldn't say we liked each other all that much. He always had to show everybody he was tougher, he could take me. We'd wrestle at recess and he'd get me in a headlock and wouldn't let go till we drew a bigger crowd of classmates, a bigger bunch of laughing witnesses. Kids who wouldn't dare laugh at me on their own would laugh along with Mato like he was just having some good fun with his best friend. After he'd finally let me go he'd throw an arm over my shoulder, and all I could do to save face was grin back at him, the good loser, my ear swollen, all the time just burning inside, wanting to smash his smile.

By the time we were in high school we were the toughest kids in San Antonio, and I'm including the Anglos, the biggest ones. We didn't give a damn about size— we'd fight anybody, anytime, kick their ass. That's when Rita came in the picture, a transfer from California. From L.A. First day there she had every guy in school walking into walls. Killer green eyes, hair like honey to her ass, great legs, skin more like a tan gringa than the Chicana she was. Sure as hell of herself, too, way cooler than most you'd ever find in Texas. Quick smart mouth on her. When the homecoming committee asked her to be one of the queen's maids of honor, she said why not, the strapless gown would show off the spider tattoos over her titties real nice. They took back the offer and she laughed every time she told the story. She was like that. Loved to shock the straight arrows. She'd been in school about a month when her and a faculty guy, an English teacher, were spotted in a nightclub, drinking and dirty dancing. The school board got wind of it and it turned into a big deal in the newspapers. The guy ended up getting fired. Rita, she just *beamed* about the whole thing. I heard she taped the news clippings to her wall, next to the movie star pictures.

I know she'd seen me watching her sometimes in the halls between classes. One day I'm at my locker and I feel somebody blow on the back of my ear, I turn around and she says, "Hey, Rudy Cortés, you don't look like such a Mister Bad-Ass to *me*." Mister Bad-Ass was what the guys

at school called me. Mato they called Killer. She was looking at me with nothing but daring in her face, those eyes
like green fire. That night we parked out in the boonies
and she let me touch her everywhere, but no more than
that. She didn't have a pair of tattoos like she'd said, just
the one: a little blue heart on her left tit.

Mato usually preferred morenas, Mexican-looking
ones, but when he saw how much I dug Rita he naturally
started coming on to her too. We told each other we were
scoring, but I don't think he was getting anything I
wasn't, not then, not yet. But her teasing was driving me
crazy. I was going around so revved up I picked a fight
for no reason with a guy on the football team and
whipped his ass in the lot behind Min's Pharmacy, where
all the after-school fights took place. Rita watched it, and
that night in the car she used her mouth on me for the
first time. I loved the look on Mato's face when I told him
about it the next day. He called me a bullshit artist but
he knew it was true, and I could tell by his face she hadn't
done it for him. That afternoon in the locker room he
made out like he was just horsing around but kept pop-
ping me good ones on the ass with a towel till I said cut
the crap. He said why don't I make him cut the crap
behind Min's at 3:15. I said you're on. It'd been coming
since way before Rita and we both knew it.

Most of the school turned out for it, even Coach Canellos, who was also the dean of boys and wanted to see
this one as much as anybody. We both gave Rita our shirt
to hold. She winked at me, smiled at Mato. I really
thought I'd take him. We went at it for twenty minutes.
I got in some good shots, but when my eyes were swollen
nearly shut, Canellos stepped in and stopped it. Great
fight, chachos, he said, then suspended us both for a

week. Rita handed me my shirt and left with Mato. A few days later he stopped by the lumberyard where I was working and told me she'd left on a bus back to California to be a movie star. He thought the whole thing was pretty funny, and in spite of myself he got me laughing about the shiners we both still wore. But the truth is, even while I was laughing I wanted to put my fist through his face.

Around that time we both said the hell with school and took up training for the Legion smokers at Roberto Zavala's Gym. Roberto put us up in the Nopales Hotel down the street with the rest of his fighters. It was a fleabag but it beat hell out of "home." Ever since my folks were killed in a car crash when I was nine I'd been living with my Aunt Concha and her two pain-in-the-ass daughters, and I was happy to be shed of that house of nags. As for Mato, his old man vanished before he was born, and his mother was a boozer with a different bum in her bed every week. When he moved out he didn't tell her where he was going and she didn't ask.

We were both natural welterweights, but I was the better boxer. I had the sharper jab, the quicker feet. I could hit too, but Mato was the real puncher. His hook to the body was like a ball bat. In those days he was always coming at you, willing to take two to give one. Roberto predicted we'd end up against each other in the semifinals, and we did. Roberto always said a good boxer could beat a good slugger any day if he was careful not to get tagged, which is a pretty big if. Stick and move and keep your distance, he told me, and you can't lose, not to a puncher, not even him. Roberto had trained us both but he worked my corner when we fought because

I'd do like he told me. Mato always did things his own way.

I could've won it easy if I'd fought the last two rounds like the first, if I'd kept jabbing and staying away from his hooks. All the judges gave me the first. But in the middle of the second he dropped his hands and laughed at me, said *Rita* could give him a better fight. So I went at him. At the bell we were both whaling with both hands but he was landing the harder shots. Roberto was having a fit when I got back to the corner. Called me fool, pendejo, every name there is. Mato grinned across the ring and shook his head to let me know how little I'd hurt him. I knew Roberto was right, that I was a jerk to fight Mato's fight, but I couldn't help it. All I wanted was to smash his face. So we mixed it up again in the third and he wobbled me with a hook to the liver and an uppercut that broke my nose. I hung on to the end of the round, but the damage was done and the judges gave it to him. After the decision, he puts his arm around me and smiles for the cameras. The picture in the sports page next day called us "Amigo Maulers." Jesus. I would've *danced* on him if he'd dropped dead. In the final, he put the other guy away in under two minutes of the first round.

A Dallas group gave him a pro contract and set him up at a training camp. I signed on with a manager who worked out of El Paso, so I went to live there. I roomed in a place on Stanton and trained in a good gym across the river in Juárez. A lot of the Mex fighters couldn't speak English and called me pocho because I didn't know but a dozen words in Spanish. But they smiled when they said it and we got along OK.

For the next two years Mato and me both kept winning and working our way up the ranks. Sometime in there I saw Rita in a skin magazine, a red-haired "starlet" now, calling herself Jill Somebody, five pages showing her titty tattoo and everything else to the world. I don't know how to explain it, but the pictures made me horny and mad at the same time. I sent her a note in care of the magazine—"Looking good kid, Mr. Bad Ass"—and then felt like a jerk for mailing it.

They matched me and Mato in New Orleans on the undercard of a televised championship fight. They talked us up as dynamite comers with identical 14–0 pro records, 11 kayos each. Mato was already #4 in the federation rankings, I was #6, but the betting line had us even. He came down to the ring from the dressing room with a crowd around him, lights flashing, music on the PA, a whole show like he's a champ already. Dances by my corner in his sequined robe and says, "Say goodnight, Rudy." *Smiles.* For six rounds it was as close as the book-ies thought it'd be. Then he butted and opened a hell of a cut over my eye. My guys couldn't stop the blood. The ref called it accidental and the ring doctor wouldn't let me go on. Mato was up by a point on two of the cards, so it was his fight. He comes to my corner and pats me on the shoulder, showing the crowd and the people in TV-land what a good sport he is. Leans in close and says, "Like they told us in school—use your head to get ahead." I called him a bastard and meant it, and he laughed.

Fourteen months later we'd both won five more, and they signed us to fight again, this time for a shot at the champ. Mato was five-to-three favorite but there was talk the smart money was on me. I was training for that fight when one day I'm jogging past this adult video store and I slow down to check out the pictures and the new video boxes in the front window—and there's Rita on the front of one called *Lila's Luscious Love*, kneeling naked on a bed with a "don't-you-wish" look on her face. I don't know how long I stood there looking at it before I got back to my run. Every night for the next two weeks I thought about going down and checking out that video but I never did. It was bad enough just imagining what was on it. I wrote her a letter one night without mentioning the video, just "Hey, how are you, what you been up to?" But I didn't know where to mail it, so I stuck it in one of my bags.

The fight was in Atlantic City and it was another close one. Most everybody scored the first five rounds even. I was at my best but Mato had come a long way. He was faster and smoother than I thought he'd ever be. He'd learned to put a twist on his jab and to use it backing up, to jump in with a combination and dance quick out of counterpunch range. He'd learned to *box* is what I'm saying.

He talked a lot the first couple of rounds, telling me how slow I'd gotten, laughing and shaking his head whenever I landed a shot, letting the crowd know it didn't do a thing. In the third I started talking back, giving him the same kind of trash. My corner told me to shut up, just fight, but I couldn't help it. Maybe if I hadn't been running my mouth so much he wouldn't have been able to snake the right over my jab in the fourth like he did. Ripped the eye wide open—same eye as before. I couldn't see squat with it for the blood. My corner worked like hell on the cut between rounds, but then he'd open it right up again. He'd tie me up against the ropes and roll his head on it, rub his glove across it, give it short twisting shots, keep working it bigger and bigger. My blood was all over us. The ref kept saying he was going to stop it after one more round, and I kept saying don't do it. Then Mato connected with the eye again in the eighth and I started seeing double. At the end of the round the ring doc took another close look and shook his head. The ref waved his hands and that was it.

Mato came to my corner and held my hand up in a grand sporting gesture. Says to me, "Gave it your best, mano, got nothing to be shamed of." Giving me that *smile*! I wanted to kill him. But then I suddenly knew the truth: I *knew* he was a better fighter than I was. And I knew I either learned to live with it or I'd be eating my guts out the rest of my life. So I shook his hand and I meant it, and his smile went sort of funny, like it was the last thing he expected. I don't know why, but his look made me feel like I'd won something.

A few weeks later the doctors told me the eye was ruined for good and I couldn't fight anymore.

Mato went on to win the title like everybody knew he would. He was a popular champ, too, always gave the fans their money's worth. The first couple of years, he defended the title every two-three months. Fighting that often not only made him rich, it kept him in shape so he didn't have to train much for a match. Some champs feel about training the way most good-looking women feel about housework—you know, it's beneath them. But after he'd beaten the top contenders, he was fighting one bum after another and putting them away inside the first couple of rounds. Those quick kayos look great to the fans but you can't stay sharp if you're training half-assed and fighting nothing but palookas. Especially not if you're playing the role all the time like Mato was doing—partying, knocking over the chicks, lapping up the attention.

Me, I became a ref. Third man in the ring. Turned out I had a flair for it, what some would call a naturally theatrical manner. I grew a bandido mustache and the fans liked the way I danced around the fighters and shook both index fingers at the fighters like pistols whenever I gave a warning. They loved the way I mugged it up big when I gestured for a fighter to keep his punches up or for a couple of huggers to knock off the waltzing and *fight*, goddamn it.

I took to chewing bubble gum while I worked and would blow a big bubble every now and then when the going was slow, just to give the fans a little entertainment and let the fighters know they were boring hell out of all of us. When they heard a bubble pop they knew they'd best pick things up. Between rounds I'd feint and jab at the girl strutting around the ring with the round-card over her head, get a grin out of her and a laugh from the crowd. If she was showing her ass in one of those little thong numbers, I'd sometimes do a double-take and grab at my heart. That always broke the place up. Some of the sportswriters didn't care for my clowning. Said it was "demeaning to the fight game" to have a referee carry on the way I did. Dig it: *demeaning*. To the *fight* game. Oh, man. The fact was, most of the fans and even most of the news-hacks got a kick out of my show, and the commission never did come down on me about it. Besides, I was a damn good ref. When I was in the ring I *ran* it. A fighter didn't do as I said after I warned him once, I quick took the point. The pugs learned quick that when I said jump they better jump. One time a couple of sluggers kept hitting fast and furious after the bell and when I shoved between them to break them up I caught a wild one on the jaw. I just looked at the pug and gave him a big shrug—like, *"That's* the best you got?"—and shook my head in disgust. The crowd loved it.

I traveled a lot, naturally, but home was in Houston. A buddy in real estate got me a good deal on a house on a bayou in Morgan's Point. I took up sailing and every chance I got I was out on the bay in my boat. I'd have to say things were pretty fine.

Then out of the blue I get a phone call from Rita. She'd seen me ref a fight on TV, then tracked me down through a magazine sports guy in L.A. She was in town and wondered if maybe we could get together for dinner, talk about old times, have some laughs. Well yeah, sure. Talk about surprised. It'd been more than eight years. I was nervous as a kid as I drove to meet her at a steak house in Galena Park. She showed up in a cab, looking swell. She smiled big and warm when she saw me, gave me a tight hug, a kiss on the mouth. Turns out things had soured for her in L.A. It was practically a closed club out there, she said, strictly who you knew and who you blew. She'd been in a couple of "minor productions," but her agent was straight from hell and she finally realized she was never going to get a break, not out there.

I didn't bring up the skin magazine or *Lila's Luscious Love.* What for? That was then, this was now. She was just passing through, she said, on her way to Atlanta to interview for a TV job. After dinner I drove her to the hotel and she asked me up for a drink on the terrace and a look at the great view she had of the city. One thing led to another. I wanted to *sing* after we made love. Next day she packed her bag and went home with me.

Over the next month I pulled out of a couple of fights

just to stay home with her. We sailed, had picnics, went to the movies, talked a little, fooled around a lot. I'd say I was falling in love. Then one night we're in a restaurant downtown and Mato shows up with his crowd. Sends a bottle of wine to our table, then comes over, all smiles and damn-small-world, long-time-no-see, how-the-hell-are-you. Wearing a white silk suit, Rolex, tie that probably cost two hundred bucks, his hair longer now, *styled*. But he looked fifteen pounds over the limit, and I figured he'd play hell making the weight for his next fight. He was in town for an athletic-shoe commercial they were shooting at the Astrodome. Get together sometime, he says, shaking my hand so-long and winking at Rita. It wasn't till then I saw how she was looking at him, and my chest suddenly felt hollow.

I told myself it wouldn't happen again, but I was just whistling. All the following week she already seemed more like a memory than somebody real and right there with me. I went off to Biloxi to work a fight, feeling empty, knowing she'd be gone when I got back. She was. Left a note on the fridge: "It was fun." *Fun*. Not long afterwards I saw a picture of them in the papers. She was hanging on his arm at some charity thing in New York.

I wouldn't say I got over it.

Two months later Mato signed to defend against Caballo Galvez in Vegas and I was picked for third man. I didn't want a damn thing to do with Mato, but I figured he'd somehow be getting the best of me if I turned the job down, so I took it.

There were two other title fights on the card that night—flyweight and junior lightweight—but Mato's was the main event, and the place was standing room only.

Galvez was a brawler out of Guatemala who'd won his last seven by knockout and had come up the rankings like a rocket. He was no palooka, and Mato had his work cut out this time. Rita was at ringside with a bunch of Mato's high-roller pals. She wore diamonds and a black dress cut to here. She gave me a smile just like Mato's, and when I didn't smile back she laughed.

The crowd was almost all Latino, but except for a bunch of Guatemalans up in the cheap seats Galvez didn't have a friend in the place. As he made his way to the ring, you could hardly hear his tico-tico music on the PA for the booing. This was Mato's crowd and the cheers shook the walls when his people escorted him from the dressing room with the *Rocky* theme blasting out of the speakers. He made his customary strut around the ring with a fist raised high, blessing the faithful with that arrogant smile. We go through the booing and cheering all over again when the announcer makes the introductions—I got the usual good hand and gave the crowd a wave and an Ali shuffle—then they closed around me in the center of the ring for last-minute instructions. "Good clean fight," I tell them. Mato smiles at me and gives Galvez a wink. When he'd heard Galvez owned a women's cosmetics business in Guatemala, he started referring to him in the papers as Chiquita, and Galvez was red-eyed fury.

It was a street fight from the opening bell. Galvez was even more of a puncher than Mato, so Mato did his best to box him—using the jab, circling one way and then the other, weaving, keeping his distance. But the Guatemalan had been around the block too and knew all the tricks, including how to cut off the ring. He cornered Mato at least once in every round and forced him to slug it out. They were butting in the clinches, thumbing, using elbows, shoulders, rabbit-punching, you name it. Both corners kept getting on me about the other guy's dirty tactics. I wasn't blowing bubbles that night.

At the end of the fifth, they were in a corner and still punching after the bell, so I grabbed Galvez from behind and pulled him back—and when I did, Mato gave him a shot to the head. Galvez was so enraged he had to be wrestled back to his corner by his seconds. His fans were hollering bloody murder but Mato's crowd easily drowned them out. I put a finger in Mato's face and said I'd take a point next time. Just loud enough for me to hear, he said, "Goddamn, I guess *that'll* make us even," and smiled his bastard smile. He raised a fist at Rita as he went back to his corner and I couldn't help looking her way. She gave me a look and a smile, blew him a kiss.

Something twisted under my chest bone and felt about to break. I could hardly breathe. I felt like I was smothering in a red haze. I stood in a neutral corner during the one-minute break and thought about nothing but breathing in and out.

Mato was a hair ahead on all three judges' cards when the bell rang for the next round, but I don't remember the first minute of it. I was dancing around the fighters and looking alert, but all I was really seeing were the smiles I'd gotten from Mato and Rita. All I was hearing was Mato's *"that'll* make us even" over and over in my head. Then I heard Mato grunt in pain and everything pulled into focus.

Galvez had him against the ropes and was banging him with body shots, trying to make him drop his hands so he could get at his head. The Guatemalan had pure murder in his eye—but he was too wound up, punching too wild. Mato countered with a flurry and got away from the ropes. But I could see he was tiring, the high life was catching up to him. He was flat-footed now, not moving as quick as before. They were fighting toe-to-toe, trading wicked shots, spraying sweat off each other's head with every punch. The place was going crazy, Mato's fans screaming for him to kill Galvez, *kill* him. Whoever said the real beast in the arena is the crowd knew what he was talking about.

With a minute-and-a-half to go Mato landed a hard combination, then tried to take Galvez's head off with a right hand from the floor. But he missed—and Galvez countered with a monster hook that buckled Mato's knees. Mato tried to cover up but the Guatemalan gave him two hard shots to the kidney to bring his hands down and then drilled him with a straight right that staggered him back into the ropes.

Now Galvez had him. He tore into him like a crazy man, punching with both hands as fast and hard as he could. He was just *whimpering* with rage. They say he landed 48 head shots in the next nine seconds. Mato's hands dropped and his head was snapping every which way with the punches but Galvez had him pressed to the ropes and wouldn't let him fall.

The crowd was on its feet and howling, some of them already yelling "Stop it, *stop* it!" I gave a quick look at Rita standing at the ring apron directly under the fighters and looking up in horror, her face and hair getting spattered with Mato's blood.

Through the quivering roar I heard them yelling, *"Stop it!* STOP IT!"

Stop it, hell. A towel came flapping into the ring but I made like I didn't see it and let Galvez go on hammering.

I didn't pull the Guatemalan away till Mato's cornermen came tumbling through the ropes. As Mato slid down the ropes to the canvas his eyes were nearly shut but looking my way. I like to think he was still conscious, that he could still see. That he read my eyes.

The place sounded like a zoo on fire. Rita was looking a little loony. I wanted to give her a big smile, a wink, blow her a kiss. I never knew what became of her after that. Never much cared.

Mato died on the table. I caught a lot of heat, of course, in the press, on TV. A lot of stuff questioning my judgment. And the commission suspended my license.

But that was pretty much it.

I'd have to say it's all about even.

TEXAS WOMAN BLUES

"Doom is the House without the Door."
—EMILY DICKINSON

I

SUGARGIRL'S DADDY

1

Dolores has been living with her aunt and uncle for six months when the letter comes from her father. Everybody can see it's from him because of the Texas Department of

Corrections envelope. Aunt Rhonda hands it to her like it's some run-over thing off the road, her face all squinched up. Dolores takes it to her room and closes the door.

The letter is written on institutional stationery. The information in the spaces at the top of the page has been provided in a large ball-point scrawl. Further down, the words of the letter stagger in the same unpracticed hand between the hard straight lines of the page.

TEXAS DEPARTMENT OF CORRECTIONS

Date <u>10/22/66</u>   Inmate No. <u>1099</u>   Name <u>Buckman stock</u>   Unit <u>Ellis</u>
To <u>   Dolores stock   </u>   Relation <u>   daughter   </u>
RFD, St or Box No. <u>380 Bowie ave</u>   City <u>Raymondville</u>   State <u>Texas</u>

TO THE PERSON RECEIVING THIS LETTER
All inmates' mail is opened, censored and recorded by OFFICIALS. Inmates may receive not more than three letters a week from any one person on their correspondence and visiting lists. These letters must be limited to two pages. You may use one sheet and write on the front and back if you wish. Please address the inmate by name and number. If these rules are not observed the letter will be returned to the sender . . .

Dear sugargirl
I'm sorry I have not writen to you untill now. They told me awhile back Hannah past away. I been meaning to write you and tell you how sorry I am but, I have been at a lost for words. I am so sorry sugargirl. I guess you dont believe me but, I loved your moma very much tho I guess I din't show it too good sometimes. I can't think of anything to say, to make up for the pain and the heart-ache I caused her, and you too. All I can say is I'm awful sorry. Please try not to think to hard of me sugargirl I know I was'nt much of a daddy or a

husband either one. Sometimes I feel like cutting my own throat for the no-count I am. I figgure god's making me pay back for that more than for what I did to that fella in Houston. I wish I could be with you now, sugargirl taking care of you like a good daddy ought but as you know I got what they call a prior oblagation. (ha ha). I hope your happy and doing good in school. They told me your living with frank and Ronda I'm glad to hear it. I never got to know frank real good for a half-brother but he's always seemed a good old boy and I guess ronda's alright too. Be sure and mine them and be a good girl. By the way do you think you could send me a litle money. I'd sure be greatful. I'm always running out of cigs and stuff. Even in this place you got to have some money ain't that a hoot. Just a few dollers would help a lot. It gets a little irratating in here sometimes but I guess thats why they call it a prison huh. (ha ha.) Well I guess that's all for now. Please write, Your father.

p.s.—happy birthday sugargirl!!! Sweet sixteen and never been kissed huh? (ha ha, not hardly huh.) I wish I had a present I could give to you.

pp.s—please excuse my bad writting.

There is no signature. Directly below the last line of the letter is a stamped circle the size of a fifty-cent piece enclosing the word "CENSORED."

She tells herself to throw the letter away, now, right this minute. Instead, she reads it all the way through once again, slowly, from letterhead to final misspelled word.

He says he's sorry. Says it right there in his own jerky handwriting. Says it . . . four times, all told. But the first time's just sorry he hasn't written to her. And the next two are sorry momma's dead. Only the last one's sorry about how he treated momma so bad. And *her* too, he says, though try as she might she cannot think of a single time her daddy ever mistreated *her*.

But she has no trouble remembering how he treated momma, and the recollection fills her with a sudden fury. Cut his own throat for being such a no-count, hell—there were bound to be lots of folk who'd be happy to do the job for him, herself included.

She is instantly appalled by the ferocity of her vindictiveness. Lord, girl, why feel so . . . *hateful* about him?

Because. Because he was a lowlife drunk and a damn whoremonger who was so god-awful mean to momma is why.

Yeah, well . . . but he was never mean to *you*, was he? Never even raised his voice at you, did he?

She recalls that voice now as clearly as if she'd last heard it five minutes ago. It had made her shiver when he hollered at momma, but oh it was such a sweet voice when he sang. Back in the good old days he used to sing to her at bedtime almost every night. "Goodnight, Irene" and "Red River Valley" and "Hush, Little Baby." And on the long drives back to Alice from the beach at Mustang Island in the yellow Roadmaster the three of them would harmonize on "Row, Row, Row Your Boat." She always loved singing the part that went, "merrily, merrily, merrily, merrily, life is but a dream." She'd always been sunburned and sandy and a little tired, but the way daddy and momma would look at each other up in the front seat and stroke each other and make each other laugh made her feel better than anything would ever make her feel again.

One time when they were driving back from the beach

she asked momma if life was really just a dream like the song said, and momma told her, "Sometimes it is, honey," and reached over and stroked the back of daddy's neck as he drove along one-handed like always and held a cigarette between his teeth like it was a little prize cigar. "Can be a pretty *sweet* dream."

Daddy had grinned around the cigarette and glanced at her in the rearview mirror. "That's right, darlin, *can* be. Or can be a damn nightmare, you ain't careful."

"Buck Henry!" momma said, slapping at his shoulder. "Don't you be telling her things like that! She's just a little girl!"

Daddy chuckled and said, "She sure enough is. My little sugargirl, ain't you darlin?" He winked at her in the rearview and they laughed together like conspirators. Momma looked from one to the other of them and shook her head, saying, "You two are *so* bad, I swear."

That was way back when, she reminds herself, and she was just a child. That was back before he started losing jobs on one rig after another. Before he started drinking so hard and getting in so many fights. Before him and momma started going at each other so bad.

No, he never did raise his voice at her, but she remembers now that he did give her a sort of push one time. It was only a little shove and only that one time. But still. You wouldn't think it would've slipped her mind so easy, considering when it happened and all. And considering she hasn't seen him since. And anyway, it was just a shove, it wasn't like he'd *hit* her or anything, for pete's sake.

Yeah, right. But he sure enough hit momma that time, didn't he? Hit her and worse. God *damn* him! How could he have *done* her like that? That low-down sorry . . .

Whoa now, girl, just hold on. Let's be fair here. Momma *did* hit him first and that's a true fact. In the face with a wire hanger, remember? And he *was* pretty drunk. Not that being drunk is any excuse at all because it's not, even if momma used to let it be, back before the excuse just flat wore out. Just the same, it's something to keep in mind, that he was drunk, because it's a fact, and you have to keep the facts straight if you're going to be fair.

That's all she's trying to do here, be fair.

Hardly a day goes by that she doesn't think about the last time she saw her daddy. Hardly a day will ever go by. A Sunday morning it was, as pretty as they come, the windows open wide and full of soft yellow sunlight, the blue curtains lifting lightly on a cool breeze. Church bells from down the street. Momma had made sugar-and-cinnamon doughnuts and a full pot of coffee for breakfast. (Her own cup had half-milk.) She was on the sofa looking at the funny papers while momma ironed clothes and hummed along to the songs playing low on the radio. Then here came daddy's old pickup clattering down the street and roaring into the front yard and braking up a spray of dirt in momma's new-planted flowerbed, his radio blasting out some Okie song before the engine shut off and the truck door banged and his big boots thumped up onto the porch. There'd been times before when he'd been gone a day or two, but this time it had been five days and nights without a word if he was dead or alive.

Back when she hadn't even started going to school yet, he'd almost always be singing when he came home from the oil field at the end of the day. The clump of his boots on the porch would make her heart jump as she ran to greet him with momma already at the screen door and smiling. Sometimes the song he'd be singing was a little off-color and momma would blush and hiss, "Buck Henry Stock!" and gesture toward Dolores. He'd hug momma tight and pat her on the rump and then give Dolores a big handsome grin and say, "Well now, who's *that* pretty li'l darlin?" He'd snatch her up and whirl her around over his head while she shrieked with delight and momma stood by with her fist on her mouth. He'd hug her so tight she could hardly breathe, but her heart would feel as swelled up as a birthday balloon. She loved the smell of him, the mingled odors of oil and sweat and tobacco and beer. And just barely detectable under it all, the hint of some fierce aroma like that of a flaring kitchen match. For the rest of her life in this tough Texas lowcountry, that mix of smells in a man will snag her like a lasso.

But the smell he carried that morning was different— a reeking tangle of whiskey and vomit and ladies' perfume. He was sort of halfway grinning, like he'd just heard a good dirty joke but wasn't real sure he should tell it to momma. You could see he was still drunk. And he had a mean-looking black eye swollen nearly shut. Once upon a time that eye would've moved momma to sufficient pity to forgive him just about anything, even being gone a couple of days, but not this time. She was way past that. When he hadn't phoned by the fourth morning, Dolores had seen by her face that she'd reached the end of her rope with him. And when the screen door slapped shut behind him and she caught the smell of that perfume, well, that did it. She glared at him and said, "You no-good son of a bitch." She who rarely cussed and had never before cussed him. The floor dropped out from under his grin and he looked like she'd spit in his face.

Suddenly it was like the world sped up to sixty miles an hour. They yelled terrible names at each other and

the little breakfast table with the coffeepot and doughnuts
tumped over and then momma was whipping him across
the face with a wire hanger, cutting bright red lines in his
face. He backhanded her into the wall and snatched away
the hanger and she clawed at his eyes and they knocked
over the ironing board as they went down fighting like
cats in the mess of doughnuts and coffee on the floor.
Dolores recalls screaming for them to stop it, stop it, recalls being so afraid for momma that she tried to pull
daddy off her and that's when he knocked her aside without even glancing at her. (She now remembers hitting the
wall so hard her head rang.) And then momma had the
clothes iron in her hand and was trying to put it to his
face and there was the hiss of its touch against his neck
and he roared and wrestled it from her and now had a
fistful of her hair and momma was fending with her
hands and the room shook with her screaming and was
full of the smell of her burning flesh.

And then momma broke free and ran shrieking out of
the house and daddy stomped over to the door and
kicked out the screen and hollered a bunch of filthy names
but didn't chase after her. The back of his shirt was
smeared with doughnuts and stained with coffee. He
turned and caught sight of Dolores huddled in a corner.
She was too terrified to move, and she could tell that for
a second he didn't even recognize her. And then he did—
and his face sagged like all the bones in it broke at once.
He stood there a minute, staring at her and crying without
sound, his tears mixing with the blood running off the
slashes on his face and dripping off his chin, looking like
he'd just crossed over to someplace he'd never be able to
get back from again. Then he turned and bolted outside
and the truck door slammed and the engine roared and

the tires spun in the grass and the truck fishtailed out onto the street and squealed away.

Then she was out the door too and running down the street and crying so hard she couldn't see where she was going and a neighbor woman caught hold of her and took her into a house where somebody was yelling into a telephone for the police and a bunch of people were gathered around momma in the kitchen and smearing butter on her hands and arms and momma was crying and crying like somebody'd died.

They never heard from him again, but they heard *about* him every now and then over the following year. Arrested in Corpus Christi for disorderly conduct. Locked up in San Antone for destruction of municipal property. Jailed in Galveston for assault. Then came the news about his really bad trouble in Houston and the thirty-years-to-life sentence in the state penitentiary at Huntsville. But they never heard *from* him in all that time. Never heard from him until *now*, with momma more than six months in the ground.

And he says he's sorry.

Naturally he says that—just look what he says right after: send me money. I'm sorry, now send me money. Of all the damn *nerve*! First time he writes to her in the nearly three years he's been behind bars and he's asking for money. It's the only reason he wrote to her, she just knows it, and she feels like both cursing and crying.

But hey . . . he remembered her birthday. Right there at the bottom of the page, see. Her daddy remembered her birthday. He even wishes he had a present for her. There he is in prison, living a life of daily torments, and still he remembered his Sugargirl's birthday.

Sugargirl. Nobody else ever called her that. Only daddy.

She feels her heart banging in her chest like a bird encaged with a snake. She goes to the window and draws deep breaths. She feels parched, but she'd rather go thirsty than leave her room for a drink of water just now and maybe run into Aunt Rhonda.

She carefully reads every line of the letter again. He's allowed three letters a week from the people on his correspondence and visiting lists. Was she on those lists? He says please write, so she must be on his letters list, anyway. What about his visiting list? Wouldn't he have told her if she was? Wouldn't he have said come visit me? She wonders who *would* be on that list. She can't think of a single solitary soul. Grandpa and Grandma Stock were both dead, and Uncle Rayburn, daddy's older and only full brother, had been in the crazy ward of the VA hospital since the Korean War and like as not always would be. And who knew where his one sister Sally Stock Brown had been these past five years. Back before she got married, Aunt Sally used to visit fairly often. She was funny and sassy about everything and could make momma laugh so. Dolores thought the world of her. Then she married a fella named Lyle Brown, a truck mechanic from Uvalde who momma thought was a peckerwood and who she could never understand Aunt Sally getting hitched to. Not six months later Sally took off on the back of a motorcycle driven by a pool player named Farley Zane and nobody'd ever heard from her again. Maybe Aunt Sally wrote to daddy from wherever she was, but not likely, since she would've written to momma if she'd written to anybody, but she hadn't. As far as Dolores knew, the only living kin daddy had was Uncle Frank.

Could be daddy had friends she didn't know about, friends who wrote him and visited him regularly, but she didn't think so. The kind of men she remembered him buddying with weren't the letter-writing sort—if they could write at all. He anyway never did have many close friends. The only two goodbuddies of his that ever dropped by the house were Everett Purdue and a huge red-bearded fella named Double John. But Everett had gone to prison about a year after daddy for armed-robbing a filling station in Oklahoma. And just a few months ago Double John had accidentally gassed himself to death one freezing night after his wife locked him out of the house and he went to sleep in his truck with the motor running in order to keep the heater going. Most likely, Dolores thought, daddy didn't get too many letters or a whole lot of visitors.

What if she *was* on his visiting list? Would she go see him if he asked her to? The question yanks her heart up into her throat. Well, now, she just doesn't know, she guesses it would just depend. She runs her finger swiftly along every line of the letter again. Nope, he doesn't say it. He doesn't say he loves her. Not anywhere on the page. A fact is a fact, and it's a fact he doesn't say it. "I loved your momma very much"—*that's* in there. But not a word about he loves *her*.

But hold on now . . . the letter *was* censored. No bones about it, either—it says so right there at the top: "All inmates' mail is opened, *censored*, and recorded by OFFICIALS." And then again at the bottom of the letter—in the big round stamp that practically hollers it at you: "CENSORED." Maybe the prisoners aren't allowed to write "I love you." Maybe that's part of the punishment. Maybe they're allowed to say they love somebody else, like he says he loved momma, but not allowed to say it to the people they write the letter to. Maybe they even censor the word "love" out of the letters the prisoners *get*, so they can't have even the comfort of being reminded that somebody somewhere still loves them. That would be terrible, she thinks . . . but even more terrible, girl, is just how damn dumb you are, because only somebody dumber than dirt would think something so ridiculous.

Yeah . . . but . . . maybe he was just too *scared* to say it. What if he thought she might be so mad at him she'd just laugh at his letter and throw it away? Just imagine how it'd feel to think your words of love might get laughed at and thrown in the garbage. She tells herself to be fair now: could she really blame him for not saying "I love you" in *this* letter, the very first one he's written her since going to the penitentiary? The first letter he's written her *ever*? Shoot, he's just waiting to see if she's going to write him back, is all. If she does—and if she doesn't tell him to go to hell—then he'll likely trust her to treat his feelings with the respect that's a daddy's due. And *then* he'll know he can go ahead and tell her what's really and truly in his heart.

She tries to imagine what it's like to have to live among hundreds and hundreds of criminal strangers, among heartless killers and robbers and awful men of every sort. What it's like to have to live in a small steel cell with bars all around and guards watching you all the time. She wonders if he shares a cell with another prisoner, and if he does, if he's gotten to be friends with him, if he's told him about his daughter who he calls sugargirl. She wonders if he ever wishes he could just go out and get in a car and drive himself someplace for a cheeseburger and a strawberry shake, or go to a drive-in movie and have popcorn and laugh at the cartoons, or go to the beach like they used to do, him and her and momma, singing all the way there and all the way back: "Row, row, row your boat . . ." She wonders if he spends his days busting rocks with a sledgehammer or picking cotton out in the hot sun. Does he go out with a chain gang and work with a scythe in the ditches by the side of the road with his shirt off and the sweat running off his sunburned back while people drive by in their cars and stare out at him without a bit of pity? Does he work in a machine shop and stamp out license plates? She knows they wear white uniforms. She once saw a newspaper photo that showed a bunch of state convicts working at a cotton farm in the valley, and one of them—a Mexican-looking boy— had his whole back covered with a big colorful tattoo of an eagle with a snake in its beak and its wings spread wide. He was smiling over his shoulder with big white teeth and looked like the proudest thing. Most of the convicts she's ever seen along the road or in pictures looked like they'd never smiled in their life.

What she wonders most of all is if he ever thinks of her.

Well, of *course* he does, you nitwit! He wrote to you, didn't he?

She wonders if he has a picture of her, and if he does, if he keeps it taped on the wall next to his bunk so he can look at it when he's lying there. It couldn't be any more recent than her seventh grade picture from four years ago. When he looks at it does he wonder how she's changed and what she looks like now? Maybe she should go down to the drugstore and get some of those four-for-a-quarter pictures from the little curtained booth in back and send them to him. She could make a different face in

every one so he could see all the ways she really looks.
Would it please him if she did that? Would he think she
was pretty? Or would he be disappointed and not even
put the new pictures on the wall?

She wonders if she's been unfair these past years for
seeing him only as momma saw him—as a no-good lowlife who wouldn't know what responsibility was if he
tripped over it on the sidewalk at high noon. And she
keeps wondering if she's going to write him back.

He *said* he was sorry, girl. What more can he do?

By the time Aunt Rhonda calls her to set the table for
supper she's made up her mind. He is, after all, her
daddy—although he signed the letter "Your father," like
he was writing to a grown woman, which she believes
she certainly is.

And he *did* say he was sorry.

And he called her Sugargirl.

And he remembered her birthday . . .

2

During supper Aunt Rhonda asks what the letter has to
say. She poses the question as airily as if she's asking if
anybody cared for more iced tea, but there's no hiding
the snoopy hunger in her voice, nor the spite Dolores has
gotten to know so well since coming to live with her.
(One minute she and momma were eating supper and
watching a *Honeymooners* rerun, and the next, momma
was facedown in her plate of red beans and rice and dead
of a stroke before Dolores could even start to scream.)

Much of her aunt's resentment toward her, Dolores
knows, comes from her dislike of momma, even though
the two women met only once, back when Dolores was
just a tiny baby. The way momma told it, that one time

was enough for both of them. She and daddy were paying her and Frank a visit, and Rhonda put on such pious airs momma couldn't stand it. So she'd turned the radio on and put it up loud on a boogie-woogie station and flashed a lot of leg at Uncle Frank as she kicked up her heels all around the living room with daddy. "That skinny tight-faced Rhonda didn't know whether to spit or go blind," momma said. "And Frank, well, you'da thought he'd never looked on so much of a woman's legs before to see how he was gawking at mine." Momma laughed, thinking on it. "But I guess being married to that priss Rhonda, he like as not *hadn't* seen a woman's legs in a *long* while. Poor fella was probly hurtin bad from lack of lovin and probly hurtin even worse now. I wouldn't be a bit surprised to hear he's took up with some little tramp one of these days." It was the first time she'd spoken to her of such things, and she gave Dolores a look. "I ain't talking too salty for you, am I?" she asked. "I mean, being your momma and all?" And Dolores, not yet fourteen, shook her head firmly even as she felt herself blushing and said, "Course not. I'm not a *baby*." Momma smiled and said softly, "Course you're not." It was one of the few times after daddy left that she heard momma mention any of the fun she'd had with him.

Dolores herself has provoked her aunt mightily by refusing to attend the Youth Prayer Services held two nights a week at the Good Shepherd Baptist Church just down the street. The one time she went she'd felt like throwing up right there in the church, the other kids were so god-awful self-righteous. They'd looked at her like they all had their own private keys to the Pearly Gates and she never would. She has since had to listen to her aunt's almost daily declamations of the hellfire awaiting the likes of her. She has endured the woman's ill will by accepting it as just another unpleasant fact of life. Like her allergy to peanut butter. Like mosquitoes in summertime. Like the dirty-talking boys at school.

She loathes living with Rhonda, but where else could she have gone? Fifteen years old and not a penny to her name, and Uncle Frank the only kin the state children's services could get in contact with. It wasn't like she'd had a lot of choice about it. But the six months she's been here seem like six years, and if she wants to finish high school, which she does, then she's got to live here nearly two more years, and how in the world can she ever last that long in this house? She has often thought that having to live here is like a prison sentence—but after reading her daddy's letter for the umpteenth time her mouth had suddenly gone dry at the thought of just how truly awful a *real* prison like Huntsville must be. He'd be in there at least thirty years and maybe a lot longer. How in the world could he stand it?

She'd had the sudden and dreadful notion that maybe the only real choice anybody has in life is whether to go on standing it or not.

Because of her own bitter feelings about her father, she has never been too bothered by Aunt Rhonda's mean talk about him. But his letter has confused her. At the same time that she feels angry about the way he treated momma, she aches to be hugged to his chest and hear him say, "Sweet dreams, sugargirl," like he used to when he'd tuck her in and kiss her goodnight.

She senses that if her aunt gets wind of what she's feeling, she'll jump at the chance to make her feel even worse. And so, when Rhonda asks what daddy ("that man" she calls him) had to say, Dolores simply shrugs and says, "Nothing much."

"Nothing *much!*" Aunt Rhonda repeats, and arches her plucked brows. "After all this time without word one to *anybody?* Without so much as a word of condolence to his only daughter after her mother passes away? Declare, I'd think he'd have a good deal to say for himself." She turns to Uncle Frank and says, "Don't you think so, Franklin?"

Uncle Frank looks up from his plate and smiles guardedly. He is a large closemouthed man who spends most of his days in his gun shop in town. Dolores has not come to know him very well but strongly suspects that for all his size and apparent toughness he is afraid of his wife. It is hard for her to believe that any man cowed by his wife could be even *half*-brother to daddy. Life, she thinks, is just full of strange jokes.

"Well, honey," he says, "I think—"

"I mean," Aunt Rhonda says, her eyes back on Dolores, "it isn't every day we get a letter at this house from a bona fide *convict,* is it?"

Dolores shrugs and busies herself with her stew. She is determined to keep the letter to herself, to keep from being baited into a show of bad temper.

"Now Rhonda honey," Uncle Frank says, his interjection surprising Dolores—and Aunt Rhonda as well, to judge by the look on her face—"why don't we let the poor girl be? A letter's a personal thing, and I guess if Dolly wants to tell us what was in it, she'll do it when she's ready to—won't you, Dolly?" He is the only one who has ever called her by that nickname which she detests.

"Didn't say much," Dolores murmurs. "Just howdy, is all."

"Just *howdy*?" her aunt echoes sarcastically. "Oh now, I'll just bet he said a lot more than *that*."

"Now Rhonda honey . . ." Uncle Frank starts to say— and then hushes at the look she gives him.

"Yeah, well," Dolores says, meeting Aunt Rhonda's eyes, "that's about all he said." She holds her aunt's stare a moment longer, then turns her attention back to her plate. Take *that*, you!

"Fine then," Rhonda says. "Be that way."

Dolores eats the rest of her meal with a great show of appetite, though the only thing she actually tastes is the rare and wonderful flavor of victory.

3

Later that evening, after doing the dishes, she lies on her stomach on the floor of her room and tries to compose a letter, writing with a ballpoint pen on lined notebook paper. She writes, "Dear Father," but the word looks as strange on the page as it sounds in her head, so she tears the sheet out of the notebook and begins again.

Dear Daddy, she writes, she was so happy to hear from him. It was so sweet of him to wish her happy birthday. She has thought of writing him a letter lots of times before but she never did because she never did know his address. *Addresses* would be more like it, since they heard he was moving around a lot, especially from jail to jail (ha ha). It wasn't till they heard he'd be in Huntsville for a good long while that she thought maybe . . . She snatches out the sheet of paper and crumples it into a ball.

Dear Daddy: how nice to hear from him after all this time. But she'd really like to know something. Why didn't he write sooner? Why didn't he write to them while momma was still alive? Why didn't he . . . She wads up this one too.

Dear Daddy: what a surprise! *So* glad to hear from him. *Especially* glad to hear he's *sorry*. Only, why did he have to wait so long to *be* sorry? While didn't he feel sorry *before*? Why didn't he feel sorry before momma's heart finally used up *every last drop* of love it had for him. Why couldn't he of told *momma* he was sorry while she was still alive? Would he have *ever* told her? *Dammit,* daddy! Why did he have to run off? Why did he have to go to Houston? Why did he have to go into *that* poolroom and fight with *that* man? Why did he have to beat him so damn *dead*?

Riiiippp!

Dear Daddy: why couldn't he say it to *her*, his daughter, his *only* daughter, his Sugargirl? It's been all these *years* and now he writes her this letter but he doesn't say it, not *once,* he doesn't even say . . .

She stands up and goes to the window and stares out at the gathering gloom. The air is still and heavy. Heat lightning flashes whitely way out over the Gulf. Her throat and eyes burn. She leans her forehead against the window frame and stays that way for a few minutes before returning to her notebook on the floor and tearing out and crumpling the page she was writing.

Dear Daddy: she doesn't like Raymondville very much. She doesn't like the school she has to go to. Most of the kids are really rude and dumb as sticks. The teachers are mostly a bunch of irritable biddies and boring old farts. Except for Mister Traven who's about the youngest teacher there and has a neat red beard and the softest blue eyes and always smells a little of oil since he works nights out at the field. He's the nicest man. Not at all like the mean boys who say they think she's pretty and everything but get all mad when she tells them she's not allowed to ride in their cars and then go around telling awful lies about her and saying she's done just the nastiest things with them. Some of the stories have got back to Aunt Rhonda and she always believes them rather than believe *her*. Aunt Rhonda can be *so* mean, daddy. Always telling her how she's going to hell and all. Always talking mean about momma and him both. Always saying how she's not worth all that her and Uncle Frank have done for her. Aunt Rhonda makes her feel like she's not worth *anything*. Has *he* ever known anybody who made him feel like that? Sometimes she wishes she was deaf so she wouldn't have to hear Aunt Rhonda anymore. She wishes there were more people like Mister Traven who once told her she's the smartest one of his students and will surely make something of herself one day.

She pauses to consider the matter of Mister Traven. Go ahead, girl, she thinks—go ahead on and tell him. It's the same as lying if you don't. Tell him how Mister Traven, that nice man with the neat red beard and soft blue eyes, stopped his car for you on the road that sunny afternoon hardly more than a month ago when you were walking home from school and offered you a ride and then stopped at the Superburger Drive-in for a couple of bottled cold drinks and then took you for a drive and said he understood how hard it was to be the new kid in school and all, how he just bet all the other girls were jealous of you because you were so pretty, and how annoying it must be to have a lot of immature boys pestering you all the time with only one thing on their dumb little minds, and how lonely it could feel when it seemed nobody knew the real you way down deep inside. Tell him, Sugargirl. Tell how it just took your breath to hear him talk like that. Tell how he drove to a woods out by the salt lake and said he wanted to know who you really were, way deep inside. Tell about how he stroked your hair so gently, how you couldn't help reaching out and touching his beard and how, when he kissed you, you could smell the faint odor of oil on his pale skin. Tell it all. Your first time. How pine cones thunked softly on the car roof and your heart was beating so hard while you did it right there on the front seat and you thought you'd die of the excitement. And how confused you got afterwards when he saw the blood smear on the seat and suddenly looked so scared as he buckled up his pants, how he didn't say a word as he drove you home and when he got you there he only said, "Be sure and do your homework, hear?" How ever since then he hasn't said three words to you and hardly ever looks you in the eye in the classroom and how you just don't understand it and how awful it makes you feel. And don't stop there, either. Go on and tell how ever since then you sometimes dream about that business in Mister Traven's car and wake up with your heart jumping like crazy and feeling the same kind of excitement you felt at the time.

Tell him *that*, why don't you? See what he thinks of his Sugargirl then.

Oh, daddy, she writes, she feels so *empty* sometimes. Does he know what she means? Does he ever feel like there's nothing ahead but more of the same awful empty feeling, forever and *ever*? Does he ever just wish he was de—

She puts down the pen and reads what she has written. And then she slowly crumples the paper. She goes to the window and stares out at the darkness for a long time.

Who you fooling, girl? If he cared the teensiest bit he would have written long before now and he wouldn't have asked for money and he would have *said* it.

But he didn't. He did *not* say it.

It is after midnight when she writes: Dear Daddy: you BASTARD.

She underlines the final word again and again until the pen point tears through the paper and mars the page beneath, and then she buries her face in her arms to muffle the sound of her crying.

After a while she gets up and blows her nose. Then she gathers all the false starts and slips out into the darkened hallway and tiptoes to the bathroom and flushes it all down the toilet.

She swears to herself she will never write to him, not ever, and the vow will prove to be both true and false. It is true she will never mail anything to him. But during the remaining ten years of her life she will on many occasions begin a letter to him in a late-night whiskey haze. These efforts will be utterly incoherent to her on the following day. None of them will ever extend beyond three or four lines, and most will go no further than the salutation: Dear Daddy . . .

II

PERDITION ROAD

1

Her dreams were frequent and bad. Sometimes, like the one she was having now, they were recollections of incidents in her life, as grainy and unreal as a home movie—

and as undeniable. She was dozing with her cheek pressed against the reverberant window of a bus hurtling south through thin morning fog, dreaming once again about the awful business with Uncle Frank, about being crushed under his bulk and gagging on the stink of him, feeling his sweat dripping on her, crying, saying don't, don't, and pushing against his pale hairless chest with both hands even as she felt an ambush of pleasure through her protests and hating herself for it, hating him even more, and yelling now, yelling in shock as she caught sight of Aunt Rhonda gaping at them from the bedroom doorway and tottering like a frail stricken bird . . .

She came awake with a gasp.

The over-rouged woman in the neighboring seat was staring at her like she thought she might be loony. Dolores tried a reassuring smile but her face must have done a bad job of it: the woman's mouth tightened and she quick turned away.

To hell with you, Dolores thought. She was still breathing hard from the vividness of the dream. The air in the nearly full bus was stale and dry. Her throat burned. She felt she might sneeze and hoped she wasn't catching a cold. As she fished in her purse for a Kleenex she felt a sudden rush of loneliness so powerful she nearly sobbed. She snatched out a tissue and dabbed her eyes and commanded herself to *stop it*. The woman beside her scooched over toward the aisle a little more.

Oh, God *damn* that man. Rhonda too, the self-righteous old bitch. Damn that whole sorry business with Uncle Frank. It had been just terrible. Awful. It wasn't like she'd ever said it wasn't. But it sure hadn't been *her* fault. After

all. Not more than partly, anyway. Well, for damn sure
not *all*.

The main thing was, she did not need anybody giving
her hell about it even one more day. Especially not Aunt
Rhonda. The woman was crazier than John the Baptist in
the wilderness, forever thumping that Bible and calling
names. ("Whore! Harlot! The sins of the mother shall fall
upon the daughter just as surely as those of the father are
visited on the son! Look upon her, Lord! Look upon this
daughter of Jezebel on her dark road to perdition!" Two
solid months of that, every damn day. And Uncle Frank,
that miserable peckerwood, sitting through it all in front
of the TV and saying not word one, like none of it had a
thing in the world to do with him. Bastard.)

"Harlingen!"

The driver's voice rasped harshly through the speakers, startling her. She pressed up closer to the window
and saw that they were coming into town. Palm trees
along both sides of the highway. A few motels and cafes.
A strip of bars all closed up tight—The Silver Cane, Crazy
Jack's, El Waterhole #2. The bus slowed as they started
coming onto traffic lights. It wasn't a real big town—nothing like Corpus Christi, the biggest town she'd ever been
to—but it was plenty bigger than Raymondville. They
passed a wide dirt lot where Mexican workers were clam-
bering aboard field buses. Filling stations and fast food
places every which way you looked. A shopping center
with an almost empty parking lot at this hour and a
movie theater sign advertising *Bullitt*. Realty offices and
car dealers. Buck's Gun Shop with bars over the windows.
An Oriental girl with hair like ink setting up a flower
stand at an intersection. Rowena's Beauty Salon. (*Rowena!*
You had a name like that, you *had* to know something

about beauty.) Hi-Way Bowling Lanes, and two old boys leaning against a pickup truck, drinking Lone Stars and the sun just starting to show itself. Chico's Barber Shop with a big handlebar mustache painted on the window. A woman sitting on a bus bench and looking at her feet. A white-whiskered man carrying a big plastic bag full of who-knew-what over his shoulder and talking to himself as he trudged along the shoulder of the road, his clothes so foul-looking you just knew he carried a smell to reckon with. A dog lifted its leg on a police car's tire in front of Maria Elena's Cafe.

The morning sun shone on the storefronts, blazed against the windows. She imagined families at their breakfast tables, kids getting ready to leave for school, getting a goodbye hug and kiss from their mommas, their daddies. She abruptly felt her mother's absence like a hole in her heart and for an instant she again thought she might cry. *Stop it!* she told herself. *This minute!* She blew her nose and sat up straighter.

Aunt Rhonda and Uncle Frank would've been up for a while by now. They would've seen her emptied dresser drawers and wondered when she'd gone. They might've even wondered where. They could go on wondering from now till Doomsday.

The only direction out of Raymondville that didn't take you into Mexico or the Gulf of Mexico was north, and the first big town you'd come to, a good long ways up the coast, was Corpus Christi. But Uncle Frank had friends in Corpus and might have them track her down if he took a mind to. Way farther north was Houston, which she didn't have enough bus fare to get to but where she wouldn't have gone anyway. It was *too* far away, for one thing, practically in another world—and she'd anyway always thought of it as the meanest town there was, mainly because of the song she'd heard all her life about if you're ever in Houston you better walk right and you better not gamble and you better not fight or the sheriff gonna get you and lock you up tight.

Daddy sure enough found that out, didn't he? Four years he'd been in the state prison in Huntsville, little more than twice as long as momma'd been in her grave. The son of a bitch. As far as she was concerned, all the things he did to break momma's heart amounted to a crime worse than killing that fella with a pool cue. She hoped he lived to be a hundred and never got paroled.

So even though there wasn't much of Texas between Raymondville and the Mexican Border, that's the way she headed—south to Harlingen on the four A.M. bus coming through from Corpus on the way to Brownsville. And although Harlingen was way closer to Raymondville than Corpus was, Rhonda and Frank didn't ever go down there ("It's nothing but wetbacks there," Aunt Rhonda said, which was what she said about every place in Texas whether she'd ever been there or not). As far as Dolores knew, they didn't know anybody there they could ask to look around for her.

Shoot, girl, they ain't about to look for you now or ever and you know it. Be glad of it.

The big bus slowed, brakes hissing and sighing, and swung into the terminal.

2

Twenty minutes later she had herself a job. Counter waitress in a bustling little cafe called The Wagon Wheel, just a block down from the bus station. The owner was a stocky bald man named Shelton. He'd put the little cardboard "Help Wanted" sign in the front window not an hour before Dolores came walking down the sidewalk with her suitcase in her hand and no idea where she was headed. One of his two daytime girls had quit that morning when her boyfriend phoned and told her he was moving to Houston and if she wanted to go with him she had till noon to get ready.

"She's a fool to go with him," Shelton said. "He ain't worth last month's want ads. Big-talkin' truck mechanic with white teeth and a head of hair. Girls today ain't got the sense God gave a barnyard hen."

He paused to take a sip of coffee and put a match to a Camel. The interview was taking place on counter stools. Squinting through the smoke, he looked Dolores up and down. "How bout you, girl? You gonna run off with the first coffee shop cowboy asks you to go to Big D with him?"

She was flustered by his lingering appraisal of her legs under the skirt that suddenly felt way too short—and by the leers and grins she was getting from the men sitting nearby. No sir, she assured him, her voice tight, she certainly didn't intend on doing anything like that.

"Yeah, yeah," he said tiredly. "Girls with your looks don't have to intend nothing. Intentions just come along and happen to you." He sighed and exhaled a long stream of smoke. "What the hell, I got to have me another daytime girl and I got to have one now. Job's yours. Dollar-and-a-half an hour and all your tips. Get paid ever Friday. I give you lunch and a half-hour to eat it. Only listen: try to look at the customers a little less fraidy-cat than you been doing. They'll most of them talk like loverboys but won't none of them bite you. You might even try smiling some, jack up your tips."

He took her into the back room and showed her where to stash her grip. He handed her a red-checkered apron and a white paper hat to wear, then gave her a quick rundown of the counter operation, showing her where everything was she might need—silverware, condiments, napkins and placemats, checkpads. She already knew how to work the register from the job she'd had at the Burger Hut in Raymondville.

"Well, all right, then," he said. "Let's get to work." He hustled back into the kitchen to help a colored cook named Willard work up a steady procession of orders for eggs, fried potatoes, burgers, chicken fried steaks, chili beans and blue plate specials.

A jukebox next to the counter played loudly and incessantly, almost all its selections country-western oldies like Hank Williams, Patsy Cline, Bob Wills, Ernest Tubb. Even Tex Ritter, for God's sake, was on there, and some customers actually played him. Frankie Laine was a big favorite with "Rawhide" and "Mule Train." In the midst of all that twangy shitkicking, only Buddy Holly and Elvis kept Dolores from going insane.

The place always smelled heavily of fried grease, diesel fumes, men in need of a shower. Even the sunlight that leaned in the windows looked oily. Most of The Wagon Wheel's trade was from men passing through, grabbing a bite while they waited for their bus. Sad-looking salesmen in stained suits. Uniformed servicemen hardly more than boys. Sunburned oil workers with bright eyes and big voices. Dusty farmhands. Old Mexes in sarapes and young ones with wide neckties and shiny pompadours. Vacanteyed drifters. Sometimes some coloreds.

The field Mexicans were always well-mannered, and

the few black folk who sometimes came in for a roll and coffee. But they never had much to spend on themselves and couldn't afford tips beyond nickels and dimes. Her best tips came from the customers she least liked to wait on—the Mexican dandies, who called her *mamacita* and ran their eyes over her like hands, and the oil field roughnecks, who liked to get a rise out of her any way they could. They liked to tell crude jokes in voices loud enough for her to hear, then laugh to see her blush, which she nearly always did. Sometimes their voices dropped low and then they'd all bust out laughing and grin at her and she'd know they had been joking about her. Or she'd catch them nudging each other and gawking at her rear end when she was bent over the cooler. She'd feel her face burn and want to shrink into herself, to make herself as small as possible so there would be less of her for them to look at and joke about.

Shelton seemed indifferent to it all, and she figured he'd think she was a big baby if she complained, so she didn't. But every time some bunch of men at the counter snickered behind her back or showed her their nasty oily grins, her anger would clench in her belly like a fist and she'd want to tell them off. Then she'd spot the dollar bills scattered across the countertop and she'd bite her tongue. And when they called for refills and ogled her up close and smacked their lips and said, "*Qué chulita*," or "Darlin, I sure do like the way you wear them jeans"— and even if every now and then one of them should reach over and pat her bottom before she quick pulled away— she'd make herself smile and they'd laugh and push a bill over to her and she'd snatch it up and put it in her pocket. She made herself think of their vulgar talk as simply unpleasant noise to put up with, like most of the jukebox selections. There was no need to take any of it personally, not even the pats on the ass. After all, it wasn't like they were actually *doing* anything to her. And she did have to make a living.

And it *was* a living, dammit, a real job, and she *was* supporting herself with it, and who woulda thought she could do that? The Burger Hut job was the only other she'd ever had, but she'd only been at it a couple of months before Aunt Rhonda suddenly decided that it was improper and made her quit. ("A decent woman's work is in the home. The heart of the whore is forged in the marketplace." That batty bitch.)

On the day Shelton hired her she had asked if he knew of any place close by where she could rent a room, and he directed her to Miss Aurora's, a boardinghouse for women, only three blocks from the restaurant. "I'm just saying it's close by and it don't charge a arm and a leg," Shelton had told her. "I ain't saying it's the damn Hilton."

The place was a musty old two-story of peeling white-wash with a front yard gone to weeds and faded flowered carpets in the parlor. Except for a retarded girl of fifteen who was the live-in maid, Dolores was the youngest resident in the place by at least thirty years. The half-dozen others were all spinsters or widows. Most of them were usually roosting in the parlor whenever she passed through, and though they always nodded politely when she smiled and said hello, the smiles they showed in return were more like looks of pain. Through the cloying fragrance of their perfumes there always seeped the odors of old closets and turned milk. None of them ever received visits from men. Their eyes would follow her up the stairs when she came in, trail her to the door whenever she left for work. She knew damn well they talked about her, and the idea of it was a constant irritant. She figured that the landlady, Miss Aurora—a skinny fake redhead who looked like she got made up by an undertaker—had rented to her only to give the biddies something fresh to talk about. Juiceless, jealous old bags. She detested the place more than she could say, but it was all she could afford that was close enough to the restaurant to let her walk to work, so it would have to do for now.

The other waitress on her shift was Rayette Nichols, a chubby middle-aged blonde who wore a girdle and the brightest red lipstick Dolores had ever seen. She was quick to laugh and had an easy way with the customers. In private, however, she admitted to Dolores that she didn't really like the job all that much. After they got to know each other better, she confessed she'd "done a little flatbacking once upon a time—you know what I mean?— for a couple months up in Dallas, way back before I ever met my husband Henry."

It took Dolores a minute to understand what she meant—and then Rayette laughed at the look on her face. "Shoot, honey, it ain't like I was committing *robbery*, for Pete's sake. I wasn't *hurting* nobody. Just the opposite. I was making fellas feel pretty damn fine, if I say so myself. I always gave dollar's worth for dollar's pay. Let me tell you, all them who look down their noses at it, they ain't never been on their own and near to starving, you can bet on that."

Dolores was fascinated by Rayette's tales of her hooking days in Dallas. Those days came to an end when a fellow grabbed her into a Lincoln Continental one night as she came out of a motel after doing a trick. The fella's name was Victorio and Rayette had heard of him but thought the other girls had been making him up just to scare her. But he was real, all right, and she nearly wet her pants she was so scared. She'd heard he once put a cigarette lighter to a girl's underarms. He told Rayette she had three choices: give him eighty percent of every dime she made from now on, or get out of town, or get nails put through her knees.

"He was offering to be my manager, you see," Rayette said. "That's manager as in p-i-m-p. I didn't even have to think it over. I was on the bus to San Antone that same night. Never done another trick again neither, no ma'am. I was lucky I got away with being a independent for as long as I did."

That had been a dozen years ago, and ever since, she'd stuck to waitressing. "But a place like this," she said, looking around The Wagon Wheel. "There ain't no future in it. Can't make any money slinging chili to these clodhoppers and blowhards." She said if Dolores was smart she'd get a job in a bar.

"*That's* where the money is," Rayette said. "I oughta know. I worked most the best bars between San Antone and the border, and I mean to tell you, honey, I was raking it in before I married Henry. Especially out in Laredo. Them Laredo boys don't know what to do with their money but piss it away in bars. Real good tippers, too. And I was *good* at my work, I ain't lying. It's something you can take a little pride in being good *at*, not like working in this place here with its two-bit tips. Why hell, even now, I lose me some of these extra pounds, and shoot, I'd be right back in business making *gooood* money."

She paused to light a cigarette, then cut a sharp look at Dolores. "So why don't I do it, right? Henry—that's why. Says he loves me just the way I am and don't want me to lose a single solitary pound. He's no lightweight,

Henry. Always stuffing hisself with biscuits and gravy, fried chicken, slugging down beers—and getting *me* to pig out right along with him. Thinks I don't know what he's up to, keeping me fat so's I couldn't get a job in a good bar if I tried. He's never said so, but I know he don't want me working in the bars again. Jealous, he's just flat-out jealous is what it is, even if he'd never in a million years admit it. I love him, you understand, but . . . well, sometimes he's just *such* a dipshit."

She blew a stream of smoke at a wall calendar with a photo of a beautiful stretch of California coastline. "You know," she said tiredly, "I'm still a young woman—damn if I ain't. But I swear there are days now when I feel oldness trying to press up against me like some bold son-ofabitch in a crowded bus. Pressing up on me and breathing on the back of my neck."

3

On the day she got her eighth pay envelope she told Shelton she was quitting. He wasn't surprised. "Fact is, you stayed longer than I'da bet on," he said. When he asked who the fella was and she said there wasn't any fella, he shrugged and said, "Right you are, sunshine, it's none of my business. Luck to you."

She caught the early-morning bus to Laredo and arrived late that afternoon and treated herself to a motel room with a color TV and an air conditioner strong enough to frost your breath. There was a little machine attached to the bed and when she put a quarter in it the bed would vibrate gently. She lay in bed and watched TV and put three quarters in a row in the machine and wished she knew somebody she could call up on the telephone and tell about this. Before she knew it she was crying. She chided herself for a baby but it still took her a while to stop.

The next morning she hiked out to the edge of town where she'd seen a strip of roadhouses as the bus came in. There were bars right there in town she could've tried, but they looked too dark and mean somehow, maybe because most of them didn't have much in the way of windows. The roadhouses she'd spotted had plenty of windows and seemed the friendlier for it. But they were a lot farther out than she'd thought—and a lot farther apart. She worked up a good sweat and was honked and whistled at by several passing drivers before she finally came to a place called The Texas Star with a big sign out front saying BEER—FOOD—DANCING. She dried her face the best she could with a handful of tissues and dusted herself off and went inside. The bartender said they didn't need anybody right now, thank you. The next two places said the same. One manager seemed real amused by her. "Come see me when you get dry behind them pretty ears, sweetheart."

She figured they thought she was too young, so at the next place, Sparky's, she added two years to her age and claimed she was nineteen. The owner said he'd have guessed a tad older, if she didn't mind him saying so. He gave her a job waiting tables, two o'clock to midnight, six days a week, starting today. She wouldn't be serving much food, he told her; his customers were mostly drinking men. She almost hugged him, she was so grateful.

She stopped at a laundromat on her way back to town and took a close look at all the handwritten ads posted on a bulletin board next to the dryers. Every laundromat she'd ever been to had a board like this. Sure enough, there were several notices for places to rent. She asked a woman waiting for her clothes to dry, a tall sallow brunette with her hair in curlers, if she could tell if any of the rentals were nearby enough to walk to. The woman studied the ads as she pushed a squalling infant in a perambulator back and forth and a dirty-faced little girl of about three clung to her leg. She pointed to an index card written in red ink and advertising a two-room cottage, furnished and cheap. "That one's just off the road about a quarter-mile down," the woman said.

Dolores used the pay phone to call the number on the card and spoke to a pleasant woman who gave directions and told her to go on out and have a look at the place— the door key was under the potted cactus plant on the back porch. If she liked it, call back and they'd settle.

Dolores thanked the brunette for her help and started for the door and the woman asked if she was going to be living out there by herself. Dolores said she was. The woman looked down at the children, both of them now bawling for her attention. She seemed weighted with an exhaustion that could never be rested away. "Sounds nice," she said.

Three hours later Dolores was in the ladies' room at Sparky's, putting on a touch of lipstick before starting her first shift ever as a barroom waitress. She couldn't stop grinning at herself in the mirror. A job *and* her own private place to live. Hot damn.

Shoot, if she'd known it was gonna be this easy to get by on her own she'da started doing it long before now. Bet your ass.

4

Unlike the transients at The Wagon Wheel, Sparky's patrons were mostly a regular crowd and lots of them worked together—ranch hands, construction workers, truckers, roughnecks. It was a rare Mexican who came in the place. Whenever any did, Sparky would unplug the jukebox and the room would get so quiet all you heard was throat clearing and chairs scraping on the floor as some of the old boys turned to give the Mexes some hard eyeballing. At such times Dolores always thought she heard something else too, a faint hum she seemed to *feel* rather than actually hear, a low keen humming of something to do with blood. None of the Mexicans who every now and then wandered into the place and ordered a beer ever stayed long enough to finish it. "Law says I gotta serve em," Sparky said. "But it don't say nothin about havin to be glad to see the sonofabitches."

Business was always light in the early afternoon, but then right at Happy Hour the guys would start arriving in bunches, dirty and sweaty and joking loud with each other. They were a lot more easygoing than the men she waited on at The Wagon Wheel. Most of the laughter she'd heard in the Wheel was nasty as spit, mean and bitter. But then, the guys in the Wheel had mostly been men on the move, rootless, men without women, men who were alone even in each other's company. Naturally they'd been bitter.

The men in Sparky's laughed with a real sense of fun. Many of them were married and had families, or at least had a steady girlfriend, and some of them, to hear them tell it, had a lot more than one. Even some of the married ones (*especially* some of the married ones) liked to brag about how much fooling around they did on the side, although Dolores was pretty sure most of their bragging was just talk. All in all, they were a rough but likable bunch, and she surprised herself with the easy rapport she struck with them.

She was a natural for the job. To the tables full of men she carried a breezy air of familiarity, a readiness to trade wisecracks and flirty banter. She soon worked up a whole catalog of retorts to their grinning propositions, an assortment of gentle rebuffs for the guys who were serious, and a set of firm putdowns for those who didn't know when to quit. ("Hey bubba! I *tole* you bout them hands. Once more and I swear I'll have those ole boys at the back table there see to it you stop doing what I don't let *them* do.") Whenever she was groped by a regular customer, which she occasionally and naturally was, she'd react with exaggerated shock but also with enough real indignation to keep the fondling from becoming anybody's idea of a privilege.

When she tended to a table of mixed company her approach was of course much more demure. She'd keep her smile bright but utterly unflirtatious, and she'd give most of her attention to the women. Even so, the mixed tables never tipped as well as the stags.

She also learned fast how to deal with the solitary drinkers. A lot of these regulars liked a quick chat or a little gossip served up with their beer. Others took their drinking more seriously and just wanted to get on with it and never mind the bullshit. She learned when to laugh with the jokers, when to sing along with the guys who sang when they got drunk, when to nod sympathetically at those who never tired of telling their life's sad story, and when to keep her distance from the guys who sooner or later started talking to themselves in accusatory tones.

The only ones who really bothered her were the silent lookers. Solitary strangers who never smiled and rarely spoke except to order a drink. They almost never took their eyes off her. Even from across the room she could feel their stares trailing her like tracking dogs. These were the true loners, and almost every night one would come in. Sometimes he'd leave after just one or two drinks, sometimes he'd stay until closing. They hardly ever showed up in the place more than once, and only rarely did two of them come in on the same night. It was like they belonged to a club and that was one of the rules— only one to a bar on a given evening. There was something about them, something seething with restrained fury like it was pacing in a cage. They drank hard but didn't seem much affected by it except in the eyes, which got brighter without gaining a thing in warmth. She avoided their eyes as much as she could—those cold hungry eyes that made her shiver.

5

Ten hours a day, from two o'clock till closing time at midnight, the job kept her busy and from thinking about things. Every night after closing she helped Wally the bartender clean up the place while Sparky tallied the day's receipts in the back room. They'd sometimes all have a drink together at the bar before calling it a night.

Sparky was over seventy years old and looked every day of it, his face dry and cracked from more than fifty years of working outdoors in the cattle business in North Texas, which Wally called Baja Oklahoma. He'd been married twice and had two daughters he never talked about except to say they were "a couple of damn tramps." He liked to talk about his cattle days, though his tales of drives to Kansas when he was a youngster were more likely rooted in pulp fiction than actual biography.

"The only cow Sparks ever really drove out of Texas was his first wife," Wally told Dolores. "Drove her right into the arms of a string band player who liked his women hefty. I heard tell they run off to Missouri. Woulda drove his second wife away, too, except she caught the pneumonia and died before she could pack her bags."

Wally was in his early thirties and still hanging on to handsome despite his barroom pallor and a beer belly that would soon be sagging over his belt. When Dolores asked him if he was married he said, "That's for me to know and you to find out," so she knew he was. He finally admitted it—after she'd turned him down for a date every time he asked during her first couple of weeks on the job. He had two kids he was crazy about and he showed her pictures of them, a boy six and a girl four, but he never talked about his wife. He'd joke with the boys at the bar about women, and every now and then he'd ask Dolores with a big grin—and with a wink at the fellas—when she was going to ask him home for a drink "or something." She'd give him an exaggeratedly vampish look with a lot of eye-fluttering and coo, "Well, I just don't know, Wally honey. But play your cards right and one of these days you just might get *real* lucky." The boys at the bar would laugh and encourage Wally to keep on trying and just generally ate the act up.

On those nights when she joined them for a drink at the bar after hours, either Sparky or Wally would give her a ride home. But whenever she didn't feel like sticking around, or whenever the two men chose to have one more for the road, she'd simply walk the two miles. She'd keep far off the shoulder of the road, preferring the risky footing of the dark uneven ground to the glaring attention of passing headlights. She did not want anybody stopping to offer her a ride. Who knew when it might be a silent looker.

The first thing she'd do when she got home was make sure the doors and windows were all locked and the window shades all pulled completely. And no matter how gritty she might be, she could not bear the idea of being naked and behind the shower curtain at that late hour of the night, and so she would not bathe until the following day. She would hurriedly slip into her long cotton nightgown and, no matter how hot the night, pull the bedsheet up to her chin. She dreaded the dark and would have preferred to leave a lamp burning, but she was afraid the glow of it might act as a lure to her window. Fortunately, she was usually so tired by the time she got home she had no trouble falling asleep before she was too scared to. And before the low moan of loneliness in the darkness rose to a sob.

6

Sundays were the worst. Her day off. She'd sleep as late as she could, until she couldn't get back to sleep anymore and finally got tired of lying in bed. She'd take a long shower and wash her hair and then fix herself a breakfast of coffee and bacon and toast with apple butter. She would wash and dry and put away the dishes. She would dust the furniture and sweep and mop the floor. She'd wash her underwear in the sink and hang it on the shower rod to dry. She'd put the rest of her laundry in a pillowcase and hike to the laundromat and when she got back she'd put it all away neatly. She'd iron her clothes for work the next day. She'd spend a long time doing her nails. And all the while the portable radio would be playing—"Happy Together" and "White Rabbit" and "Love Is Blue."

Sometimes her backdoor neighbors, the Santiagos, would have a cookout that filled their yard with dozens of relatives, and Joselita, a mother of five at age twenty-two, would come over and in her broken English invite her to join them. Dolores did so once, but the warm ties of the Santiagos and their kin and all of them talking mostly in Spanish only made her loneliness feel the keener and thereafter she always turned down their invitations with some lame excuse. She'd sit at home the rest of the day and hear the sounds of music and laughter from the Santiagos' yard while she chain-smoked Marlboros and leafed through one of the *True Romance* magazines she'd found stacked in the closet—left by the previous tenant, probably—and thought what dopes the women in the stories were and tried with all her might to ignore the loneliness hanging in the room like a noose.

7

She awoke in the dark middle of a drizzling Sunday night. Her throat was hot and tight. Silent lightning lit the window curtains blue. She was awake for several minutes before she realized she was crying.

All right, she thought, all right. You best *do* something.

Like what?

Like what do you *think*?

Well . . .

About time you faced up to it, girl. You know damn good and well what you're wanting. You ought admit it instead of going on trying to fool yourself.

Well . . .

Go on now, face it.

Dammit, I'm not no *trash*. I'm not!

Whoa now, girl, who said anything about *that?* Aunt Rhonda? What's *that* crazy old bitch know? Not a thing, that's what.

Well . . .

You just got a bad headful of her mean mouth is all. You ought not let it keep you from having a little fun. It ain't right to do yourself like that. You *deserve* some fun.

Well . . .

You *know* you do. We're just talking a little fun, for Pete's sake, a little company. There's not a thing in the world wrong with that.

Okay.

About time you faced it.

I *said* okay.

Well . . . ? Who's it going to be?

8

She decided on Wally. He wasn't bad-looking and he was always joking with the boys at the bar about hoping to get lucky with her someday. So why not? But first she went to a clinic and got fitted for a diaphragm. She'd been awful lucky with Uncle Frank and didn't ever want to push her luck like that again. She felt her face burning with embarrassment the whole time she was in the clinic, but the doctor himself seemed bored with it all and the nurse didn't bat an eye.

A few nights later she stayed for a drink with Wally and Sparky after closing, then asked Wally for a ride before Sparky could make the offer. When he stopped the car in front of her place she asked if he'd like to come in for a beer. Her pulse throbbed at the base of her throat and her tongue felt slightly swollen. He had long since quit trying to get asked in on the nights he drove her home, and her invitation seemed to puzzle him for a moment, as if she'd spoken to him in a foreign language. Then his grin practically lit up the car.

She let him into her bed five nights in a row. He was always clumsy, always quick, always left her feeling like—*knowing* that—it would be just terrific with somebody who really knew what he was doing. It was her tough luck that Wally wasn't him. Even so, she might have given him more time to try to get it right with her if he hadn't started talking about his wife.

He didn't mention her until Friday night, after he was dressed again and she was in her robe and they were sitting at the table over nightcap mugs of coffee. His wife didn't really know him, he said, she didn't understand him. He did not refer to her by name until Dolores asked him what it was. *"Marion,"* he said—like the word was raw garlic in his mouth. She had no sense of humor, he said, she hated sex. If it wasn't for the kids he would've left her a long time ago.

Dolores felt like she'd read this story in a hundred magazines. Listening to him talk about his wife the way he did was a little like watching somebody draw a beard on a woman's picture. The woman might be a total stranger but you still felt sorry for her somehow. And you knew the person doing the drawing just had to be a real ass.

When he came around the table to kiss her goodnight she put up a hand and said, "No. No more."

He grinned like she was joking and reached for her.

She pushed his hands away and backed out of reach. "I said *no*, Wally. It's done with."

It took him a moment to get what she meant, and then

he said, "What you mean, *done with*? Done with how come?"

She told him she was sorry. She said the whole thing had been her fault. She said she should have known better than to do this with him in the first place.

"It was fun," she lied, "but let's leave it at that. I . . . I just don't feel right about it anymore."

"How come? Because I'm *married*? Well hell, I'm gonna get a divorce, didn't I tell you? I am! It might take a little while, but—"

No, please, she didn't want to hear about it. A divorce was his own business and she didn't want to be any part of that. His being married didn't have anything to do with it, really it didn't.

"Ah now, darlin, come here to daddy." He reached for her again but she hastened around the table and over by the stove. He let a long breath through his teeth and flung his hands up in frustration. And then suddenly backhanded a coffee mug off the table and it ricocheted off the wall without breaking.

"God damn it! What do you take me for? Some kid to dick around with?"

"I want you out of my house," she said. "Right now." She was scared but absolutely refused to let it show in her voice.

"Bullshit!" He kicked over a lamp table. "You don't tell *me* to get out!" He flung magazines around the room. He upturned the table with a crash. He picked up her little radio and was about to fling it through the window when she snatched up the pot of boiling coffee and told him to put it down and get out—*now*.

He stared at her with his mouth open, then set down the radio and stepped toward her. She cocked the hand holding the coffeepot and said he was going to have a hell of a time explaining the burns to everybody.

For a moment he looked like a confused boy, and she nearly felt sorry for him. Then his face clouded over again and he said, "You fucken bitch!" He spat on her floor and stalked out and slammed the door so hard the only framed photo she owned—a picture of her mother in the dunes at Mustang Island—fell off the wall and its glass pane shattered.

She locked the door behind him and set the furniture right and picked the mess off the floor and then sat at the table till dawn, smoking and sipping coffee and thinking things over.

She was a good person, goddammit, and she had rights just like everybody else. She was proud of the way she'd handled herself with that peckerwood. She guessed she showed him. N-O spells "no" and don't let the door hit you in the ass, bubba. Damn right. The same goes for the rest of you.

9

The next one was a pimply good-natured kid named Joey who wasn't much older than she was. He was new to Laredo, a mechanic at the Ford dealership. He'd been in Sparky's only a couple of times before and it was obvious to Dolores he never in the world expected his flirting with her to get him as far as it did. He'd seemed so stunned by her smiling acceptance of his whispered proposition that she was truly surprised to find him waiting for her in the parking lot, as she'd suggested, when she got off work. They sat in his truck for a while, kissing and running their hands over each other and he told her she had the nicest titties he'd ever touched.

On the drive to her place he dropped a lighted cigarette between his legs and narrowly missed hitting a parked car when the truck veered off the road as he groped wildly under his crotch. By the time they got to the house her nerves were nearly as frayed as his.

In the bedroom he turned off all the lights before getting undressed and joining her in bed. He was sweating like his bones were on fire. He smelled of motor oil. He was so nervous none of the right things happened and he apologized in a high strained voice. She told him it was all right, just relax, don't worry about it, he was just tense, they had all night, everything would be okay in a while, he'd see. She said maybe they ought to take his mind off it by talking about something else, but all he could talk about was fishing or the stock car he and his cousin were building and planning to race at the dirt track in San Antone and she was asleep in five minutes.

He woke her an hour later with an erection as hard as a tap handle. Before she was fully awake he was in her and grunting like a man at work. Within seconds he was thrusting wildly and moaning on a rising note and her breath caught and her back arched and her mouth went wide with pleasure for a brief wonderful moment that was not quite long enough to deliver its promise of release before he cried out and fell away from her, sighing like a tire going flat. A moment later he was snoring. She lay gasping, her fingers working at the dampened sheets, and was not able to go back to sleep until a long while later.

In the morning he overslept and had to hurry if he was going to get to work on time. His acne was worse than she'd realized. As he was lacing up his work boots she noticed the gunk under his fingernails—and the pale band around his ring finger. He saw her looking at it and grinned sheepishly and took the ring out of his pocket and slipped it on. He shrugged and said yeah, he was married, but his wife didn't understand the first thing about him and he never in the world would've married her if she hadn't got pregnant. He had a baby daughter twelve weeks old.

That was it for Joey.

That was it for roadhouse pickups. Pete's sake, you couldn't even see them all that good in that dim yellow light. Only a puredee fool picks out somebody to go to bed with in worse light than you'd insist on for picking out a new blouse. No sir, no more of that. She swore to herself that the next man she did it with would be single, *clean*, and interested, by God, in *her*, not just her titties. Neither Wally nor the Joey kid had asked the first thing about her, about what she liked to do or the kind of music she preferred or anything. Neither one had given a damn is why. Next time it would have to be somebody who cared.

10

She was walking home every night now, passing up the after-hours drink at the bar rather than hang around waiting for Sparky to call it a night and drive her home. About six weeks had passed since she'd turned Wally out of her house under threat of boiling coffee, and his close-mouthed sullenness toward her had lately begun to give way to mooning looks and small tentative smiles. The dumb Okie's pride was apparently close to fully recovered and beginning to nudge him to give her another try. She realized he was not only foolish but stupid besides. Just the same, she didn't want to antagonize him all over again by refusing the offer of a ride home—or worse, by accepting the ride and then fighting off any moves he might try to make on her in his car, where she wouldn't be likely to have a pot of hot coffee handy. So she'd been keeping her distance from him during work hours and leaving for home as quick as she could after they turned the CLOSED sign in the front window.

One night she came out after closing and was halfway across the dimly lighted and nearly empty gravel parking lot when somebody grabbed her from behind. Her immediate thought was that it was Wally trying to be cute, and she tried to wrest herself free more in irritation than in fear, wondering how he'd managed to slip out ahead of her. Then she recalled that Wally had left hours ago, right after receiving a call from his wife about one of the kids getting awfully sick and needing to go to the emergency room, and Sparky had taken over behind the bar for him. Suddenly terrified, she twisted around in her attacker's grasp and saw his face—the face of a silent looker she'd served bourbon and branch to for most of the evening and who she'd seen go out the door an hour ago. His eyes were huge and furious and he was pulling her toward an idling pickup truck a few yards away. They struggled wordlessly, the only sounds those of their gasping and the scraping of their feet in the gravel as he wrestled her closer to the truck. She finally thought of screaming, and she did, even as she remembered that Sparky was tending to the books in the little office way in the back part of the building and probably wouldn't hear her. The man punched her in the face and she saw stars and her knees gave way. Just like the cartoons, she thought, feeling herself being dragged by the arm for a moment before the man let go and she heard yelling and the sounds of running feet. She looked up and saw the man jump into the truck and slam the door just as two men in cowboy hats ran up and one of them kicked the tailgate as the truck leaped forward in a rooster tail of gravel and the other bounced a beer bottle off the back of the cab as the truck swung onto the highway with tires screeching and shot away down the road.

"Goddamn coward yellow sonofabitch!"

One of the cowboys was tall, one short, both lean. They helped her to her feet. Was she all right, could she walk, did anything feel broken? The little one was asking all the questions. His voice seemed to come from inside a barrel. The left side of her face was partly numbed, and she discovered that her elbow was torn and bleeding. She wasn't crying but her nose was running something awful. The little one gave her his bandanna. He said they best take her to the hospital, but she said no, she'd be all right, just give her a minute and she'd be fine. She tried to walk unassisted, swayed, started to fall, and they caught her by the arms again and the little one said they really ought to take her to the hospital to get looked over. No, please. She was just a little groggy, really. She'd be okay in a few minutes, she knew she would. Well, all right, but they for damn sure would at least see to it she got home safe and sound.

They helped her to their car, a magnificent white Cadillac convertible. The top was down and the car shone like the moon. She sat between them and gave directions to her place. Her head began clearing as they sped through the cool night air. She thanked them for their help. The tall one just kept on driving and the little one said think nothing of it, darlin, and they took her thirty miles out in the boonies and raped her.

11

At first she tried to fight, but the taller one pinned her arms behind her, and the little one, the one named Mort, licked her ear and whispered into it that she best cut the crap if she knew what was good for her. And in that instant she knew he was right—knew right then and there that she either did what they wanted or they'd make her do it anyway and be all the rougher about it. So she quit the fuss and did what they wanted.

They were at it for a couple of hours, having fun with her every which way and passing a bottle of Old Crow between them, making her take a drink every once in a while herself. "It's a party, sunshine," little Mort said. "*Ever*body drinks at a party."

When they'd finally had enough they drove her home. Tucson, the tall ropy one, did the driving, pushing the Caddy up over ninety on the long stretch of highway back toward Laredo. She hoped with all her might that a state trooper or a Ranger would spot them and pull them over, but of course there wasn't a cop to be seen.

Mort snuggled up close with his arm around her on the drive back and asked if she was all right. She nodded and kept her eyes straight ahead, watching the dark road zooming under the Caddy's headlights.

He pressed some money in her hand. "Here honey," he said, "buy yourself some new things, okay?" They had made a mess of her clothes. She'd seen Tucson tuck her panties into his pocket. Mort added to the money in her hand and said, "Some *real* nice things, okay?"

In front of the house he held the car door for her like a little gentleman. For a moment she had the awful feeling he was going to walk her to the door, maybe kiss her goodnight. But he simply got back in the car and tipped his hat and said, "Thank you, honey, thank you," like the whole thing had been her idea for cheering up a couple of lonely trailhands.

Tucson, who'd humped on her like he was trying to kill something with a stick, never said a word. Just drove fast and raped hard and stole women's underwear. Mort was something slimy she'd like to see run over by a car, but Tucson was something else. He was something she wanted to see tied up tight and then have at him with a steak knife and book of matches.

She stood at the side of the road, clutching her torn shirt to her sore breasts, and watched the Caddy drive off into the morning mist. She was afraid to curse them yet, even in her mind, for fear they might somehow hear her thoughts and wheel the Caddy into a quick U-turn.

She locked her jaws against the pain and made her way to the door. Before going inside she wadded the bills in her hand and flung them into the shrubbery under the front window. She went in the bathroom and bent over the toilet but finally had to put her finger in her throat to make herself throw up. In the mirror she saw that her cheekbone under her left eye was swollen darkly. She brushed her teeth for fifteen minutes, then undressed and got under a steaming shower and scrubbed herself thoroughly with a washcloth as hard as she could stand it.

And standing there with the shower cascading over her head, she cried. Cried loudly and long, wailing and sobbing and gasping for breath and wiping webs of mucus from her nose. Cried from the depths of her battered heart.

The humiliation! It felt like something jammed in her windpipe. Just took what they wanted. Like she was nothing but some . . . *thing*. Some thing they could do whatever they wanted with. No asking, no nothing. Just *took* it.

Worse. Let's face it, girl, it was worse than that. They'd both seen it. Seen it and heard it. That goddamned red blazing moment when she'd suddenly arched up under that Tucson bastard and dug her fingers in his back. They'd seen it and they'd heard the sound she made and they'd known it wasn't pain.

God *damn* them.

Them? God damn *her.* Filthy, weak, stupid . . .

Why didn't she just go back inside and ask Sparky to take her home?

Christ's sake, she'd been hit in the face, she couldn't think straight.

She was clear enough in the head to appreciate that nice Cadillac car.

Get them. Get the bastards. Call the police. Right now.

Yeah, sure, the police. *Real* good idea. Two words against one.

Call them anyway. Do it.

Are you simple, girl, or what?

All her idea, your honor. And if you don't mind us saying so, the lady had herself a real fine time for a fact. She didn't hardly want the party to end. She wasn't the least bit put out till afterwards when we paid up. Claimed it wasn't enough. Damn if it didn't seem like a lot to us.

And the judge: I know the story, boys. Heard it a thousand times if I heard it once. Lots a these working girls don't know when to leave well enough alone. You, girl: don't let me see your painted face in here again.

Case dismissed. But the boys wouldn't be happy about her putting them through all that. They'd sure enough come around to discuss it with her. How stupid can you get, girl, showing them where you live? Letting them bring you right to your front door?

O lord, they'd probably come around to see her again anyway, since they'd seen how much she enjoyed it and all. When they'd seen it touch her, Mort had kissed her on the nose and laughed.

What to do?

You kidding? *Go.* Hit the road. Skeedaddle. Ride, Sally, ride.

She stayed under the shower until it turned cold, then dried off and did the best she could for the shiner with makeup. She put on her best skirt and blouse and packed the rest of her clothes. She tucked her tightly-rolled savings—two hundred and twenty dollars—into the toe of a spare shoe and slipped the shoe in the suitcase.

She went out the back door and crossed the yard and knocked on the rear door of the Santiagos' house. Joselita and Moise were having breakfast, already dressed for work. They said they would be very happy to give her a ride to the bus station in town. She had a cup of coffee with them and said she was going to visit her grandmother in Houston. They said that was nice, families should always stay close. They politely averted their gaze from her bruised eye.

She finished her coffee and went back to the house to get her suitcase. She took a last look around, made sure all the lights were out and all the taps turned off tight. She was halfway across the yard again when she stopped, set down her bag and went around to the front of the house. She knelt on the wet grass and probed the shrubbery under the window—pricking her finger on a thorn and staining the hem of her skirt—and soon found the wadded money. Six twenty-dollar bills. She stood up and folded the money carefully and slipped it into her bra.

I mean, she thought . . . after all.

III

GENTLY DOWN THE STREAM

1

Dolores is drowning.

The murky water is bloodwarm and tastes of salty copper. Far above her upturned face the surface glimmers dimly. She flails weakly with exhausted arms, kicks feebly against a bottom of soft mud. She can hold her breath no longer and her lungs begin to rip. She tries to scream and the foul water rams into her mouth like a boot heel . . .

She bursts awake—pushing up on her elbows, gasping, kicking at the sheets entangled about her legs, for a moment longer still feeling her chest being crushed under a lack of air before she realizes where she is.

She falls back on the sweat-damp pillow with a huge inhalation which she releases in a long hissing sigh.

Oh man. Oh that damn dream.

Her heart hammers on her ribs. Her throat burns. A headache hacks at her skull like a hatchet.

Easy, sweetie. It's only morning. Calm down.

An oily cast of orange sunlight oozes through the window blinds and casts black stripes on the opposite wall. Already the bayou humidity has begun to congeal the air. She is sheathed in sweat.

She turns her face from the window and stares at the open closet door. The closet seems larger than usual somehow. She puzzles over this for a minute before she understands.

Billy Boy's clothes are gone.

Wake up, girl. Things are happening here.

She tries hard to recall the night before, fuzzily remembers drinking bourbon from the bottle while she watched TV. She hadn't seen Billy Boy in, what, two days . . . no, three. And now she vaguely recollects reeling into the bedroom and . . . *oh yeah* . . . Ellis Corman, the next-door neighbor . . . peeking over into her bedroom again from his bathroom window, the hairy-ass peckerwood. So this time she left the blind up and turned on both dresser lamps to give him better light to see by and turned the radio on loud and dropped her robe and danced all around the room in just her panties to the Kinks' "You Really Got Me," kicking her legs up high and shaking her ass and titties and just generally giving that horny sonofabitch a hell of a show, letting him drool over what he couldn't have . . . And then . . . and then Della Corman was at her own bedroom window and looking over at her with her mouth open big enough to hold a watermelon. And then Della was gone from the window and a second later busting through the bathroom door and Ellis nearly jumped five feet in the air with his eyes like golf balls as Della came in whacking at him with both fists and he was all hunch-shouldered and ducking and sidestepping and finally managed to get around her and out of there and Dolores remembers standing naked at her window and laughing . . .

And then Della Corman was at the bathroom window hollering "You filthy *whore!*" and yanked the blind down and snapped off the bathroom light.

The fat-assed bitch. Dolores had been of a mind to go over there and snatch her bald headed but decided to have another little drink first . . .

She remembers nothing more.

Billy Boy must've come in after she passed out.

She sits up and swings her legs over the edge of the

bed and kicks over a nearly empty bottle of Jim Beam as a bolt of red pain flares in her skull. She cradles her head in her hands and watches the bourbon spread and vanish in the cracks between the floorboards.

Sweet Baby Jesus. The little sonofabitch did it. Got his hat and gone.

She stands up, sways dizzily for a moment, then staggers naked across the hall and into the bathroom. She reemerges wearing a man's blue workshirt, only slightly too big for her, and goes into the living room. The kids are sitting on the floor watching television cartoons. Bugs Bunny.

The volume of the little black-and-white is barely audible. Bugs Bunny gnaws at a carrot. The kids don't even smile at the action on the set, just watch it blankly while they eat sugar-coated cereal by the handful from the box set between them. On the screen Yosemite Sam is hopping with rage and shaking a cutlass in Bugs' face. Bugs does not look too concerned. The kids don't even glance at her.

She goes into the kitchen and sees a note stuck to the refrigerator door with a pink wad of chewing gum.

Just like him to use gum. Goddamn bubblegummer. What else can you expect from somebody named *Billy Boy*, for Christ's sake?

Sorry slim. No more for me. Your probly sick of it too so I guess I'll move on down the road. You got great looks, you'll do all right. I'm a low life I know. Luck to you and the kids.

Little prick didn't even sign it. Lowlife is right. All of you. Lowlifes. Good goddamn riddance.

On the kitchen table is a loose-leaf sheet of paper beside an empty Old Crow bottle. She steps over for a look. "Dear Daddy" is scribbled in a barely legible hand across the top line. The rest of the sheet bears a big X. She crumples the page and tosses it in the direction of the full garbage pail.

Yesterday's pot of coffee is still on the stove. She gives it a shake and finds it's yet holding about a half-cup, so she turns on the burner under it. On top of the three-day pile of dishes in the sink are two empty bottles of Pearl. She just bets he didn't bring them in with him and goes to the refrigerator and looks inside and sees that, sure enough, the little bastard drank her last two beers.

She goes to the kitchen doorway and leans against it, her head throbbing. "You kids see Billy Boy this morning?"

They remain fixed on the screen, seem not even to have heard her, though she knows they did.

"*Hey!* I'm talking to you! You seen Billy Boy today?"

"Yesssss," the girl says without looking away from the TV. Nearly six years old, she is older than her brother by a year.

"*Well?* What'd he say?"

"Nothing much."

"Mary Marlene!"

The girl cuts her a fast look. "*Nothin!* He give me and Jesse fifty cent apiece to keep real quiet and not wake you up."

She suddenly thinks of the car. She strides quickly to the front window and pulls aside the curtain and sees through the screen that the Ford is gone from under the big magnolia in the front yard where she always parks it for the shade. The bastard said the car was hers, he got it for her. Liar. Oh how they lie. She catches the fragrance off the white blossoms. A ship's horn blares sonorously out on the channel. Purple thunderheads are already building high over the gulf.

She turns back to the girl. "What else did he say? Mary Marlene! *Look* at me when I'm talking to you!"

The girl glares at her mother, her mouth in a tight little line.

"I want to know what else he said. Tell me exactly."

"*Nothin!* Said he hadda go to Houston or someplace. Give me and Jesse fifty cent each and said we could spend it on *whatever we want!*"

"I've told you about taking that tone, missy."

The girl shrugs and turns her attention back to the television. Beside her the boy watches the screen with his jaws slack and snot shining under his nose. That one's a dummy for damn sure, Dolores thinks, a purebred fool. And she feels an immediate rush of familiar guilt. What kind of mother thinks such things about her own child?

But he does look like a fool, damn it, he *does*. Acts it, too. If he at least looked a *little* like his daddy, but . . . he doesn't . . . he *doesn't*.

She tries to ease the guilt by thinking that she really does love them like a mother should, deep down inside— but this time the trick lie doesn't work. It's bullshit and she can't pretend it isn't and she's by Jesus had her fill of bullshit, even her own.

Oh, she supposes she *did* love them once, back when they were just babies. But now the girl's a smart-mouth pain in the ass and the boy's a scary retard and the fact of the matter is that she wouldn't mind a bit if they both vanished tomorrow. *Poof!*—gone, just like that. Wouldn't that be nice?

The guilt bores into her heart. But the truth's the truth, damn it, and no bullshit in the world will change it.

"Listen to me, Mary Marlene. He say anything *else*?"

The girl sighs with theatrical emphasis—and for an instant Dolores sees herself picking up the TV and hitting the girl over the head with it. She puts a hand to her aching forehead and thinks maybe she's crazy. Only crazy people think things like that.

"He said he liked Road Runner best of all."

"What? He watched cartoons with y'all?"

"Only just while Road Runner was on. Me and Jesse, we like Sylvester Cat the best. We wanna see him catch that Tweety bird and eat his head off."

Judas Priest. Ain't he the one? Watches cartoons cool as you please before he runs for it.

"That's it? He didn't say nothing else? *Mary Marlene!*"

"Whaaat?"

"Did he . . . oh hell, never mind."

"We turn it up now?"

Without answering she returns to the kitchen and pours the half-cup of heated coffee and sugars it and then pushes the coffee away and slumps against the counter and mutters, "God *damn* it." She goes back to the bedroom and falls across the bed—and a second later flinches when the TV volume suddenly thunders through the house.

"YE LONG-EARED VARMINT! SAY YER PRAYERS!"

"Mary Marlene!"

"EH . . . WHAT'S UP, DOC?"

She's on her feet and stomping to the bedroom door, ready to scream at the girl to turn the thing off—*off*, not just down, goddamnit—when she remembers the title. The title to the car is in her name.

She wheels toward the closet and gets down on hands and knees and digs through the pile of clothes and shoes and old magazines until she finds the small toolbox in the back corner. All her important papers are in this box. She'll just by God show that title to the laws and they'll run the bastard down and make him give her the car back, maybe even lock up his sorry ass for a while for car theft. She's almost chuckling as she sits on the bed and opens the toolbox.

The title's not in there. Her certificate of marriage to Buddy is there, and her daddy's letter from Huntsville, and her passbook showing a balance of sixty-three dollars and two cents. There's her emergency roll of cash held tight by a rubber band. A few small tools. A gun cleaning kit and a half-full box of cartridges. Her blued Colt revolver. But no title. The sonofabitch must've taken it. Likely get a goodbuddy somewhere to notarize it, then get a new title in his own name.

That sorry lowlife.

Cartoon music clamors. Looney Tunes.

She takes out the pistol and box of cartridges and sets them on the bed, then slips the rubber band off the roll of bills and counts eight twenties and eleven tens. Two seventy. Plus the sixty-three dollars and four cents in the savings account makes . . . what? She never could figure in her head worth a damn. Three hundred something. And two cents. Whatever it is exactly, it ain't a fortune. Still it's *something*, which is a lot more than she's had a time or two before. She's not real surprised to find the money still there. Billy Boy wasn't a thief. Just a two-timing peckerwood and a liar and an Indian giver is all.

She rolls the bills tightly again, puts the rubber band around them, drops the money back in the toolbox and puts the box back in the closet. She sits on the bed, only vaguely aware of the blaring theme music of Casper the

Friendly Ghost, and wonders what she's going to do. To-morrow. Today. In the next five minutes.

After a while she catches sight of herself in the big mirror over the dresser and she goes over to it and leans in close to scrutinize her face.

Not too bad, she thinks, not yet—if it wasn't for this, anyhow. She puts a finger to a small scarred bump high on the bridge of her nose. That was from Smiling Jack, who put an end to a period of her life she's never told anybody about except her husband Buddy . . .

2

She'd arrived in San Antonio on the bus from Laredo and checked into a motel and for the next three nights in a row put on a short sexy yellow dress and sat on the bed smoking and thinking about what Rayette Nichols had said back in Harlingen when she asked her once what it was like to go to bed with men she didn't even know.

It mostly didn't feel like much of anything, Rayette told her. You were just letting some fella poke at you and grab at you and slobber on you for a few minutes is all. "Feels about the same, I guess," Rayette said with a grin, "as for most women doing it with their husband." Oh yeah, a few of them were fun, she said, but she'd be lying if she didn't admit that with *some* of them, well, it was like rolling in shit, they were so nasty. But even with the nasty ones you could go home afterward and take a nice hot bath and be just as fresh and clean as before—*plus* be money ahead.

"Hell, honey," Rayette had said, "all they are is men."

On her fourth night in San Antone she finally worked up the nerve to go out to a bar and sit by herself. Hardly an hour later she was back in the motel and in bed with a man who paid her thirty dollars for the privilege. She'd been so nervous the fella couldn't help but notice, but he'd been so understanding about it, so gentle and nice, she would've forgot all about the money if he hadn't taken it on himself after he got dressed again to count it out and put it on top of the TV. He advised her to get the money first from now on because you never knew when some guy might crawfish on the deal after he'd had his fun. That made good sense and she thanked him for it. Later on she would think that if that first one hadn't been so nice maybe she wouldn't ever have done it again.

Or if that good-looking young Mex cop six weeks later had been rougher on her, had rattled her sufficiently, that might've got her out of the trade soon enough too. She'd taken him for a trick and they left the bar with their arms around each other and when they got outside he showed her his badge and told her to take it on out of San Antonio or next time he'd run her ass in. And her ass was way too nice to get all worn out on the work farm, he said, giving it a pat and smiling like he meant it. She thanked him for the break and was on a Trailways to Austin that night.

She thought the capital was a nice town, prettier and a lot cleaner than San Antone. But there was too much competition from free stuff, from all those horny government secretaries and all those university coeds. After a few weeks she hopped a bus to Houston, where she thought she'd do better.

And she did. She rented an efficiency near the interstate and bought some nicer clothes. She worked the downtown hotel bars mostly and over the next two weeks made more money than she'd thought it possible to make so fast. The first few days she did but a couple of tricks a day at thirty dollars a throw, but by the end of the week she was charging forty-five bucks and getting away with it. She once turned six tricks in one night and felt rich as the Queen of Sheba. She bought more clothes, sexy new underwear, a radio for her room. She got a little toolbox to keep her money in and cached it in the closet.

She was scared of course, every time, all the time. But her luck held well. Nobody got rough with her or tried to cheat her or force her into doing anything she didn't want to do—and some of them would ask her to do some godawful things.

She'd been working Houston a little over two months when a man took the stool beside her at the bar of the Prince Travis Hotel one late night and introduced himself as Jackson Somebody. She'd been about to go home after another profitable evening, but figured what the hell, one more wouldn't hurt anything. Especially one so handsome and nicely groomed and expensively dressed. And so she accepted his offer of a drink. He had dark bright eyes and black hair, a deep tan, a soft Louisiana accent and a glorious white smile. When he discreetly slipped her a hundred-dollar-bill her heart jumped up and clicked its heels and they exchanged winks and left the bar arm-in-arm.

Up in his room he asked if she would think him depraved if he sat and watched as she undressed. "Few visions are so sensual," he said in his lilting accent, "as that of a lovely young woman shedding her clothes in preparation for the act of love. I have always found it enrapturing."

She'd smiled at his odd way of talking and held his face in her hands and kissed him on the lips and backed away a few feet and started taking off her clothes. He sat on the bed and watched her, smiling, smoking a dark sweet-smelling cigarette. Then she was down to her yellow bikini panties and she stepped out of them and struck a pose—hip cocked, head tilted, one hand over a breast, one hand extended toward him with the panties dangling from her fingers. She giggled and playfully flicked the underwear at him.

Still smiling, he snuffed the cigarette and stood up and took a pair of black gloves from his jacket.

"You *are* a *lovely* girl," he said softly as he fitted the thin gloves carefully over his fingers, this man she would evermore think of as Smiling Jack. "But precious . . . anybody working as an independent in my territory is stealing from me . . . and what*ever* made you think you could do that?"

Her heart felt like it was tumbling down a flight of stairs. She wanted to tell him she was sorry, she'd meant no disrespect, she'd pay him whatever he thought she owed him, she'd leave Houston and never come back to this town again—wanted to beg him please not to hurt her, but before she could get the first word out of her mouth he was on her like a hard wind out of hell . . .

A policeman named LeBeau came to see her in the hospital. He wore a stained yellow jacket and a porkpie hat and looked fed up with the world. All she could tell him was the man's description and that his first name was Jackson. Her head felt misshapen. Her voice sounded strange in her own ears. LeBeau put away his notebook and smiled at her with nothing but his mouth. Not likely they'd catch him, he said. And even if they did, it wasn't likely he'd go to trial. And if he did, it wasn't likely he'd be convicted, not with it being his word against hers.

"I'll tell you something, darlin," LeBeau said, "just between us and not as a member of the Houston Police

Department." He stood and hitched up his pants. "Nobody gives a shit what happens to whores. Any girl sells her ass is trash and just asking for trouble. Who you think cares she finds it?" He wagged an admonishing finger and left.

She lay in the hospital another two days, congested with rage and humiliation. And fear. She'd remembered Rayette saying all they are is men, but she'd forgotten—more likely chosen not to recall—the business about Victorio. Well, no more of it, no matter what. Better to go hungry than have to deal with any Victorio or Smiling Jack or God-knew-who. Next time could be nails in her knees. No, *thank you.*

And as she lay there in her bandages and watched some local news show on the wall TV she realized it was her birthday. She was eighteen.

Smiling Jack had taken all the money she'd had in her purse, and she told the hospital she was broke. She had to sign a paper promising to pay off her bill when she was able. As soon as she got back to her room she packed her bag and got her money from the toolbox. An hour later she was on a bus to Texas City, ignoring the looks the other passengers gave her battered face.

And when everything was finally healed—the cracked ribs, the concussion, the bruised breasts, the broken finger, the various cuts on her face—the only vestige of Smiling Jack's handiwork was the small scarred bump on the bridge of her nose.

3

"Pretty face," she says softly, assaying it in the mirror. "Yes it was."

But no more. Too much the worse for wear. No wonder Billy Boy went packing.

Cut the shit, girl. Wasn't the face and you know it.

What was it, then. Answer me that.

Nothing but you, sugar. Y-O-U. You know that too.

Oh. Yeah.

She goes over and sits on the bed, picks up the pistol and twirls it on her finger like a movie cowboy. It's a .38 caliber Colt Cobra with a four-inch barrel, finished in blue and fitted with a checked walnut stock. It weighs seventeen ounces and is eight-and-a-half inches long. She has owned it since shortly after her episode with Smiling Jack.

She learned to shoot from Uncle Frank. She'd been living with him and Aunt Rhonda more than a year by then and hadn't exchanged more than a dozen sentences with him in that time, but he'd lately begun paying her more attention. One afternoon when she was walking past his gun shop at the edge of town he came to the door and said hi and asked if she'd like to come in and look around. She'd never seen so many guns. He handled them with an easy familiarity she couldn't help but admire. She'd recently seen the movie *Bonnie and Clyde* and had wondered what it felt like to shoot a gun. She loved the feel of them. When he asked if she'd like to shoot one sometime, she said oh yes.

They'd go deep in the woods behind the house and shoot bottles and tin cans. He showed her the proper stance for facing the target, the way to hold the piece in a two-hand grip, how to aim and squeeze—not jerk—the trigger, how to accept the recoil. He let her fire his shotgun too, a pump-action Remington. But her love right from the first had been his two revolvers—a Smith & Wesson four-inch .38 and a huge .44 caliber Remington with a barrel about as long as her forearm, an ancient cannon of a piece he said his grandaddy had taken off a dead bandido when he was riding with Pershing's cavalry down in Mexico, hunting for Pancho Villa.

It was during those shooting lessons that he started with the touching. "No, Dolly, turn a little more this way," he'd say, correcting her stance with a hand on her thigh, on her hip, on her rear. "Straighten your back," he'd say, his hands spread on her ribs, thumbs nudging her breasts. At first she'd been unsure what to do, thought she ought to say something, make some gesture of objection, but then figured what the hell. It wasn't like he was *hurting* her or anything, for Pete's sake. And truth be told, she didn't really, well, *mind* it all that much. It was actually kind of exciting in a way, all that pretending they weren't either one of them aware of what his hands were really and truly doing. Together with the excitement of the gunfire and the kick of the pistol and the way the tin cans whanged and jumped and the bottles busted in sprays of glass—well, sometimes it all just made her feel like rubbing herself up against something.

In the absence of any resistance, his touches of course got bolder, and one late afternoon he finally pressed on her the most intimate touch of all, right there on a layer of pine needles.

She liked it, she can't ever deny it, but even though she didn't object, she knew it was wrong and swore to herself it wouldn't happen again. But of course after it happened once it was bound to happen some more. And it did, the very next day, out on the pine needles again. She wanted to tell him no, wanted to say they ought not be doing this, but, lordy . . . it was *so* exciting.

The next day she was reading in bed and Aunt

Rhonda was off at her sewing club meeting when Uncle Frank came into her room, undoing his belt and saying a bed would sure beat pine needles for comfort. Before she could give it a thought her shift was bunched up above her breasts and her panties tangled around one ankle and they were at it again, only this time he was so rough about it she got scared and tried to push him away, but she was also enjoying it in spite of herself and even as she pushed at him with her hands she was pulling him in with her heels and she was scared and furious and all mixed up and more excited than ever . . .

And that's when Aunt Rhonda showed up at the door.

4

She releases the revolver's cylinder and swings it out, sees that all the chambers are empty, then turns the gun around and peers into the bore as she positions her thumbnail under the breech to reflect light up into the barrel. The inner surface of the barrel gleams, the lands and grooves spiral cleanly, without a pit or speck of dust. Still, it's been a few weeks since she last cleaned it, so she fastens a brush tip to the end of a cleaning rod and runs it through the barrel a few quick times. Then she unscrews the brush from the rod tip and replaces it with a button-tip fitting. She stuffs a small patch of flannel into the muzzle and thrusts it all the way through the barrel with the rod. Next, she moistens a flannel patch with oil and shoves it through the barrel. She reexamines the inner barrel and smiles at its gleam. She removes the button tip and attaches a slotted tip in its place, then fits a fresh flannel patch in the slot and runs the patch through each of the six cartridge chambers. When all the chambers are sparkling, she snaps the cylinder back in place with a jerk of her wrist, then spins it with her fingertips to test its action. The cylinder whirls smoothly. She has always loved that rapid ticking. Now she applies a light coat of oil to all the exposed metal, then wipes the gun clean with a silicone cloth. The weapon shines.

She dumps a handful of bullets out of their box, picks one up and regards it closely. Hardly bigger than a peanut. But no goober in the world can do you the damage one of these can. She drops the round back on the bed and aims the pistol at the blank wall across the room where she now envisions Aunt Rhonda's face. You ugly hateful old bitch. The hammer snaps down with a clear flat *click* and Aunt Rhonda's face dissolves. She lowers the gun and lets out a long breath.

Hell, why shoot *you*? It wasn't you humping his own half-brother's daughter, his own half-niece.

The word "incest" intones lowly in the back of her mind and she feels her face go hot.

It *wasn't* that. It can't be that except with a daddy or a brother and he wasn't either one. It wasn't *that.*

On the wall hangs a framed black-and-white photo of Billy Boy wearing his usual cowlick and lopsided grin. His freckles clear and sharp, making him look like Howdy Doody at age 37. Squatting beside a billygoat at the petting zoo of the county fair, where a roving photographer took the shot. Dolores paid a dollar for it.

She takes aim on his right eye.

Click. That's for all your lies, you bastard no-count.

The sight sets on his left eye.

Click. That's for all your damn cheating.

She aims at his big front teeth.

Click. That's for breathing the same air as me.

Click . . . click . . . click.

She opens the cylinder again and slips a round in a chamber and closes the cylinder and spins it. She places the muzzle against her breast and feels her heart thumping wildly up against the pistol barrel.

Go ahead, girl. Try your luck. One little squeeze.

She eases her finger off the trigger and lowers the pistol to her lap. Her breath is wedged in her chest and her pulse throbs in her throat.

You damn crazy woman.

She suddenly remembers the old boy back in Alice who couldn't stand it anymore and took a shotgun to himself. A *shotgun*, for Christ's sake! How can anybody botch it with a damn shotgun? But he did. Took off half his face and a fairsized portion of his brain and *still* lived through it. If you can call it living to be damn near totally paralyzed. That poor fella laid in bed for months with no control over bowel or bladder, his head wound constantly seeping pus and god-knows-what. All he could move was the one eye he had left, that and his nose. He was fed through a tube in his arm. They said he passed his days soiling the sheets and shedding tears out of his one eye and snorting up snot. His sister had to spend much of her day mopping up his messes. Not long after they left Alice they heard she'd choked him to death and been sent to prison for it.

You do not want *that*, she tells herself. Besides, who'd take care of *you* if you botched it? Who'd change the sheets when you made a mess in bed?

"Who's gun's that?"

Startled, she jerks around to see the two kids at the bedroom door, their eyes fixed on the revolver in her hand. She had not been aware of the television's silence.

"Whose *gun's* that?" the girl repeats.

"Well, not that it's any of your business, Little Miss Nosy, but it's mine." She slips the pistol under the rumpled sheets. "What you-all want?"

"We wanna know can we go to Ruben's and hep him build a treehouse."

"*Ruben's?* Just yesterday you said Ruben Harris was the stupidest boy in the world."

"His daddy gave him a big buncha lumber and we wanna go hep him build a treehouse."

"So now you don't care he's the stupidest boy in the world?"

The girl shrugs irritably. "We're gonna go hep build a treehouse," she says, and turns to leave.

"Hold it right there, missy! You don't tell *me* what you're gonna do, I tell *you*. What do you know about building a treehouse or anything else, anyway?"

The girl glares at her. "You said if we asked we could do stuff. You *said*." The boy steps closer to Mary Marlene and takes hold of her shirt. His eyes big on Dolores. The boy was more tight-lipped than ever lately. Hardly ever spoke anymore except in whispers to his sister.

"First you get the word right. It ain't *hep*, it's *help*. I told you a hundred times. You want to grow up talking like some ignorant ranchhand? Now say it, say *help*. H-E-L-P. *Say* it!"

"*Help!*" the girl snaps. "You said if we asked and I done *asked*!"

"Dammit, Mary Marlene," Dolores says through her teeth, "what'd I *tell* you about sassing me?" She'd like to smack the girl's face. She's never once hit either of them, but lately the impulse to do so has been constant and almost irresistible. And has terrified her.

The girl looks as though she wouldn't mind smacking *her*, either, her eyes blazing with rage. How does it happen, Dolores wonders. How do they get this way, those darling little babies?

"Aw hell," she says, feeling a sudden exhaustion right down to the bone. What's the damn point of arguing with a smart-mouth brat anyway? "Go ahead on."

They streak through the living room and screech the front screen door open wide on its rusty spring as Dolores calls out, "Don't let any flies in or slam the—" and the door bangs as loud as a pistol shot.

She gets up and goes to the screen door which as always remains partly opened and latches it against the entry of any more flies. Then goes to the kitchen and contemplates the pile of dishes in the sink, the shiny patches of cooking grease on the stovetop and the wall behind it, the dustballs on the floor.

Used to be you kept house some better than this.

She takes the now cold half-cup of coffee to the little kitchen table and sits and sips at it. The room is quiet but for the buzzing of the circling flies.

The next thing she knows she's still at the table and the coffee is still in front of her, but she's aware that time has passed because the sunlight has completely withdrawn from the window over the sink and is now streaming through the windows on the other side of the house. She's obviously been asleep but doesn't see how it's possible for somebody to sleep sitting on the edge of a straightback chair and not fall over. Maybe she wasn't asleep, maybe just in a trance of some kind. The thought scares her, but she doesn't know why, and her confusion makes her angry.

"Damn it," she says, and starts to stand up and realizes that her bare ass has been pressed for so long into the hard edge of the chair it has gone numb.

No wonder I been in a trance—my brains are paralyzed.

The shift of her weight on the chair has renewed the circulation in her buttocks and now they burn. She moans and stands up slowly, massages her ass with both hands, limps into the living room.

Everything's so *quiet.* The room seems utterly alien to her and she feels a momentary confusion before the furniture regains its familiarity and she spies the open box of Sugar Pops on the floor where the kids left it, and one of Mary Marlene's frayed sneakers poking out from under the sofa, and the usual sloppy pile of *Cosmopolitan*s next to the ripped armchair in the corner.

I know this place, she thinks, her heart sagging, and she sits on the sofa and puts her head in her hands.

The low coffee table is spotted darkly with cigarette burns, littered with several issues of *TV Guide,* a scattering of matchbooks, nearly empty paper cups of Kool Aid, a blackened banana skin. The two ashtrays on the table are full to overflowing with cigarette butts. She looks around for cigarettes but sees none anywhere and does not feel like getting up and going into the bedroom to search. She picks through both ashtrays until she's found the longest butt, then straightens it the best she can and lights it with a match. She takes a deep drag and exhales with a huge sigh.

In the dust coating the coffee table a fingertip has traced the shape of a heart containing the inscription "M. U. + R. H."

Mary Underhill and Ruben Harris.

Not even six years old and she's already a fool for love. Little idjit. She'll see.

5

Buddy once carved a heart with their initials in it. Into an oak trunk in Texas City. B. U. + D. S. It was a late afternoon and the sunset blazed red as fire in the oil-fumed air. It was the first time she'd permitted him to walk her to work, the first time she'd ever been in his company outside of The Fiddlesticks, the roadhouse where she worked as a waitress. For over a month he'd been coming in the place every day after work at the refinery to have supper and a few beers and to talk to her. He'd been doing this ever since the night he came in with a bunch of friends and saw her for the first time. The talk between them was easy and full of laughter without him ever getting raunchy like the others. After the first week he wasn't even trying to hide how he felt about her. She could see it all over his face. The whole place could. His bubbas made good-natured fun of him—calling him a goner, saying love had done poleaxed him for sure—but he didn't mind their ribbing at all. She'd blush whenever they kidded him about being so sweet on her, and Buddy would beam at her all the more. Every time he came in he asked her for a date—asked her to go dancing, to a movie, for a beer and sandwich someplace, for a walk along the bayshore. And every time, she turned him down.

It had been nearly six months since she'd fled Houston with her battered face. Her flesh and bones had since healed, but her nerves were still beat up. She lived in fear of things she couldn't even name. She'd wonder sometimes if maybe the Houston cop LeBeau had been right, if she really was no damn good, and such wondering would make her angry at herself. Of *course* he wasn't right. What did *he* know about her anyway? She was as worthy of respect as the next person, dammit. She was.

But her self-assurances could not dispel the fear. And now this nice fella, this good-looking Buddy Underhill, was bringing that fear to a head by wanting to get to know her. She knew that if she let him get close to her she'd soon have to lie to him about her past and then live in the terrible fear that one day he'd find out the truth. Or she could tell him the truth herself. Tell him right off the bat. And watch him run the other way.

He was so gently and so sweetly persistent that she finally relented a little and said all right, he could walk her to work—but that was all. Don't think about walking her back home, that was the condition. A walk *to* work was one thing, a walk home *from* work was something else altogether different and she wasn't having any of that.

Fine, he said, no problem, any way she wanted it.

Late the next afternoon, he was waiting for her on the sidewalk in front of her little rented cottage, his hair combed wetly, his face freshly scrubbed and grinning at the sight of her when she came out the door. They walked along making small talk and were halfway to The Fiddlesticks when he paused under a huge oak blazing red in the sunset and gently took her hands and smiled into her eyes and told her he loved her.

She busted out crying. "No, you don't!" she said. "You can't *do* that to me!"

And right there by the side of the road, in a shame-faced sobbing fury, she told him everything there was to tell about the brief part of her life that ended in a Houston hospital room after her run-in with Smiling Jack. She talked and talked and the sun dropped behind the trees and he never once interrupted her. And when she was all through talking, the sun was down and an overhead streetlight had lit up and stretched their shadows across the road and she was very late for work and Buddy was holding her in his arms and saying don't cry, baby, don't cry.

He told her none of it mattered, not anymore. All that mattered was right now and tomorrow and the day after that. He told her again that he loved her, and he kissed her. And she kissed him back. And for a minute she got scared all over again because her heart was racing so fast and her breath was so hard to catch and her throat was so tight—and then she stopped being scared because she realized all it was was happiness. Because—talk about luck—she loved him too.

And while she fixed the ruined makeup on her happy face in a little pocket mirror in the glow of the streetlight, he carved the heart with their initials in the roadside oak.

They were married six weeks later in a small Baptist church in town. They had a five-day honeymoon in a rented piling house on the beach at Gilchrist and got tanned as dark as Mexicans. They swam in the Gulf and ate boiled shrimp and fried catfish and oysters on the half-shell and drank ice-cold beer by the quart bottle. They took the ferry to Galveston and rode the rides at Stewart Park and at a shooting gallery he won a prize for her, a little ballerina made of blue glass. They made love a half-dozen times a day.

Back in Texas City they rented a house on a bayou and bought some linens and cookware and were given lots more stuff by their friends. They didn't buy their own home because his job as a rigger would keep them on the move from one oil field to another all over this end of the state. When she unpacked her things and found the .38, she said she guessed she'd sell it, but he said no, keep it. He'd lost his own gun in a poker game a few months before and hadn't got another one yet and it was good to have a gun in the house. You never knew when you might need it.

Buddy wanted a family and she wanted to please Buddy—and so she was pregnant when they moved to Liberty. When she gave birth to Mary Marlene, Buddy kidded her for a teenage mother. The baby was four months old when they moved again, this time to Baytown, where eight months later Jesse was born.

She was happy. There was no other word for it. She was loved and in love and they had a home and a family and all the bad things were in the past. They made long Sunday trips to the beach at High Island and sang "Row, row, row your boat" on the evening drive back home. They went on picnics in the parks and played games with the kids. They went to drive-in movies and before the end of the second feature the kids would both be asleep and she and Buddy would be necking and groping each other like high schoolers.

They agreed not to have anymore children for a while and so she went back to her diaphragm. Some of their old friends from T.C. had come to work in the Baytown patches too, so they had plenty of old friends and new ones, both, and they all went honky-tonking together a couple of nights a week.

Who—she often asked herself as she fed the babies or checked on supper or hung the wash or held Buddy's

head to her breast in the night—would've ever thought it
could happen?

Happiness is a damn funny thing, she thinks as she
picks through the ashtrays in search of another long butt
to light up. You get to where you're sure you'll never
have it—and then one day it falls on you out of the blue.
You know damn well it doesn't happen to many and that
you best not ask too many questions of it and just grab
on with both hands and hold to it for all you're worth.
But even while you're happier than you thought it was
possible to be, you're afraid, too, because you can't help
thinking something could happen to make it go away. But
if after a while it doesn't go away, you little by little stop
being afraid of losing it. A year goes by, and then another
and another, and little by little the feel of happiness starts
to become as familiar as the smell of shaving cream in
the bathroom or the sound of special laughter coming
through the front door at the end of the day or the touch
of a certain hand on your skin in the night. You reach a
point where you don't even realize how much you've
come to take it for granted—it's like the air you breathe—
and so you stop paying close attention to it, and that's a
real shame because, afterwards, it's so hard to remember
everything about it as clearly as you wish you could, and
it seems to have gone by so fast it's like you hardly had
it for any time at all . . .

They planned a big party for Mary Marlene's fourth
birthday but in the rush of things Dolores forgot to buy
ice cream. She'd picked up everything else—the cake and
cold drinks and candles and decorations and balloons—
but somehow the ice cream slipped her mind. Buddy got

home from work just as the neighborhood kids were arriving for the party. They played pin the tail on the donkey and Mary Marlene opened her presents and then the candles were set in the cake and ready to be lit and Dolores handed out paper plates and plastic spoons and went to the freezer for the ice cream and that's when she realized she'd forgotten to buy it. Mary Marlene went into a snit, and Jesse, already taking his cues from his sister, started up a steady whimpering.

"What the heck," Buddy said. "The kids are right. What's a party without ice cream? Be right back." And he got in his truck and drove off to a convenience store on the highway just a few blocks away.

The way they told it to her, later, he'd walked into the store just a couple of steps ahead of a pair of uniformed state policemen who'd stopped in to get cigarettes. A holdup was going on. Two nineteen-year-olds with magnums who opened fire the instant they saw the cops. Guns went off all over the place. Three people were wounded. One of the troopers would be paralyzed the rest of his life. The two robber boys were shot dead. So was Buddy.

He was the best part of her life, the longest, the quickest to go by.

6

You never got a Buddy when you need one.

She recalls a song her momma used to sing: "I-I-I-I ain't got no *bodddd*-eee."

Or no *Buddd*-ee either.

Ah hell, listen to me. *Poor little me.* Boo damn hoo.

She goes back in the bedroom and stands before the mirror and studies herself. Front view's not bad *at all—*

especially for somebody pushing twenty-five and with two kids and a few too many rough nights that are maybe starting to show in the face some. She takes off the shirt and tosses it aside. But now just look at that. Hardly no droop at all to those hooters—for sure not enough to hold a pencil under them. And only a teensy roundness to the tummy. Waist still slim as a girl's and curves right smoothly into lean tight hips. Thighs nice and firm and not a hint of those riding-pants bulges so many women have, even the young girls. When she flexes a leg—like this—or lifts one out to the side—like this—what you see is lines of muscle and tight flesh and nothing else. No sag, no flab, not on this girl.

She turns her back to the mirror and cranes her head to look over her shoulder. Ladieeess and gentlemen . . . presenting the sweetest little ass in Texas. Round, tight, dimpled over each cheek. More than one man has told her it's the best he ever saw and the nicest he ever put a hand to. A college professor she once did business with in a Houston motel told her it was a classic. That was the very word he used, "classic." Get told something like that by a *professor*, well, who was she to argue? She turns around to face the mirror squarely once more, slides her hands up her thighs and over her belly and up to cup her breasts.

No question about it, baby doll, you're *still* a fine-looking thing.

She takes Billy Boy's framed picture off the wall and holds it facing the mirror. Take a good look at *that*, mister. That's what you're giving up. Don't it just make you wanna cry, you dumbshit huckleberry? You said you *loved* these tits.

She sees herself crying in the mirror and the sight

infuriates her. She slams the photo against the edge of the dresser, spraying glass over the dresser top and onto the floor, then flings it across the room. It bounces off the wall and lands faceup on her rumpled robe, the frame still intact. She stalks over to it and kicks it spinning under the bed to strike the wall on the other side and flip up and prop itself crookedly against the baseboard. Billy Boy's grin is still in place.

Her big toe hurts. Blood seeps from under the toenail. She leans against the wall and hammers it with the bottom of her fist until her hand aches, then she sits on the bed and sobs.

A minute later she giggles through her tears and runny nose.

Oh man. I can't even whip the little bastard's *picture.*

A car turns onto the driveway next door, wheels crunching through gravel. She gets up and goes to the window and sees Della Corman's blue Belvedere. The driver's door swings open and Della Corman works her ample girth out from under the steering wheel, pausing to tug the skirt of her Value Drugs uniform back down over her gelatinous thighs. She opens one of the car's rear doors and lugs out two large sacks of groceries, then bumps the door closed with her hip and lumbers up the steps to her screened kitchen door. She struggles to brace the sacks against her chest while she gropes for the door handle.

I hate you, Della Corman. Hate you, loathe you, despise you, wish you were dead. You *and* your Peeping Tom husband.

She retrieves the pistol from under the bedsheets and aims out the window at Della Corman, setting the sight squarely in the center of her large rump. As Della manages to hook a finger in the door handle and awkwardly pull the screen door open, Dolores squeezes the trigger.

Click.

The small dry sound of hammer striking empty chamber stuns her. She is suddenly aware of the tension in her outstretched arms and tight two-hand grip, of her readiness for the gun's recoil.

Sweet *Jesus,* girl.

She unlocks the cylinder and lets it swing out and sees the sole bullet snug in its chamber . . . the chamber that had been poised to roll up under the hammer with the next squeeze of the trigger.

She gently closes the cylinder and sets the pistol on a pillow and stares at it as if it were a frightening note in an illegible scrawl.

Need us a damn drink, what we need.

Still naked, she goes into the kitchen and rummages through the cabinets until she finds a bottle with something left in it. She pours the remaining Old Crow into a jelly glass and raises the glass in a toast. "To *me,* you sonsabitches!"

The glass is nearly half full, and she gulps it down in two huge swallows. The bourbon hits her stomach with the force of a punch. She staggers back against the edge of the sink, unable to draw breath, gagging—and then her lungs suck air in deeply and she is seized by a violent fit of hacking. The glass slips from her hand and bounces on the floor. Her eyes flood. She sags slowly to the floor with her back against the cabinet doors.

She tries to say "Ahhh!" but can manage only a weak gasp. So she settles for thinking it: *Ahhhh!* That's the joke, isn't it? *Ahhhhh, that's gooood stuff!*

She brushes webs of mucus from her nose and mouth

with her fingers. Yessir, *gooood* stuff. From where she sits she can see that all the sunlight has left the living room windows.

Time sure flies when you're having fun.

Now she catches the odor of her own flesh and sniffs herself more closely.

Hmm. Somebody round here does not smell of roses. C'mon, girl, let's clean you up some.

7

She'd read somewhere that porpoises had been known to save men at sea—shipwrecked sailors and men who went topside for a breath of air in the middle of the night and fell overboard without being noticed. The man would be treading water way out there with no land in sight, all alone and helpless, getting weaker by the minute and absolutely sure he was going to drown, and then a porpoise would show up and keep him afloat with its nose, and nudge him along toward the nearest shore, sometimes for days, sometimes for hundreds of miles. Nobody really knew why a porpoise would do such a thing. Some said it was because porpoises were good by nature. She has often thought of Buddy that way—like a porpoise good by nature who kept her from drowning in herself, in her own weakness, which sometimes feels to her as deep and frightening as an ocean. Too bad he didn't get her all the way to shore before he died. And even if he never could've gotten her to shore, even if that was asking too much, even of him, he could've at least kept on keeping her afloat.

She'd mourned and mourned and Buddy's friends had mourned with her. But as the weeks turned to months the friends stopped mourning and half a year after they put Buddy in the ground they started making moves on his widow. And she'd been so sick at heart still, so afraid of tomorrow, so terribly lonely in the sleepless nights, so desperate to touch something, anything, *anybody* that had been a part of his life and therefore a part of him—and drinking so steadfastly every night—that she surrendered to them. All of them. She went to bed with every man she'd known to be Buddy's friend and even with some who simply claimed they'd been.

It went like that for month after month. And all the while, her heart cried for her lost good man—and for herself, who could not stay afloat without his help.

One night she and some guy she knew was married but whose name she wasn't sure of—a guy who'd told her he'd been best friends with Buddy when they were teenagers and worked on the rigs in Luling—were stumbling around drunk in her bedroom and struggling to get out of their clothes and the fool lurched hard against the dresser and her little glass ballerina tumbled off and shattered on the floor. She knelt in the broken glass and fingered the pieces and began to cry. The fella said he was sorry and put his arm around her to try to comfort her and she started slapping at him and cursing him and throwing things at him—a lamp, the bedside clock, her shoes. The man quick grabbed up his boots and shirt and hustled out of there, looking back at her like she was some kind of crazywoman.

The next day she loaded the truck with as much of her belongings as she could fit into it and moved with the kids to Beaumont.

She rented a little house near the park close to Willow Marsh Bayou and got herself a job as receptionist at the Ford dealer's. She didn't have any experience at that kind of work but the interviewing manager told her he just knew she'd get the hang of it right quick. It was all he could do to look away from her legs in the minidress.

She made it a point to be at work on time every morning and by the end of her third day she knew everything there was to know about being a receptionist. After two weeks the manager gave her a three-dollar-a-week raise and said she was the best receptionist they'd ever had. Every day after work she picked the kids up at the home of a neighbor woman who took care of children for a dollar a day while their mommas were at work. She cooked a good supper every evening and watched TV with the kids and tried to make conversation with them during the commercials. She tried to find things to do with them on weekends. She kept away from the booze. She was trying with all her might to be the good person she kept telling herself she truly was.

But she couldn't keep from remembering something she'd heard her momma say—that there's no changing what you are and only a damn fool thinks there is. Dolores lay awake nights wondering how big a fool she was. Talking about daddy one time, momma had said that a leopard can try all day and night to make itself a zebra, but won't none of its spots ever turn to stripes, not ever.

The job bored her damn near to tears. The fake smile she wore the day long felt like some awful mask. The salesmen all came on to her—every one of them married but acting like he was hot stuff and she ought to be thrilled he was asking her to sneak off to a motel at lunchtime. She told them she was engaged, that her fiancé was in the army and stationed in Germany but would be coming home in about three months. And still some of those peckerwoods persisted.

And she'd now begun to face the truth that she really didn't like her kids. She'd had them for Buddy's sake and no other reason. Now Buddy was gone but they were still with her and every day it was harder to go on pretending she cared about them like a mother should. She could see in their eyes that the kids sensed the truth. Was it any wonder the girl was such a pain in the ass, the boy a mute little freak? What could be worse for a kid than knowing his momma didn't love him? She tried not to think what *her* momma would say if she was alive and knew how she felt. Guilt fed on her heart like a mangy dog. She started allowing herself a couple of drinks before bed to help her get to sleep. Before long she was having more than a couple.

After three months she gave up all pretense. She quit the Ford place and went to work in a bar called The Lucky Star and shortly thereafter began bringing home men. Most were a one-time thing, some she got together with for several nights in a row. She didn't stick with any of them for as long as a week.

It was like Baytown all over again, only now she was drinking much harder.

It went on like that until three months ago, until the morning she woke up while it was still dark outside and the radio was blaring "Hello Walls" and one of the dresser lamps was on and there was a naked man sleeping on either side of her and she had no idea who they were. The big one on her right had a crude tattoo of a coiled snake on his back. The bedroom was an unholy mess. Empty beer cans littered the floor, a few gleaming whiskey bottles. Clothes strewn everywhere. Spilled ashtrays. The room was miasmal with the thick tangled smells of whiskey and ashes, sex and sweat. She vaguely recalled meeting these two in some bar, riding with them in their truck, that they were from Vidor, just up the road. Her lack of clear memory added to her fear. She eased out of bed and went to the closet and slipped on a robe and got the .38 out of the toolbox, then went to the blasting radio and turned it off. The sudden silence seemed to plug her ears. She kicked the mattress hard and the big one groaned and pulled the sheet up over his head. The other one snorted and mumbled and cracked one eye open and finally saw her standing at the foot of the bed in a shooter's stance with the cocked pistol in both hands and pointed at his head. His eyes widened and he raised up on one elbow and said, "What? *What?*"

"Get him up," she said. "And you get your asses out of here. I mean *now.*"

He shook the big man until he came up from under the sheet snarling, "*Quit,* goddammit!" Then he saw her with the gun and got big-eyed too—but only for a second. He sat up and laced his muscular arms around his raised knees and grinned at her. His arms and chest also carried tattoos, all of them poorly rendered. Jailhouse art. She'd come to know it when she saw it.

Lookit here, she thinks, at the fine company you're keeping. You really come a long way in this world, ain't you, girl?

"The fuck you doing, sweetpea?" the big man said. "Put that thing down before I ram it up your ass."

He scared her so bad she couldn't stand it.

"Ram *this.*"

The gunshot rocked the room as the bullet passed over their heads and through the bedroom wall and ricocheted off the block wall in the bathroom and whanged against a pipe.

They threw up their hands and gaped at her with eyes big as boiled eggs.

O lord, she thought, it'll be cops all over the place in a minute.

She pointed the piece at the big one's chest and drew back the hammer.

"You shitheads got ten seconds to get out of my life." Her voice sounded far away through the ringing in her ears.

They scrambled out of bed and snatched up about half their clothes and nearly ran through the walls in their haste to depart the premises.

She followed them to the door and kept the gun on them till they'd got into their pickup and roared off down the street and their taillights disappeared around the corner.

She'd expected to see the neighborhood porchlights blazing, to see people at their doors and gawking toward her house. Expected to hear sirens closing in. But all along the block the houses remained dark under a sky just now dawning gray. Not a soul in sight.

What made her think anybody'd give a damn?

She went inside and locked the door behind her and then went to the bedroom, trying hard not to let a single thought into her head because whatever the thought might be she knew it wouldn't be a good one.

She was cleaning up the mess when she caught sight of the kids at the door, watching her. The boy was sucking his thumb and holding to his sister's T-shirt and looked like he'd been crying. Mary Marlene looked pale and scared and like she was trying hard not to show it. Dolores felt her heart turn over in her chest. It's your doing, girl, she told herself—*your* doing they have to go through this. The girl would never again appear to Dolores as vulnerable as she did at this moment, nor would her voice ever again quaver as it did now when she asked, "Momma? The party over?"

8

She's heard it said that life is not one damn thing after another—it's the same damn thing over and over.

Got *that* right. And whoever said what goes round comes round. For damn sure right on that one too.

The question is, what are you supposed to do when that same damn thing that keeps coming round gets so awful you just can't stand it anymore? What then? *That's* the question. Been the question for a while now, and she ponders it under the steaming shower until the water turns cold.

She dries her hair as thoroughly as she can with a towel, then goes to the kitchen, where a small breeze is coming through the window, to let it finish drying and to do her nails. She sits at the table and puts each foot in turn up on a chair and very carefully applies a coat of Crimson Kiss to the nail of each toe. Then she does her fingernails. While she waits for them to dry she listens to the radio. Oldie-goldies. "Summertime Blues" and "Be My Baby" and "Hit the Road, Jack" and "All Shook Up."

She now goes to the bedroom and stands at the dresser mirror and stares at her face and decides not to apply makeup. *That's* your face right there, girl, Smiling Jack's keepsake and all. You can paint it all you want but it won't change a thing. For the next ten minutes she brushes her copper hair till it hangs softly, brightly on her shoulders. Then she picks through the dresses in the closet and she finds the one she's looking for and slips it on.

She checks herself in the mirror again and thinks, Well, now, ain't I something? The beauty in the mirror gives her a saucy wink. She's changed stations on the radio and Ray Charles is singing about the girl with the red dress on who do the boogie-woogie all night long, yeah, yeah. Her hair jounces in time to her nifty little dance steps, the little dress rising high on her thighs as she executes a side-scissor-step across the floor and follows it with a spin and a wicked left-right-left combination of hip thrusts. Yeah, yeah!

Her breasts swell above the low neckline of the little cocktail dress, her nipples jut against the fabric. Buddy bought her the dress for their first anniversary but didn't see it on her until they got home—and when he did, he said he'd made a mistake, that he hadn't realized it was going to look quite like *that*, and he sure didn't want her wearing it in public because he'd be in one fight after another with all the guys who were bound to look at her in ways he wouldn't be able to let them get away with. He said he was sorry, he knew he sounded like a jerk, but that was how he felt and there was no way he could lie about it. She kissed him for his sweetness and promised she would wear it only at home, only for him, and they had enjoyed the hell out of this dress many a time, yes they had. This is the first time she has worn it in, what, nearly two years.

Two years. Is that all it's been? Not quite. A hair shy of two years, actually.

Which means that *exactly* two years ago he was still alive and she'd been married going on five years and if she was to think real hard about it she might be able to remember exactly what they were doing two years ago, her and Buddy, but all she knows for absolute sure is what they *weren't* doing. What they *weren't* doing was expecting him to be so goddamn dead so goddamn soon and leaving her all by herself for the world to make whore soup out of all over again—that's what they absolutely for goddamn sure were *not* doing . . . and if you start to cry now, you little cooze . . .

Okay, all right, I'm fine. See? No crying. No tears here. All smiles am I.

Two years . . . Might as well be two hundred.

Quit it! That was then, this is now. And anyhow, just look at you. Damn dress never looked so good. You ain't getting older, honey, you're getting better.

Yeah, right. I ain't rightly sure I can stand any more of this kind of better.

How about some pukey self-pity? You stand some more of that?

Believe I had my fill of that too, thank you.

She also believes a drink would help plenty right about now but then remembers there's not a drop left in the house. No help there.

Oh Lordy, where's some help?

Roger Miller is singing dang him, dang him, they oughta take a rope and hang him.

She knows exactly what would help right now. More than a drink. More than anything has ever helped except for Buddy.

To shoot something.

That would do the trick, she knows it would.

She can feel it in her bones.

9

The day after she ran the two Vidor dickheads out of her house at gunpoint, she packed up the truck and took off with the kids again, heading east for the Sabine River and Louisiana just on the other side of it, not thirty miles away. Like she'd heard some old boy say in the bar one time, the only thing worth getting out of Texas is your ass—and she was dead set on both changing her luck and getting as far out of Texas as her meager grubstake would take her.

But she'd gone only a dozen miles when the truck overheated and the motor started clattering and black smoke came pouring out the tailpipe. By the time she pulled into a garage in Orange she'd burned up a bearing. The mechanic said he could have it fixed in ten days or so but the bill was going to be a whopper.

She'd felt like sitting down and crying right there on the floor of the garage. Fixing the truck would cost all the money she'd been counting on to get settled in New Orleans, maybe, or in Florida, better yet. But there she still was in Texas, with the Sabine within spitting distance, practically. She asked the mechanic if he knew of any jobs in town and he said no ma'am he sure didn't. A young woman waiting to get tires put on her car overheard her and asked if she'd ever worked as a cocktail waitress. Dolores sighed and asked if there was any other kind of work in the world, and the girl laughed and said she knew what she meant. She said there was an opening where she worked, at The Barnacle, in Port Arthur, just on down the road. Two hours later she had the job. An hour after that she used the last of her money to rent the little frame house off Proctor Street.

Over the next two weeks she felt like she could never

quite get her breath, felt as if she had something small but as ashy and compact as a chunk of coal lodged in her chest. Her pulse raced constantly. She knew it was fear but she told herself she didn't know why she should be so afraid, and the lie only made the fear worse, because what she was afraid of was that she would have to go on being herself, and she didn't believe she could stand much more of that.

And then she met Billy Boy Renfro in The Barnacle one night and he asked if she'd like to have pie and coffee with him when she got off work. He was the first who'd ever asked her to join him for something other than a drink, and she was caught by such surprise she said sure, why not, more out of curiosity than anything else. She'd reached a point where not much made her curious. He was short and wiry, a welder at the shipworks, and he was funny and sweet and behaved like a gentleman. By the time he dropped her off at her place at two in the morning and kissed her goodnight and said he'd see her tomorrow, she was dizzy with the idea that maybe she still had a little luck left and maybe it was about to turn.

She'd known it wasn't going to get far with him, known it in her bones. But when you feel like you're drowning—feel it not just in awful dreams at night but even when you're awake and walking around in the broad daylight, feel it when you're having coffee in the morning or staring at your kids from across a room or suddenly catching a look at yourself in the mirror—when you're always feeling like that, like you're not even sure you're going to be able to draw your next breath . . . well, it's no surprise you'll grab at anything drifting by, grab at it and hope it'll keep you from going under just yet . . .

They got together almost every evening. He'd come

to The Barnacle just as she was finishing her shift for the
night and they'd do some drinking and dancing for a
while in the company of some of the other waitresses and
their boyfriends. Then they would go to her place where
the kids had much earlier put themselves to bed and
they'd make love into the night.

One time they saw her neighbor Ellis Corman watching them from his bathroom window and Dolores shook
her breasts at him like a stripper and Ellis suddenly remembered to turn off his bathroom light and they
laughed and Billy Boy pulled down the blind.

They'd been seeing each other for six weeks by then
and she said he was spending so much time at her place
he might as well live there instead of with his Uncle Ray-
mond like he did. He said he didn't know about that. She
said she did—and put a nipple to his mouth while her
other hand roamed over him brazenly. The next day he
brought his clothes from his uncle's house and hung them
in her closet.

He seemed always to have plenty of money and he
didn't mind spending it. He told her that besides his
welding job at the works he played poker twice a week
at Purple Jim's garage up in Bridge City and had been on
a run of luck lately. "Course now," he said, "there's times
it goes the other way, too, no matter how good you are,
and when it does, well, that's when you get by with
drinking beer ruther than Jim Beam and eating hot dogs
ruther than steak."

He said she ought to be driving something nicer than
that rattletrap truck and so she traded it in on a yellow
Ford two-door and he paid the rest in cash.

She was astonished to see how well he got along with
the kids. Dolores hadn't seen them take a shine to any-

body since Buddy. Mary Marlene couldn't get enough of fawning on him, and Jesse, wonder of wonders, would sometimes get in whispered conversation with him. She asked once what the boy said to him and Billy Boy just grinned and winked at Jesse and said, "That's our little secret." It was one of the few instances in the past two years she'd seen Jesse smile.

The first couple of times he went to play poker at Purple Jim's after moving in with her, she came home from work and took a hot bath and waited up for him, freshly powdered and wearing sexy new underwear under her robe. But he both times came in a little too drunk to do much about it. Even though she was angry she kept it to herself, but after the second time she didn't bother with the fancy undies and the bath powder anymore.

The following week, when he didn't come home till dawn and then announced with a chuckle that his luck had gone a little sour and he'd lost nearly three hundred dollars, she got furious.

It was partly because of the money, of course. Hearing him talk about losing three hundred dollars, *laughing* about it, like there was no chance at all the world might ever do him harm, made her angry in ways she couldn't have explained if she'd tried. *She'd* never been able to laugh about money, goddammit. But it was something else too—a sudden, inexplicable surge of fear. She was so frightened, and so furious *because* she was frightened and didn't know why she should be, that all she could think to do was tell him what a dumb sonofabitch he was to waste his money that way and come in too drunk to even give a proper fuck to the best-looking woman *he'd* ever have.

He looked at her for a moment like he was trying to see if she was joking, but she could see in his eyes how her face must look, and he lost his smile quick and said he didn't much appreciate her talking that way to him.

She said she wasn't really all that interested in what some drunk money-waster did or did not appreciate.

He said she ought to have more respect for her kids, if not for him, than to use that sort of language in the house.

She said she would talk any fucking way she pleased in her own fucking house and her fucking kids were none of his fucking concern, thank you very much.

And he was out the door and gone.

Real smart, girl. Let him see you for what you really are, that'll wow him for damn sure. She felt like howling.

He came by the next day just before she left for work and they told each other they were sorry and they kissed and made up and sealed the reconciliation with a quickie before she had to rush off to the job. But damage had been done. She saw it in the shift of his eyes, felt it in his touch. She heard it in the vagueness of his voice.

That night when she got home he was watching a late movie on TV, and she got a beer and joined him on the couch. They watched the movie for a while and then during a commercial he told her they'd just been given an extra-special job down at the shipyard, a priority job for the Coast Guard, and he'd be working double shifts for a time, round the damn clock practically, and so like as not he'd most of the time eat and bunk right there at the yard. She said that was good news, the extra work—and even as she told herself to keep her mouth shut and not say anything more about it, she added, "Oughta help some to make up for that three hundred dollars, huh?"

He gave her a look she couldn't read and then turned back to the TV without saying anything.

She didn't see him for the next ten days. And now she began to have the drowning dream nearly every night—the dream of treading water way out in the Gulf, so far out that the shoreline was no more than a dark line on the horizon. She'd have no idea how she got out there, rising and falling on the swells under a vast gray sky and looking toward the distant shore and knowing she could never swim that far. She'd be exhausted from the struggle to keep her head above water—and then a wave would close over her and she'd be sinking, face upward to the receding silver surface, feeling her lungs starting to tear as her feet touched the soft mud bottom and sank into it and her mouth opened for air and filled with the coppery strangling water . . . and she'd waken in a soaking sweat and with her heart lunging hard against her ribs.

The first time she'd had the dream she was so scared by it she started drinking at midmorning and was passed out by late afternoon and did not go to work that night. When she called in sick with a hangover for the third time that week the manager told her if she was going to be all that undependable he'd have to let her go. "Well, I guess I'll just let *you* go, mullethead!" she said—and banged down the phone as hard as she could and hoped she'd blown out his eardrum.

She was drunk as a coot when Billy Boy came in just after sundown but not so drunk she couldn't smell the perfume on him or see the lipstick on his shirt. The next day her memory of the fight was vague. Lots of yelling and cursing. A dim recollection of going at him with both fists and landing a couple of good ones. Of glaring at him while she caught her breath—and him standing there and fingering a bloody lip and looking at her in such a pitying way she wished she had the strength to hit him again. Of telling him if he was so hot for other women he could go fuck them all and when he was done with them he could damn well go fuck himself.

She had clear memory of the sound of his car driving away.

That was three days ago.

Since then she'd sat home all day, drinking and knowing he'd come back because he'd left his clothes and a man leaving for good does not leave his clothes behind.

And then this morning his clothes were gone.

Took his clothes and her car.

Left her nothing except all to herself.

10

She is sitting on the front steps watching the lowering sun set the sky aflame. The air is hot and shrill with cicadas. It smells of dust. The Spanish moss dangling from the oaks tilts slightly in a small waft of air. The shadows of the trees now stretch nearly across the street.

Almost suppertime. Before long the neighborhood will resound with the high cries of mothers calling their children home, and with the distant echoes of "Coming, momma! *Commm*ing."

She has never joined in the evening's communal call for kids. Her children won't anyway come home till just before dark, as always, after everybody else in the neighborhood has sat down to supper.

Her children . . . The words have an alien sound. Smart-mouth Mary Marlene and closemouthed little Jesse. Jesus. They deserve better. Had the best daddy in the world but no momma worth a damn.

Ain't but one way, girl. You know it.

What about them? Be awful for them.

Can't be more awful than what they got now. A momma who don't love her children . . . *that's* an awful thing. Anyhow, Billy Boy maybe don't give a damn about you but he won't let nothing happen to them.

She regards the way the leaves on the trees shine bright as red glass with the sun just above them.

"I hate to seeeee . . . that evenin sun go downnnnn." She snorts with a half-laugh, half-sob, and tells herself to cut it out. She feels like most of the air has been let out of the world and it's all she can do to achieve the next breath.

The sun is almost touching the trees now. Heat rises off the ground like a slow exhalation.

All right. Enough of this.

She stands up and feels the dress clinging wetly to her belly and the backs of her thighs, then goes inside. The house is full of shadows. In the bedroom she peels off the dress. The radio is playing "You Don't Have to Be a Baby to Cry." She notices dark smears on the dress and is puzzled and then looks in the dresser mirror and sees mascara rivulets on her cheeks. She is surprised, because she certainly doesn't *feel* like crying, not now, not anymore.

As she washes her face over the bathroom sink, a euphoria such as she's never before felt in her life swells in her chest until she aches with the sheer pleasure of it. She pats her face dry with a towel. The bathroom mirror fills with her grin. She regards the smiling fresh-scrubbed look of herself and can hardly believe how good she feels.

Maybe this is how it feels to people who have cancer and then get it cut out and are all cured again, something like this. She feels wonderful because for the first time in longer than she can remember she does not feel afraid. She has lived in fear for so long that, now, in its sudden absence, she feels almost happily drunk, the way you do in about the middle of your fourth quick drink.

She goes into the bedroom and gets the pistol off the pillow and then goes to the front window of the living room and looks out at the reddened evening. In long keening voices, mothers are calling their children home.

For some reason she will never understand, she thinks of her father. Pictures him in his little cell at Huntsville. Lying there in his bunk and feeling his worthless life wasting away heartbeat by heartbeat behind those prison walls. She wishes now she'd at least sent him a postcard.

"Dear daddy—wish you were here."

You were here, you son of a bitch, I'd sure enough shoot *you*.

No, not true, I wouldn't. That'd be the biggest favor anybody ever did you in your whole entire life. Leave you in that damn prison is what I'd really do. And you'd go right on dying little by little, breath by breath, over all the years to come. Because you're too much of a coward to do anything else but. Because you're way too damn much of a coward to do *this*.

Naked at the window in the dying light of day, she puts the muzzle in her mouth. She hears a fly buzz as she squeezes the trigger.

There is a sudden loss of sound except for a faraway hum—and in that instant her skull feels abruptly stuffed with cotton.

There is a slight muted thump somewhere at the top of her head.

And—all in the same instant—she feels a wild exhilaration.

Whoooooeeeee!

And then that instant passes and the next begins and—

BLAM!

She is knocked backwards from the window and falls against the sofa and tumbles to the floor and plunges into the deep end of the world's vast pool of pain—pain that annihilates all possibility of definable sensation. It overwhelms everything except the roaring in her skull.

And then the roaring stops. Everything stops.

No sound. No pain.

There. All done. Dead.

Hmm . . . Not quite.

Dead people don't itch.

Her nose itches.

She is aware of the smells of piss and gunsmoke.

She finds herself on her hands and knees.

Something oozes along her breast, bunches at the nipple, drops to the floor in a viscous gob. Hard to tell what it is because she can't see too clearly at the moment. She tries to wipe her eyes and falls on her face. The jolt seems to dislodge something in her head, but, except for the stirrings of a faraway ache in some distant region of her skull, there is still no pain, no sound.

Back up on all fours. More drops of goop hit the floor. They're coming from her head.

Pieces of my head, she thinks. Why ain't I dead?

She tries to shout that question but when she opens her mouth what emerges is a gargling dark-red rush of blood.

One eye comes clear and she sees the gun lying a few

feet away. She crawls to it, clutches it. She swallows blood, and it occurs to her that the taste is much like the dirty-penny taste of the loneliness.

She's upright now, leaning her shoulder against the wall, her hair sopping, the floor slippery under her bare feet. She's having a devil of a time trying to work her finger into the trigger guard and onto the trigger. The pistol seems to weigh forty pounds and feels like some alien tool she's never handled before.

The idea, of course, is to shoot herself again. Do it right this time. No more of this half-ass stuff.

You'd think she was an old lady with bad arthritis to see all the trouble she's having getting her finger on the trigger again. Blood in her eyes doesn't help much. Or the dizziness.

The room abruptly tilts way over and she staggers forward and crashes into the screen door and falls out on the porch, scraping her chin on the rough wood planking and losing her grip on the gun, which goes spinning over the edge of the porch and out of sight.

Damn.

She wants to go down and get the gun but she can't move. She's lying on her face, cheek pressed into the edge of the porch, looking down at the top step six inches down.

Voices distant and close. Screams. Faraway and practically in her ear.

She regards the step, sees with absolute clarity the pattern of its texture, the dark knotholes, the sharp splinters, the grooved grain.

Blood is dripping onto the step and flowing slowly in thin red ribbons along the sinuous grooves of the plank toward its outer edge, where it begins bunching into tremulous drops.

And watching those winding ribbons of blood, she feels herself floating along with them, *in* them, simply floating . . . for the first time in a long time . . . floating gently down the stream.

ABOUT THE AUTHOR

James Carlos Blake is the author of four novels, including *Red Grass River: A Legend* and *In the Rogue Blood*, which won the *Los Angeles Times* Book Prize for Fiction. His short fiction has received accolades and awards and has appeared in a variety of respected literary journals.

Mr. Blake lives in Florida and Texas.